SWEET OLIVE

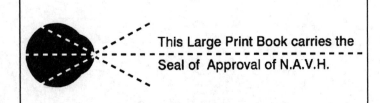

This Large Print Book carries the
Seal of Approval of N.A.V.H.

A TRUMPET AND VINE NOVEL

SWEET OLIVE

JUDY CHRISTIE

THORNDIKE PRESS
A part of Gale, Cengage Learning

GALE
CENGAGE Learning®

Detroit • New York • San Francisco • New Haven, Conn • Waterville, Maine • London

GALE
CENGAGE Learning

LIBRARY OF CONGRESS CATALOGING-IN-PUBLICATION DATA

Christie, Judy Pace, 1956–
    Sweet olive : a trumpet and vine novel / by Judy Christie. — Large print
edition.
        pages ; cm. — (Thorndike Press large print clean reads)
        ISBN 978-1-4104-6548-1 (hardcover) — ISBN 1-4104-6548-9 (hardcover) 1.
Large type books. I. Title.
PS3603.H7525S94 2014
813'.6—dc23   2013040994

Published in 2014 by arrangement with The Zondervan Corporation LLC

In memory of
Charlie R. Pace
1914–1975

CHAPTER 1

Camille Gardner debated whether to use valet parking as she approached the winding driveway, aching to be somewhere else. Anywhere other than Samford, Louisiana. Her head had not stopped pounding since her uncle had yanked her out of the Houston office late yesterday. With a threat and a jab at her honor, he had thrown her to the one town she had vowed never to visit again.

She glanced down at her heels, already pinching her feet, and felt her back grow damp against the scratchy truck seat. The damp September air, mixed with teenaged memories, made her claustrophobic.

Unsure about how she would be received at the fancy oil-and-gas gathering, she hesitated. If she self-parked, she'd sweat through her silk shift by the time she arrived at the door. If she surrendered her keys, she'd have to stand around and chit-chat with people she didn't know when she got ready to leave.

A Mercedes sedan with an LSU sticker and a Lexus SUV with a tiny Ole Miss flag pulled around her and interrupted her pondering. A BMW convertible with a license plate that read *TOY4VAL* followed, the driver tapping her horn.

"Sorry." Camille offered a wave. The striking driver acknowledged her with a slight frown and a toss of long, blond hair.

The pickup looked like a mule compared to the purebred sports car, and Camille exhaled. Her contact lenses burned her eyes, and her short hair stuck to her neck.

She confirmed that the puny air conditioner was set on maximum cool and watched young men in black pants and white shirts park cars and run back up the hill, like participants in some sort of sporting competition.

For a moment, she wished she could trade places with them — but running wouldn't bring peace. She had tried that, dashing from this assignment to those all over Texas, New Mexico, Oklahoma, Arkansas, anywhere J&S wanted to send her.

And still she had wound up back here.

She might as well get this over with.

Letting her foot off the clutch, she shook her head and coasted past the regal house, envying prime parking spots occupied by luxury cars and shiny SUVs.

As guests strolled by, she inspected their clothes, relieved to see her short dress and high-heeled slingbacks would blend right in. The engraved invitation had read *Louisiana casual,* conjuring up an image of shorts and camouflage T-shirts, but this was most assuredly not that kind of crowd.

Her corporate wardrobe, purchased for the job she hoped she hadn't lost for good, should handle Samford perfectly. Jewelry was the only real difference between her attire and that of the women who walked past. Make that *Jewelry* with a capital *J.*

Camille preferred to spend her extra money on art and relied on a single strand of pearls for these events, a gift from her uncle when she had closed her first big deal. But even Uncle Scott's blustery generosity could not temper her irritation at his bullying these past few days.

After two blocks with no hint of a parking spot, Camille eyed the clock on her cell phone and conceded her mistake. Tossing her keys to a valet, even in the ancient pickup, would have been more professional than a tardy hike up to that imposing entrance.

With gritted teeth, she whipped onto a

9

side street.

A dead-end street.

Cars lined both sides, and Camille allowed herself a groan.

In the time it took a moth to flit across the hood of the truck, she considered returning to her hotel room.

But that sort of thinking had gotten her shipped here in the first place. Her goal was closer than the vehicles jamming the boulevard, and she refused to give up now. She could do this.

Identifying the most welcoming home on the block, a Craftsman-style cottage, she pulled into the driveway. The house had a screened porch and an oversized hanging basket exploding with impatiens.

A lone lamp shone from a front window near the porch. A large bright painting hung over the sofa — a primitive watercolor, although the distance and dimness made it tough to tell more.

A gnarled magnolia tree covered in glossy green leaves sat near the driveway. Even after fifteen years, Camille recalled the light and lemony smell of the blooms in summer and was tempted to roll down her window.

Before she could act on the thought, though, a movement caught her eye.

A man knelt to adjust a lawn sprinkler a

few feet from her and turned just as she noticed him.

Muttering a "sorry" he couldn't possibly hear, she gave a quick wave and put the vehicle in reverse. Popping the clutch too quickly, she lurched and killed the engine.

She gave what she hoped was an "I'm not a nut" smile, started the truck, and coasted back a few feet, unsure of her next maneuver.

The vehicle might be a collector's dream, but it had the turning radius of a cement mixer. She couldn't wait for her corporate SUV with its rearview camera, power steering — and frosty AC.

The guy in the yard watched, his eyes hidden by a pair of classic Ray-Ban sunglasses, as Camille rolled back a few more inches, pulled forward, rolled back, and then pulled back up a few feet to reposition the vehicle.

Between her agitation at running late, handling this monstrosity of a vehicle, and the amused stare of the man, Camille felt sweat trickle down her arms. She didn't have to look to know her shift was now wrinkled.

She put the pickup in reverse and sucked in her breath, as though that would help squeeze through the tight space.

"Stop!"

In surprise, she slammed on the brakes, skidding across a patch of carefully tended grass. Her purse slid off the seat, emptying onto the floor. She glanced down to see her lipstick roll out of sight, while the truck moved an inch or two closer to a crape myrtle, its blooms the color of a slice of watermelon.

"Wait! Stop!" the man in the yard yelled again and threw a hand up. He started toward the truck, gesturing for her to lower the window. Camille fumbled for a button to ease it down before realizing she had to use the old-fashioned handle. The stubborn crank brought the glass down about an inch before sticking.

Fooling with the handle, she let off the clutch again, causing the man to take a quick step back when the truck lurched forward. Her face felt flushed.

"Sorry." She turned off the motor. She threw her weight against the heavy door and shoved it open a few inches, breathing as heavily as if she had just run a race.

"No offense," the guy said, ambling closer, "but do you know how to drive that thing?"

His southern voice didn't sound as aggravated as Camille, infused with embarrassment, would have expected.

In his thirties, probably a year or two older

than she was, he wore a baseball cap, cargo shorts, and a T-shirt advertising a New Orleans triathlon. Tanned and trim, he seemed to be holding back a smile.

Camille swatted the steering wheel with the palm of her hand. "What a lousy week!" she blurted — and immediately would have traded her favorite sculpture to have the words back. Glad she couldn't see past his sunglasses, she delivered an apology so convoluted that even she didn't know what she was apologizing for.

"No big deal." He let loose a smile that made his face even more appealing. "This isn't an easy street to navigate. With that fund-raiser around the corner, it's chaotic."

His words — delivered again in that delicious, deep drawl — relaxed the knot in her stomach.

She exhaled an unsteady breath. "I traded my car in . . . This is a company loaner." She tapped on the steering wheel, annoyed anew at the trick Uncle Scott had played. "Me and the White Witch haven't exactly bonded."

He tilted his head, as though puzzled. "That's not your usual corporate vehicle."

"Not your usual corporate assignment," she said, her tone light. "I'm only in town for a few days, and my SUV will be delivered

13

after that."

Knowing she was babbling, she opened her mouth to introduce herself, but before she could speak, he glanced at the sports watch on his tanned wrist.

"I'm sorry. I'm holding you up," she said.

He threw another of those knee-weakening smiles at her but didn't disagree. "If you cut your wheels hard, you'll miss that tree and that line of cars."

Camille turned the key in the ignition and inched back, stopped, inched back more, and looked over at the guy, checking his watch again.

"Why don't you let me . . ." His voice trailed off as he gestured at the street.

Camille, despite another feeling of defeat, nodded.

He offered his hand to help her out of the cab, his touch sending a tingle down her spine. She smoothed her skirt when she got out.

"Nice." He eased into the driver's seat. She thought for a second that the compliment was aimed at her, but then she noticed him rubbing the old leather on the steering wheel. "She's a stunner."

Camille folded her arms across her chest and muttered under her breath, resenting for an instant how easily the man maneuvered the truck.

When he jumped out, he held the door for her. "Don't feel bad about this. I flattened that recycling bin once in my father's pickup." An easy laugh accompanied the words. "My brother will never let me live that one down."

"I owe you." She gave a small salute as she climbed back into the truck. "Thanks for the help."

"Any time."

She turned her head as she drove away and watched him walk into the house. With his killer smile and almost palpable charm, he was the antithesis of the people she was about to encounter. She wished she were spending the evening on his porch.

Camille made the block and approached the party with renewed resolve, feeling like a general headed into battle.

Drawing from her mother's kindness and her uncle's tactics, she'd be out of Samford in a few days, back to her corner office, and shopping for her first house, about a tenth the size of this place.

She smiled when the college-aged valet opened the truck's heavy door, claim check in hand. "Cool. What year is it?"

"Older than you and me."

15

"It's a beauty." His eyes widened as he looked inside. "Three-on-the-tree?" He didn't wait for her answer, hopping into the truck as though it were the Porsche in front of them. "Long-bed too. You don't see many of those anymore. Sweet ride."

"Lucky me," she murmured and then spoke louder. "It's a 1970. Give it a little extra gas to get going."

Watching the blue-and-white Chevy sputter down the hill, Camille headed toward the entrance. *Sweet ride.* She'd have to tell her mother that one.

As she approached the entryway, a large man in a brown sport coat stepped out. A woman who looked like a middle-aged hippie trekked up the hill. A younger, Hispanic man stood at the massive front door, his sleek tux complementing his rugged good looks.

"I'm Camille . . . Camille Gardner." She looked from the handsome guy to the man in the sport coat. "Thank you for hosting me this evening."

The older man swiveled, a half smile on his face. With the look of an over-the-hill college football player, he was one of those men whose age was hard to determine. "The famous Camille Gardner!" He grabbed Camille's hand, jerking her arm up and down as if it were a pump handle.

"I'm Senator Slattery Richmond. Welcome to Louisiana!" His deep, gravelly voice sounded both hoarse and booming at the same time, almost like a barker at a fair.

"Thank you, Senator Richmond." She plastered on her civic-function smile. "I'm here to represent —"

"I know exactly who you are. You're that hotshot trouble-shooter from J&S Production." He looked around and lowered his voice. "It's about time you got here. With our deadline, we need action." More loudly, he said, "Call me Slattery."

Camille ran her hand through her hair, noting the curious stares of those nearby. "Tonight's about raising money for a good cause . . . and thanking Louisiana for all its support." She threw him a pointed look. "There will be plenty of time to talk business in the next few days."

She gazed past him to the hippie woman, who had made it to the top of the hill and looked as out of place as Camille had felt in the stranger's driveway. "I'm Ginny Guidry," the woman blurted out, as though called on in class.

Wearing a flowing skirt that almost touched the sidewalk and a pair of Birkenstocks, she was younger than Camille had

17

first thought, maybe in her early forties. Her brown eyes were framed by classic black horn-rimmed glasses, which added a scholarly look.

Ginny's large mouth, with bold red lipstick, moved into a tentative smile. She dabbed her forehead with a Kleenex as she spoke. "We hoped J&S might send someone tonight . . ."

Her southern drawl trailed off when Slattery stepped closer, nudging her out of the way. "If you'll step inside . . ." He turned and headed up the brick steps.

With Ginny on her heels, Camille fell in behind him, but she stopped midway and held out her hand to the man in the tux, giving him a smile. "I'm Camille Gardner from J&S."

Taking two quick steps down, Slattery, agile for his size, stepped right in front of her. "That's Larry," he said, as though the man were one of the stone lions that flanked the walkway. "If you need anything tonight, let him know."

Uncomfortable, Camille stepped around her host, extending her hand again.

For a brief second, Larry stood rigid, his brown eyes going from Camille to Slattery. Then he shook her hand, his palm calloused. "My pleasure," he said in a voice so

18

deep it felt like it tickled her ear, a trace of a Spanish accent underneath. He threw Ginny Guidry a quizzical look as he spoke.

Ginny laid her hand on Larry's arm for a second as she moved past, her rumpled blouse brushing against the shoulder of his flawless tux.

By now a cluster of guests had stacked up, and Slattery cleared his throat. "If I may?" he said, his tone impatient as he grabbed Camille's arm. The old-fashioned gesture struck her as an effort to corral her, but she forced a smile and stepped into the home.

Slattery steered Camille as though her elbow were a rudder, doing a quick round of introductions to the crowd a few feet inside the Richmonds' door.

Camille said little more than "hello," smiling as she studied the crowd. The Guidry woman had stopped a few feet away, fidgeting with a cocktail napkin from a small mahogany table. She glanced from Camille to Slattery and back to Camille, her expression even more unsure than it had been out front.

Camille, who had spent more than her share of time alone in the midst of a crowd, considered how she could break away to chat with Ginny. When Camille smiled, though, Ginny merely peered at her through the glasses and meandered off, scanning the room as though looking for someone.

Slattery's gaze followed with a frown, and he *harrumphed* under his breath. Then he turned his attention back to Camille.

Their procession through the large foyer, with its marble floor and crystal wall sconces, stalled with the arrival of each new guest, and Camille studied the space as Slattery called out to one person and then another.

What attracted her attention the most was a large landscape painting in the stairwell and a smaller modern piece on the landing above. She tried to step closer for a better look, but Slattery herded her toward a bar in the formal dining room.

"I haven't seen this much excitement over an oil-and-gas deal in decades — and the party . . . what a touch." Slattery beamed. "Leave it to Scott Stephens to come up with something like this."

"Louisiana has been good to J&S," Camille murmured.

"Stephens says you'll do damage control — and make us a lot of money."

Camille cocked her head. She'd pegged Slattery Richmond correctly from those first moments out front. The man wanted something.

This part of the business she would miss. She waited.

"My colleagues down in Baton Rouge are watching a little too closely," he said. "How soon do you expect to drill?"

"That depends on the landowners," she said mildly.

"Those crazy artists can't hold out forever." Slattery punctuated the sentence with a smug smile. "You'll be the perfect person to handle their attorney."

"I understood they didn't intend to retain counsel." She kept her voice steady, although her mind was whirling. The addition of an attorney would likely make the deal harder — but thankfully that part of this mess didn't involve her.

"Someone convinced them they needed a lawyer to get a better deal." Slattery gave a slight shake of his head. "You may get a little trouble out of him."

"Sounds interesting."

The faint vibrating noise of a cell phone interrupted them, but before she could check her purse, Slattery pulled his phone from inside his jacket. He glanced at the screen and back at her.

"Excuse me," he said, grabbing a drink

from the bar as he passed. "I need to take this."

As he walked away, Camille stepped into the living room and forced her attention to the handful of polished guests. Most people threw her openly curious looks, but no one approached. She kept her expression neutral.

The only noise in the room came from a cluster of men in a nearby corner, most in suits and ties. Each held a drink, and a few nibbled on hors d'oeuvres. The group argued loudly about the prospects of a bowl game for the LSU Tigers, with the occasional diatribe against the University of Alabama.

Crown molding and antique furnishings accented the space around them, with original art sprinkled throughout. While Camille didn't covet the diamonds many of the women wore, she would love her choice of the paintings.

"Would you care for a drink?" Larry, she thought his name was, appeared so quietly that she started.

"Maybe later. Thanks."

He studied her for a long moment, his eyes intense, before moving back into the crowd, a tray of full wine glasses in his hands.

As she glanced back into the dining room, Slattery stepped out of a door near an enormous china cabinet, pocketing his phone with a scowl. While greeting guests, he looked past them until he saw her.

He switched on a smile and steamed her way, stopping only long enough to say something to Larry.

"Sorry for abandoning you," Slattery said as he neared. "Stephens wanted to clear up a thing or two."

"Stephens?" Camille hated the wary note in her voice. She hadn't regained her confidence since the misstep two weeks ago.

"That man says you can get ink on a deal better than anyone he ever saw."

"He's full of it."

Slattery let out a loud laugh. "He assures me you'll have this cleared up in a week or less."

She certainly hoped so. Even a few days in Samford, with its painful memories and her uncle's good-old-boy network, would be too long.

She was spared a reply, though, when a burst of laughter erupted from the men across the room. Slattery gripped her elbow and propelled her in their direction. "Here's the person who can get you those Sugar Bowl tickets, fellows," he said as the circle widened to let them in.

Man after man welcomed her, sounding like a chamber-of-commerce roster. Real estate. Ophthalmologist. City official. Each murmured his name and job, going around the circle.

"Camille's a production specialist for J&S," Slattery said, as though he had personally recruited her. "One of the best."

"No land deals tonight." She watched the men inspect her. "J&S just wants to say thanks."

"The good senator sure knows how to get things done," the eye doctor said. "He was plenty hot after that national TV report a couple of weeks back."

Her face grew hot. "That was unfortunate, wasn't it?"

CHAPTER 2

Camille drew a relieved breath when the party's attention shifted away from her, and the circle of men offered good-humored welcomes at the arrival of a handsome newcomer in a suit.

"What are you all so worked up about?" he asked, moving easily into the crowd. His gaze landed on her as he spoke, and his eyes widened.

His suit was tailored. His shoes shone. Camille had a mental image of a valet leaning over and giving the leather one last buff before he stepped into the party. His hair was dark brown, with a hint of curl. His eyes were almost the exact color of the hand-blown cobalt-blue vase sitting on a nearby end table.

His perusal made her heart beat faster and hers confirmed that he was, indeed, the guy from the driveway.

"Be careful of this one, Camille." Slattery

poked the man in the arm as if they were in a high-school locker room. "We're still trying to figure out whose side he's on."

"Now, Senator . . . ," the man said, "if you're not careful, you're going to start sounding like my mother."

The words elicited a quick frown from Slattery. "This lady is Ms. Camille Gardner." Slattery sipped his cocktail. "Isn't she the best-looking landman you've ever seen?"

Camille, agitated at the appearance of the good-looking stranger, tried to hold back a groan at the tired joke and emitted a choked cough. Her eyes watered, and she knew her face was red.

The man gave her a quizzical look before handing her the glass he held. "Rough day?" he asked, his calming smile and enticing voice the only remnant of their earlier encounter.

She fingered the pearls around her neck and took a sip. "You're quite the lifesaver, Mr. . . ."

"Marshall," Slattery blared, as though speaking into a megaphone.

"Mr. Marshall, thank —"

Before she could finish, Slattery chuckled. "Marshall's his *first* name."

"Marsh Cameron," the man said, extending his hand. His grip was solid, a whole-

26

hearted kind of shake. "It's good to see you again."

Slattery's eyes narrowed as he looked from Camille to Marsh. "You two know each other?"

"Not exactly," they said at the same time.

She took another swallow of the club soda. Despite Marsh's starched look, Camille felt as though she had discovered a friend in a sea of strangers.

The daydream had not fully taken shape, though, when the lovely woman from the BMW sashayed their way, Ginny edging nearer at the same time.

With ash-blond hair swept back from her face and curled below her shoulders, the other woman glowed under the chandelier. Her lips were colored deep coral, and her green eyes were open wide. Her posture was perfect.

Wearing heels twice as high as Camille's, she stopped to give "don't-smash-my-outfit" hugs to a trio of women. "Valerie, this gala is *wonderful!*" one woman said, making the last word sound almost like a cheer. Camille tried to recall if she'd ever heard the word *gala* used in a sentence.

"Oh, darling, how gorgeous you look," a society maven with an expensive cashmere suit said. "You are stunning this evening," another called out. "Absolutely stunning."

"The lemming chorus speaks," Ginny muttered under her breath.

Camille was unable to resist staring. Not one inch of the woman's body seemed left to chance. Her hair must have been professionally styled, her nails manicured, her makeup heavy — and, in spite of all of that, she was classically lovely.

The way she carried herself, she could have been on a fashion runway, and she glided into the knot of guests as though working a receiving line.

"How's everyone doing?" Her tone was warm, but her eyes were cool as she looked from Camille to Marsh to Ginny. A light floral scent followed her.

Slattery stepped forward and gave her a peck on the cheek. "Here's my girl. I've hardly seen you tonight."

"Hi, Daddy." She barely acknowledged him before turning her back on Ginny and moving closer to Marsh. "We missed you at the beach," she said in a syrupy voice. "Your mother was so disappointed you didn't make it."

"Hi, Val." Marsh repeated the quick kiss her father had given her. "Duty calls and all that . . ."

"Oh, don't give me that 'I'm too busy'

speech," Valerie said, a hint of a pout on her mouth. Then she smiled and swirled her chiffon skirt. "Your mom helped me pick out this outfit. She knows you've always liked me in orange."

"Very nice," he said.

Camille's morale drooped, although she wasn't sure why. Maybe because Marsh and Miss Louisiana seemed to be in some sort of a relationship.

Wearing the smile of a proud father, Slattery put his hand on Camille's shoulder.

"Camille, meet the woman who keeps me on track — as long as I don't complain about the cost." He gave a hearty laugh, joined by the men nearest him. Marsh's expression was unreadable. "My daughter, Valerie, gets the credit for putting tonight's function together."

"All while working on her tan," Ginny said in a low voice.

Camille bit back a smile at the snarky comment and stepped forward, her hand extended. "Thank you for handling the details." She refrained from mentioning that the fund-raiser had been her idea.

Valerie brushed her fingers against Camille's with the quick flutter of a hummingbird in flight. The gesture came with a restrained *thank you.* "You must be new to

Samford."

She inspected Camille from head to toe, the way one might consider a cow about to be bought — or passed over — at a West Texas auction. "Are you visiting someone?" Valerie looked around the room as though hoping someone might step forward and claim Camille.

Slattery's face was rapidly approaching the color of the glass of red wine he now held, and he took a hurried gulp before he spoke. "Honey, I thought you knew." His volume brought stares from guests around the room. "Camille's our guest of honor."

Valerie flipped her hair back, the blond strands settling into place as she gave a light stamp of her foot. "What are you going on about now, Daddy?"

"Valerie! Camille is Scott Stephens's right-hand man — or person or whatever." He patted the sweat on his forehead with a handkerchief. "J&S sent her in from the Houston headquarters."

"They *transferred* someone in from Houston?" Valerie threw Marsh an injured look. "Were you in on this?"

He gave his head a quick shake, his eyes on Camille.

Valerie put a proprietary hand on his arm. "Of course you weren't. You want to settle this deal as much as we do."

Ginny adjusted her glasses. "My, my. J&S is full of surprises." She ran blue-painted fingernails through her brown hair, as wild as Valerie's was styled. "So you're the one who charms landowners. The people over in Fort Worth told me about you."

Valerie's attention whirled to Ginny. "If you had signed when you should have, we wouldn't be having this conversation." She wore the look of an angry dog straining at its chain. "You and that group of Sweet Olive hillbillies ruined everything."

Camille opened her mouth to respond, but Ginny beat her to it.

"You're wrong, Valerie." Ginny shook her head, her long, curly hair swishing back and forth. Beaded earrings reached nearly to her shoulders and bounced with the movement of her head. "It's J&S who will ruin everything."

"Ladies," Marsh jumped in. "You don't want to do this." His lips were set in a grim line.

Valerie cast a bold, hostile look around the room. Her gaze stopped before it reached Camille.

"Sorry, Marsh." Ginny fidgeted with a wide plastic bracelet. "The artists will have plenty of opportunities to talk about this."

31

"You can only drag your heels so long," Valerie snarled, the leash on her temper apparently having snapped.

"J&S isn't the only company interested in us." Ginny narrowed her eyes.

"Val, Ginny." Marsh's tone grew ominous.

Guests across the room stared, their eyes wide. Slattery looked like a man trying to guide in two planes at the same time, signaling for Larry to refill glasses and gesturing maniacally for the guests to move closer. "Come on over, folks, and we'll do this right."

At his words, the low hum of conversation grew into louder chatter, and the space became crowded.

"Daddy . . ." Valerie said.

Slattery held his hand up. "Be patient." The smell of his cologne was strong as he moved his hand to Camille's shoulder.

Ginny drummed her fingers on the back of a chair and leaned forward. Valerie assumed a smile that looked like she had just had dental surgery and couldn't operate her lips properly. Marsh had the look one might acquire upon stepping in dog poop.

Camille, now jammed in the middle of the crowd, tried to step forward but didn't make it a foot or two before Slattery spoke again. "Good, good," he muttered. "As you all know, J&S Production Company is making a sizable donation to the Samford Foundation this evening, to be used for many of your projects."

Restrained applause rippled through the room.

"The check is being delivered personally by Camille Gardner." Slattery looked expectantly at Camille, who was having a hard time getting past the anger in Marsh's gaze.

As the silence grew, she drew a breath. "Thank you, all. I can assure you J&S plans to do lots of business here." She met Marsh's eyes. "But tonight is about giving back to the community." She handed the J&S corporate check, fished earlier from her designer handbag, to Slattery. "May this help make North Louisiana a better place to call home."

She had scarcely finished speaking when guests surged forward to thank her before breaking off into small groups of animated conversation. Within a few minutes, she found herself wedged against Marsh.

"I didn't realize we'd be working this closely together," she said.

Marsh, a good six inches taller than Camille, probably close to six-three or -four, looked down at her with a hard stare. "So that's why you showed up at my house today."

"What?" Camille tilted her head in confusion.

"You're the ace who courts the landowners."

"No. I mean, yes, I put together land deals, but I'm here to help Sweet Olive understand why —"

"The old truck," he interrupted and snapped his fingers. "That's your 'deal mobile.' To think I nearly fell for it." Disdain marred his features. "J&S is up to its same old tricks."

"That's not the way I operate." She planted her high-heeled shoes firmly in front of his wingtips. "But if I want to drive a tractor, I don't see that it's your business."

His blue eyes locked on hers. The smile Camille had found so charming a few minutes earlier looked smug.

"Well, Ms. Star Landman, you clearly didn't do your homework. I'm the attorney for the Sweet Olive landowners." Marsh paused. "We intend to fight J&S every step of the way."

CHAPTER 3

If it weren't so late — and if the stupid pickup wasn't prone to overheating — Camille would leave Louisiana tonight. She could be in Houston in five hours or in Amarillo by daylight, having breakfast with her mother.

Camille rolled down the Richmond driveway with a prickle of anxiety and attempted to appreciate the big oaks arching over the street. Shifting gears, she turned down a neighborhood boulevard.

Her recollections of Samford were of an older, more rundown place, but tonight it looked like a bayou village. Spanish moss draped from a few trees. Lights shone from inside lovely old homes. She especially liked the screened porches, a feature seldom seen on Houston homes.

But the charm did not lessen her urge to get back to Texas, and she was beyond peeved that Scott hadn't returned her three calls, each placed surreptitiously from the bathroom at the Richmond house.

A wave of homesickness hit Camille, sweeping from head to heart.

She didn't even know what she was homesick for.

Her mother's brick house in Amarillo, where she'd seldom lived? The familiar, if sterile, corporate efficiency in Houston? Mostly she yearned for a home of her own, filled with art, a spot where she would finally put down roots.

She blamed the sentimentality on being back in Samford and pulled to the curb and dialed.

"How's my girl?" her mother's soft voice asked.

Camille paused. "I'm in Louisiana."

"Oh my. North or south?"

"In Samford." Her heart gave an extra beat. "The trip came up at the last minute."

"Are you okay?"

"I'm good, Mama."

Her mother cleared her throat. "Does Samford look the way it used to?"

"More or less. I drove in from Houston and didn't have much time to look around."

"Have you been over to Trumpet and Vine?"

Camille snorted. "No, and I don't intend to."

The line grew silent for one moment, then two.

"I know it can't be easy on you. I wish you were here so I could take care of you." Her mother's voice trembled. "I'm so sorry, sweetie, that I let you down that day."

They had not spoken of this in years, and Camille's stomach fluttered. "It was a bad day, but you didn't let me down. You never have."

"You're my best girl."

"You'd better stock up on the good groceries, Mama, because I'm visiting as soon as I wrap this up."

"And you're sure you're okay?"

"I will be if you make chicken and dumplings and buy ice cream for the cobbler."

Her mother gave a small laugh. "It'll be waiting for you . . . but why are you in Samford?"

"We hit a snag, so Scott decided I was needed to clear up a few things. It shouldn't take long."

"Hmm . . . I know you're disappointed, honey."

"It's not so bad." Camille hoped she was telling the truth. "Scott says I'll learn a lot about dealing with the executive side of things on this assignment."

"I don't like you gallivanting all over the country by yourself."

"You fret too much."

"You never let me take care of you."

"Give it up, Mama." Camille chuckled, comfortable with this familiar nagging. "I'm the most careful thirty-year-old in the world."

"Did they work out that bug in your fancy company car?"

"It should be ready by the time I get back to Houston."

"I wish you'd fly. It's much safer than driving. You could spend some of that money you keep sending me —"

"Mama," Camille said, drawing the word out. "Once I'm settled at headquarters, I'll travel less." She infused her words with cheerfulness. If Camille sounded happier, her mother was happier — and Camille never wanted anything to hurt her again.

"Scott called today. He was traveling and had time to kill."

Her mother's words landed in Camille's brain with a thud. "What did he say?"

"He bragged about you and said he'd rather have you out in the field. I told him you'd earned a chance to settle down . . . He'll come around."

Camille watched a light go out in a house down the street. "Did he happen to mention where he was?"

"Not that I recall. He did say he was headed out of the country."

"Off the continent would be better. I need as much distance as possible until I get settled in Houston."

Her mother was quiet, and Camille rubbed her neck. "Am I doing the right thing, Mama?"

"What do you think?"

"I'm afraid that if I don't do it now, I never will."

"Maybe that's your answer."

"But I've always done what Uncle Scott expected . . ." Camille tried to put the words together. "He's been so good to us."

"Once he sees how good you are at headquarters, he'll take credit for the idea." Her mother laughed. "My brother may be stubborn, but he's not dumb."

"I haven't ever worked the desk side of things. What if it doesn't work out?"

"Change is tough," her mother said softly.

"Is that supposed to reassure me?" Camille added a little laugh to take the edge off her words.

"You're my smart, creative girl. Trust God, and do good. It'll work out."

"It's not that simple."

"It can be."

"You need to get to bed, Mama." Camille held back a sigh. "And I need to track down Uncle Scott."

Clicking off the phone, Camille leaned against the door and surveyed the street, dreading the conversation ahead.

Everything she had seen that night made her new life seem further away.

Even the stars, shining through the old trees, reminded her of a painting she had on hold at her favorite art gallery.

Once more Camille's frustration with her uncle flared. During the past few years, her rare vacation days had been split between her mother's house and the gallery, where she volunteered as much as possible. Her new corporate job would allow time to attend Allison's art classes and help with openings — plus, she would build her personal collection. The idea brought a sense of excitement long lacking.

The gallery owner, Allison Carney, had been a graduate student when Camille was at SMU and had pursued her art dream while Camille paid her family debt.

Allison was holding her latest purchase since Camille had offered to run Allison's new community program in the spare time she was so hungry for. "I'll display it until you find a house," Allison had said. "But I don't want to hold it too long."

Camille had fallen in love with the oil painting, a landscape of a marshy coast with offbeat colors. Allison had come across this latest artist on a buying trip to Miami and predicted he'd be famous one day.

"I knew you'd like his work," Allison said. "You always go for the primitive stuff." She prided herself on snapping up inexpensive artwork and "building art careers."

"It's charming." Camille put her hands on her hips, her khaki slacks and oversized shirt a contrast to Allison's standard black dress.

Allison put on a pair of half-glasses from the counter and studied the piece. "I never cared for amateur clichés." She sighed and removed the glasses. "But a handful of my customers want primitives, so I keep an eye out for them."

Camille couldn't hold back a grin. "Not everyone grew up in Highland Park and spent summers in Beaver Creek. These artists show life from a different angle."

"Now that you're going to be around the gallery more, you'll grow to appreciate the new classics. They're the future of art."

"I like it all." Camille drank in the array

41

of paintings, placed where the lighting was perfect and the variety enticing. Her eclectic taste was a mystery to her, but it enriched her life in a way few things did. A blessing, her mother called it. A gift for art, her father had said before he left them.

Art was permanent and lovely, what Camille longed for. What her life thus far had lacked.

She had scrimped and saved from high school on to buy pieces from flea markets, art fairs, and the occasional gallery.

With the corporate position, she could retrieve her collection from her mother's house and hang it in carefully chosen spots in the home she planned to buy within a matter of weeks. She had narrowed her search via the Internet, during long, lonely nights on the road, and knew the cozy cottage she wanted.

Before she had unpacked the boxes in her new office, she'd signed up for Allison's weekly art lectures and started planning the new community program, something Camille had longed to do since college.

The news that she would have to leave after working only two Saturdays and one reception didn't please Allison. "I thought you were committed to this," she had said, her sleek black hair not moving as she shook her head. "I suppose I'll have to go to my Friends of the Gallery list."

"I'll only be gone a couple of weeks. I have one more deal, and my promotion will be sealed."

"You've had 'one more deal' since college." Allison picked up an empty frame. "You have a little gypsy in you, don't you?"

"Absolutely not." Camille snatched the frame from her hand and placed a watercolor in it as if putting a baby to bed. "I just need to wrap up this Louisiana job." She fiddled with the print for a moment before looking up. "Is this right?"

Allison adjusted the print by a fraction of an inch, her pink nails tapping against the ebony frame. "I held off on the new docent program because you said you would be available in the fall. I've set things in motion, and I need someone to run it."

"Just give me a couple of weeks, and I'll be around here so much you'll get sick of me."

From the Samford street, Camille closed her eyes and thought of the new painting. She imagined herself following the narrow dirt road through a stand of thick fir trees, coming out on the marshy coast.

The image eased her tension. She would

43

not let this job keep her from her dreams again.

She pulled out her phone and did an Internet search for Marshall Cameron, attorney-at-law.

CHAPTER 4

The fluorescent lights of the hotel lobby were harsh after the dimness of the parking lot, and Camille halted inside the heavy wooden door so her eyes could adjust.

She'd spent so many nights in homogenized places like this that she could have navigated to her room with her eyes closed. Breakfast area on the right. Desk clerk on the left. Seating area straight ahead with the ubiquitous businessman on a computer.

Her eyes widened as she got a better look at the businessman. "Uncle Scott!" The young woman behind the desk jumped at Camille's exclamation. "What are you doing here?"

Wearing his uniform of wrinkled khakis and a knit shirt, her uncle set his laptop aside and stood.

Scott Stephens looked more like a middle-aged door-to-door salesman than the head of a flourishing oil-and-gas company. His once-blond hair had turned into a mix of gray and brown, and his face was leathery from years of outdoor labor. Short and muscular, he exuded a cocky confidence that some people labeled arrogant.

"Camy! I was beginning to think you had decided to stay out all night."

She stood just past the registration counter, unable to make herself step forward. For a split second, her mind was filled with unwanted images of the last time he had met her in Samford.

She shook her head, desperate to dislodge the picture.

"That party you sent me to was like a horror movie," she said after a moment. "Senator Slattery Richmond's a cross between Boss Hogg and Napoleon."

Scott gave a bark of laughter. "That's exactly the way I remember him."

She stared at him without blinking, a technique he had taught her. "What are you up to?"

"Not even a hug for the old guy before we talk business?" Scott, favoring his bum knee, lowered himself into a chair.

Camille strode over to the sofa but didn't sit.

"You look nice," Scott said. "High heels and everything."

She crossed her arms. "This is part of my new *corporate* wardrobe."

"I prefer you in jeans and boots, with a little less attitude. Maybe you're not cut out for an office job."

"I messed up. Message received, loud and clear." She sank onto the couch. "I make one mistake, and you kick me to Samford."

"That interview made us look like a bunch of weak tree-huggers."

She bristled. "It made us look like we have a heart. People care about the environment. If you want the Louisiana leases, J&S has to show it's not like Bienville Oil."

He didn't reply, popping his knuckles, one by one. He twisted each of his wrists for an added pop.

She ran her fingers through her hair. "Did you know they've hired a lawyer?"

"The Cameron fellow, right?" Scott's eyes narrowed. "We've not dealt with him before. What's he like?"

"Charming. Handsome. Confusing."

"I'm not trying to get a date with him," he snapped. "What kind of negotiator will he be?"

"Ambitious," she admitted. "Determined. He's tight with the Samford movers and shakers, works for an elite firm based in Baton Rouge." She tried to reconcile the friendly guy in shorts with the lawyer at the party. "His name has come up as a potential candidate for a state commission. He doesn't strike me as the kind of lawyer to take a little case."

"That bothers me."

"I don't get it either. We know the Sweet Olive land is only a small piece of the Samford field. Even if he gets top dollar for them, he won't make much."

"Maybe he thinks he'll get on national TV."

She glanced down at the floor, moving the toe of her shoe on the floral carpet. "With any luck, there won't be any more publicity. I'm going to sit at my desk, keep my mouth shut, and make sure all of our leases are in order."

Instead of responding with one of his usual smart-aleck comebacks, Scott rose and walked to a tray of cookies on a fake-marble counter. He picked one up and broke it in half, standing over her as he chewed. "You've dealt with his kind a dozen times."

"And hated every one of them. I like working with good-natured landowners who know I'll treat them right."

Scott chuckled. "They never expect some-one as sweet as you to strike a hard bargain."

He popped his knuckles again, the sound reverberating through Camille's nerves, and glanced at a manila envelope on the top of his briefcase.

Her heart jumped into her throat. "No. Nope. No way. N.O."

"Camy," Scott said in the cajoling tone he used on no one else. "It's more complicated than expected."

"No. I'm the new executive-in-training, remember? You gave your word."

"This won't take long. We have a nice office here, and you'll be through in a few weeks."

"Weeks!" she exclaimed, earning a chiding look from the desk clerk.

"In this economy, Sweet Olive's crucial." Scott's lowered voice sounded like he was quieting his favorite mare at his West Texas ranch. "I have everything you need right here." He patted the familiar, oversized envelope. "It's only a dozen, maybe fifteen tracts."

"I was sent here for a dog and pony show. A fund-raiser, a luncheon or two, buttering people up so you could close the deal. You're much better at these tricky ones."

"I can't stay in Louisiana. I'm just making a quick stop on my way to Calgary."

"A quick stop in Louisiana. On your way

to Canada."

"You're the person I count on."

She gasped. "The pickup. That's why the garage gave me the old truck. You planned this all along." She practically spit the words out. "You told Slattery I'm in charge of this deal, didn't you?"

"I might have mentioned it. I can't recall."

"You haven't forgotten an oil deal since you were in college." She swallowed. "Please don't ask me to do this. I screwed up by talking to that television reporter, but I'll become the best VP in the history of oil and gas."

"You're thirty years old! You have years to sit in an office."

"I'm tired of living out of a suitcase. I'm tired of arguing with lawyers and trying to make men like Slattery Richmond happy." She closed her eyes, knowing they were heading into a familiar argument. "I've been on the road for seven years. I want a normal life."

"*Boring*'s more like it. You're worse than my sister. I can hire anyone to handle a desk job, but you have a special touch with the deals. They're in your blood."

She plastered on the expression that had made the company so much money. "If you push me, I'll leave J&S."

Scott's eyes widened, but then he gave a sheepish smile. "You had me there for a minute . . . You're good."

Camille gave her head a quick shake. "I'm not bluffing this time."

"Don't be ridiculous." He plopped back into the chair. "I know you don't like Louisiana, but I'll make it worth your while. A few weeks, Camy. Is that asking too much?"

"You've promised me a Houston job every year since college. I don't love this like you want me to."

Scott made a sound almost like a growl. "You owe me."

"I know." She recited the litany for the thousandth time in the past few years. "You've given me one opportunity after another. You've been there for me every step of the way. You rescued me from a dump at a street corner, kept Mama and me from being homeless."

"Surely that's reason enough to —"

"Not Samford." She squeezed her eyes shut.

"Your father would be ashamed of you."

Her head jerked, bouncing off the back of the couch.

"He may have had his weaknesses, but he did everything I ever asked of him." Scott faltered for a split second. "He cared about this company."

"As my uncle, you should understand. I want to buy a house, make friends."

"You're talking about that craft store, aren't you? You'd throw away everything we've built for *art.*" He snarled the word.

"I'm not throwing J&S away. And it's an art gallery — one of the finest in the South-west. I want to own a gallery one day. You know that."

"Of course I know. I'm the one who paid for that art degree."

"*After* I finished the geology program."

"Which I also paid for."

"I know you paid for my college. I know you rescued us when Daddy abandoned us. I know you bought Mama that house. I know. I know. I know." She paused for a breath. "But I've paid back my obligations."

"Come on, Camy." Scott switched to a softer tone. "A handful of rinky-dink landowners are making us look bad. At least take care of Sweet Olive."

"J&S has more than enough wells."

"There are never enough wells. You're going soft on me."

"In the past seven years, I've closed some of J&S's biggest deals. I'm done."

"I need Sweet Olive." He clenched his teeth.

"Bypass Sweet Olive. Cut the landowners off. Drill on a neighbor's land. Make them wish they'd signed."

He was shaking his head before she finished the sentence. "We need their water and locations for the well pads. Without those, we'll lose millions. We've got a use-it-or-lose-it lease down here, and I need to stay in Slattery's good graces."

She held up her hand. "Don't tell me this is another of your questionable deals."

"That's another good reason for you to stay. You can make sure things are done on the up-and-up. And you can throw around J&S money, host parties, sponsor those worthy causes you love. You can make us look good, even explore some of that environmental mumbo jumbo."

"I can help from Houston," she conceded. "I'll do computer research and develop an exit strategy for Sweet Olive. We can spin it."

"How are we going to *spin* a roadblock that costs us millions?"

" 'J&S Bows Out in Deference to Landowners and Environment.' Think of the headline. We'll be heroes, instead of corporate thugs." Her voice rose with each word.

"I won't *bow out,* as you so poetically put it. I intend to drill there. I need you — my best — to buzz in and get the mineral leases and surface agreements."

"Why not a local person?"

"She botched it by trying to push the landowners around."

"Imagine that," Camille murmured.

"The news coverage made it worse."

"I was trying to improve our image," she said. "I made a bad situation worse and I'm being punished. So fire me."

"This isn't punishment. This is the perfect deal for you."

"You've said that about the last ten deals I've handled."

"This one's different. You'll deal with a small group of cranky artists who think we're ruining their *heritage.* Your kind of people."

Camille tried not to show her interest.

"Once you do this, you can waste your skills in an office and play at that craft store for as long as you want." Scott patted his heart. "Do this one for the family. Call on a few little old ladies. Sign them by the end of September. Think how much fun you'll have tearing that attorney apart."

Even through her irritation, she felt herself wavering.

"I'll match the bonus from the Fort Worth and Muskogee jobs."

She stood. "If I do it — and I'm not saying I will — my bonus will be double what it was last time. And if that truck breaks down, you'll owe me triple."

Scott pushed himself out of the chair, a satisfied smile on his face. "My office has taken care of all the details. That truck's going to make us a lot of money."

Camille grimaced, Marsh's words in her mind.

"I'll expect you down here at eight tomorrow to develop our strategy." He stepped into the elevator and turned to face her. "I knew you wouldn't let me down, Camy."

She watched him disappear as the door closed.

For fifteen years, she had done everything he asked.

CHAPTER 5

Camille plugged an address from the note card into her GPS and waited for Miss Priss, the annoying mechanical voice, to direct her.

Her qualms at venturing out into Sweet Olive on a Sunday afternoon were overridden by the fear of her calendar. She didn't have a day to waste.

Scott had vanished before their morning meeting, texting her that he needed to take care of a problem at the home office before heading to Canada. He left the J&S envelope with detailed instructions at the front desk.

Camille considered tossing it in the trash but ripped it open and, over a free continental breakfast, immersed herself in maps, contracts, and notes, some in her uncle's handwriting.

As much as she hated to admit it, this job appealed to her.

The few holdouts couldn't be that hard to

work with, and she might work in time to explore the regional art — likely the cutout wooden hearts stuff sold at craft shows, though. The bonus money would supplement her mother's income and help Camille make the down payment on the house.

She scrutinized the GPS, surprised to see her destination was closer than she remembered. Sweet Olive was only fifteen miles up Vine Avenue, just beyond the city limits of Samford. The drive took her north on Vine, past the street where the party had been, and through a small shopping area with a handful of restaurants and boutiques.

When Vine veered, Camille double-checked her directions and was relieved to head the opposite way. She'd prefer not to explore to the left.

The houses grew progressively bigger, separated from the road by a fancy wrought-iron fence. A massive gate, with brick columns, had the words *Cotton Grove* spelled out in metal, with a keypad for entry.

Just beyond that, the road narrowed.

Staring at a new gas well, Camille took a sharp curve a little too quickly, nearly sending the truck into a field of brown stems. Dust from the shoulder stirred.

A tiny road in the middle of a cotton field led to a giant tower that looked like an industrial Christmas tree. A line of white pickups and tanker trucks clustered around it, resembling wasps buzzing around a nest.

From her notes, she thought that would be well number 291903, a Bienville Oil site. She was in the right vicinity — and the old truck fit right in.

Across the two-lane highway, showing signs of wear from the equipment, concrete had been poured for another pad. J&S had held the lease on this parcel for decades, and the discovery of the Cypress shale field provided, as Scott had said, the much needed opportunity to drill. This, one of their first new wells in Louisiana, would be a model of the wells Scott wanted in Sweet Olive.

A dirt-moving machine groomed the red Louisiana clay where trees had been removed. A dump truck beeped in reverse, accompanied by the loud banging noise of another piece of heavy machinery. A pile of branches and what looked like pieces of an old house smoldered in a heap. A collection of men in hard hats roamed around.

A fleet of J&S pickups, with the familiar red logo, congregated on the edge of the site. "Those are your grandchildren," she said grudgingly, tapping on the dashboard of the truck.

A sign reading "Water for Sale" had been tacked to a tree near the rutted road, and beyond that someone had placed another sign that said "Water NOT for Sale."

She checked the GPS again and took a right turn onto a two-lane gravel road.

Two ponds flanked the intersection, their water levels low. A small herd of horses grazed in the pasture to the left, but the grass was stubby. An old barn, listing slightly, sat on the edge of the field. With its weathered boards and rusted tin roof, it fit into the countryside as though it had grown there.

A primitive hand-lettered sign was attached to a split-rail fence. "Welcome to Sweet Olive, Where Living Is an Art." *Corny but sweet.* Her neck tensed.

Speeding up, she had no trouble locating the address she was looking for. The numbers were painted in baby blue on a mailbox decorated with an assortment of pink and tangerine butterflies.

The house was equally colorful, if somewhat worn, stuck in the middle of a yard so big it looked like a field. Painted lime green with orange shutters, it looked like it belonged in an amusement park instead of on a dusty Louisiana back road. A beat-up minivan sat under the carport.

J&S scouts had characterized the Procells as "flakes," but they certainly weren't the retiring type. What must the neighbors think of the bright decor?

A few acres away, she saw a small, white church, its steeple outlined against the sky. Next came an electric blue house . . . and a purple house? She couldn't make out the objects in their yards, but something hung on the trees, and the sun created an almost hypnotic glow.

Her attention down the road ended, however, when her eyes fell on an army of massive metal whirligigs, lined up on poles in the Procells' side yard like colorful sentinels, intricate figures perched on top. The sight produced the giddy, breathless feeling Camille got when she saw a piece of appealing art. She pulled into the driveway, her gaze running around the yard.

A wide, uneven porch sat across the front of the house, and a rusty tin roof matched that on the barn at the turn. Whatever grass might have grown in the yard had given way to dirt. A birdbath sat to the side, and spindly petunias filled an iron kettle.

Picking up a file folder, Camille jumped out of the truck and slammed the door, hoping the noise would summon someone from the house.

A barking dog rounded the corner and stopped to sniff the truck tire before lying down in a wallowed-out spot under a willow tree. She hoped the homeowner would be as easy to deal with.

Throwing her head back, Camille looked up at the figures. At least a half-dozen scenes swirled slowly around, like elaborate weather vanes. Some had a span of six feet or more, while others were only a couple of feet across. Enamel paint, in all colors, shone as sunlight hit.

A farmer and a herd of cows gathered at a red barn in the scene nearest her, and Camille clutched the pole to steady herself and study the details. A chicken pecked and a bucket moved with the hint of a breeze.

As she admired the craftsmanship, a whiff of a light, sweet scent teased her nose. Unlike anything Camille had ever smelled, the faint fragrance was an odd, delicate blend. She inhaled, and an unexpected feeling of calm settled on her.

She remembered her mother's words last night about trusting God and whispered a quiet "thank you." She would work on that trust thing when she was settled in Houston. She had never moved her church membership from her mother's church in Amarillo where it had rested all these years.

Tempted to linger, entranced by the scent and the fascinating figures, she thumped the file folder and made herself march to the porch, where the delicate smell intensified.

Camille smoothed her black slacks and adjusted her black-checked blouse. The dress code for calling on landowners was tricky. Too dressy, she was tagged a snob. Too casual, she didn't show proper respect. She frowned at her feet. The pumps not only pinched but looked as out of place as an oil well in a playground.

Camille reached for the doorbell, but electrical tape had been put over the spot. A small, smeared note said "Use Bell" with an arrow pointing down. A metal cowbell lay on the porch rail. Tentatively, she picked it up and rang it, producing a clacking noise.

When no one answered, she shook it again and finally knocked on the aluminum storm door, drawing a halfhearted bark from the dog. Voices and laughter came from inside, and she opened the outer door, trying to peek through a trio of small windows without being obvious.

A woman with long curly hair looked over the shoulder of a child painting at an easel. While Camille watched, the woman bent to listen to something the young artist said.

The child laughed.

The moment was so personal that Camille stepped back, letting the storm door swing shut. She hesitated and stepped off the porch, moving toward her truck.

"Hello?" a southern voice called, more in question than greeting.

Turning, she saw Ginny Guidry standing with the door ajar. Ginny had looked like a hippie last night and was downright country today, except for her bright red lipstick. She wore denim overalls, and her brown hair sprang from her head in a disheveled heap. Her eyes, behind the black frames, didn't look welcoming.

"I should have known you'd show up first thing," she said.

Taking a step back at the hostile tone, Camille held up the folder in her hand. "I didn't realize you lived out this way."

"Right."

Camille moved back another step. "Maybe you can help me. I'm looking for Todd Procell. J&S must have the address wrong."

"You won't find Todd here, that's for sure."

"Do you happen to know where I can find him?"

Ginny nodded and gestured down the road. "He's buried about a half mile from here. In the Fellowship Cemetery."

"I don't understand."

"He was killed six months ago in a car wreck on his way home from work."

"How horrible," Camille murmured. "Was he a friend of yours?"

"My brother. His house is right there." She pointed to another small house, this one green, half hidden behind the carport. "This is our family land."

"I'm so sorry . . ." Camille looked at the ground, unsure what to say. "I know how hard it is to lose someone like that."

Ginny focused on Camille's face and shook her head. "I doubt it."

Camille's eyes widened.

"You come out here all dressed up, wanting to sweet talk me into signing over our land." Ginny made a dismissive snort. "I've got a sister-in-law who's gone off the deep end, a niece and nephew who don't understand why their daddy died, a mountain of paperwork, a dead brother, and a dead husband."

She stopped for a breath. "As soon as I heard who you were last night, I knew you'd come calling. I'm handling the estate." Ginny gestured at the yard. "Although only a lawyer would call this an estate."

When she ran her hands through her hair,

it looked even more like a pot-and-pan scrubber. "Todd worked for J&S, and they're fighting us every step of the way on his benefits." She paused. "But I don't have to tell you that."

"This is the first I've heard of this," Camille said quietly.

Ginny rolled her eyes.

"I was looking for the Procells." Camille tried to disguise her defensiveness.

"I'm Ginny Procell Guidry. Art teacher and accidental community activist."

"That's why you were at the party." The pieces were beginning to make sense.

Ginny made a noise that stopped short of being a laugh. "That's not exactly the crowd I usually run with."

"They did have nice art," Camille said.

The wild hair flopped as Ginny surrendered a small smile.

"As do you." Camille waved at the whirligigs. "These are spectacular."

After walking over to a scene of a cat chasing a dog, Ginny touched the pole lightly. "I like everyday scenes."

"Me too. Who's the artist?"

"I am."

"You designed these?" Camille's mouth fell open. "They're fantastic." She moved to the pole where Ginny's hand still rested.

"The details are simple but powerful —"
She stopped. "Sorry. I can get carried away
when it comes to art."

Ginny gave her a curious look.

"You're a folk artist." Camille couldn't
keep the awe out of her voice.

"That's a highfalutin term. I play with
metal. People put them in their yards to see
how the wind's blowing."

They watched in silence as the wind
picked up and the figures whirred.

"It's like an unseen hand put them in motion," Camille whispered, her gaze going
back to Ginny.

Ginny nodded, a trace of a smile on her
red lips. "My grandpa — the one who first
made these in our family — said God's
Spirit moves through us in that same way."
She spoke slowly, as though remembering
her grandfather when he'd first pointed it
out. "That Spirit stirs us."

"My mother would like that." Camille
tilted her head back for a better view. The
artwork made a humming noise, building
speed as the wind picked up. With each
piece in motion, they resembled a charming
ballet.

"I've never seen anything like this." Camille shielded her eyes for a closer look. "Is
that tin?"

"All of that metal comes from a junkyard." Ginny chuckled lightly. "They cost next to nothing to make."

"How do you keep the pieces from bumping into each other?"

"Each object has its place. If the pieces are in the right place, they do what they're meant to do — chop, run, swim, whatever."

"They never collide?"

Laughing softly, Ginny shook her head. "Not if they're where they're supposed to be."

"That looks tricky."

Ginny looked up at a scene of a fish swimming, a wave moving simultaneously. "I've had lots of practice. Grandpa taught Daddy. Daddy taught me. Grandpa called them windmills. Most folks call them whirligigs nowadays."

"But how do you put them together?"

"The way I do everything — trial and error." Ginny's expression was a blend of sadness and humor.

Camille touched the pole closest to her. "I love art, but I didn't inherit an ounce of talent."

"Everyone's got talent. The good Lord created us to be creative."

Camille gave an uneasy laugh.

"Everyone's supposed to create something." Ginny tapped the iron pole with her index finger, her blue nail polish chipped.

"I'd love to buy a piece."

Ginny's momentary goodwill vanished, and she eyed Camille suspiciously. "Nice try. Oil companies act like they can throw money at us and we'll jump up and down with joy."

Camille took a step backward. "Your work's unusual. I really would love to own a piece."

"If you say so."

"You think I'm lying?"

Ginny's face tightened. "We've been lied to more times than I can count."

"About your mineral rights?"

"Yep — the real reason you came out here today."

"That's true," Camille said quietly. "But I didn't know this was your house."

Ginny squeezed her eyes shut for a second. "You might as well come in." Her voice was heavy with what sounded like dread.

Chapter 6

Marsh started his vintage MGB convertible in the parking garage, appreciating the hum of the engine for a moment before he cranked up the classic rock and roll. Maybe the clash of loud guitars could blast him out of the confusion that had settled over him last night.

He had slipped out soon after Camille left, the party flat with the same people telling the same stories and his guts churning at finding out who Camille was. For those few minutes in his driveway, he had felt a spark long missing in his life.

Then Slattery's gut-punch announcement came.

Gossip about Camille had zoomed around church that morning with a flurry of opinions on why she had come to town. He hadn't needed the sly looks to know his job had gotten more difficult.

"Well, if it isn't my favorite attorney," a

familiar voice said over the music. Marsh put the car back in Park and turned off the radio. He glanced at his watch, then unraveled his tall body from the car.

Leaning in for a hug, Val gave him a broad smile. Her straight, white teeth so close to his face brought to mind the day she'd gotten her braces off. He'd kissed her that day, a mistake that led to years of disastrous on-again/off-again dating and his mother's relentless hope, even now, that he and Valerie would marry.

"You got away in a hurry last night," she said. "Your mother was disappointed."

The sentence wasn't worded like a question, but Marsh could tell Val was waiting for an explanation. A familiar pout appeared when he didn't reply.

"You know we always have an after party with our close friends." She moved nearer as she spoke the word *close.* "I missed you."

"It was quite the shindig."

"I wouldn't go that far." Valerie straightened his collar. "Did you really not know J&S was springing some awkward cowgirl on us?"

Marsh shook his head. Camille Gardner, with her pixie haircut and sparkling amber-colored eyes, was about as far from an awkward cowgirl as he could imagine. She exuded spunk, moving through the crowd with an intriguing warmth. "You, of all people, know I'm not on the J&S grapevine. I was as surprised as you."

"I doubt that."

"Camille seems nice enough." Or at least she had when she'd wrestled with that Chevy pickup in his driveway. "Your father was pleased to see her."

Valerie's mouth curled. "Daddy's all excited because she's supposedly the best of the best and that kind of rot."

"I look forward to the challenge." He rubbed his hands together and added a teasing grin.

"She doesn't belong here any more than you belong on that Sweet Olive case."

Valerie might be right. Despite his best intentions, he had let himself become entangled in the Sweet Olive drama. He tried to shake the case, citing everything from an overloaded calendar to a potential family conflict of interest.

Ruthless litigator or not, he had lost every argument — in part because of paternal arm-twisting and in part because in his heart he believed in them.

The artists had latched on to his time within hours of his acceptance, marching up to his office like a ragtag band to say

71

there was no one they'd rather have on their side. Their compliments were liberally laced with outlandish notions about how to fight big oil and fervent notions about not taking oil-and-gas money.

Marsh glanced at his watch again, agitated. "Are you hanging around the parking garage for a reason?" He threw in one of the smiles that usually soothed Val's nerves.

"Picking up a couple of files for Daddy." She didn't meet his eyes. "How about you?"

"Playing catch-up for a few minutes before lunch."

"I hope you've got some paying customers. You're getting the shaft on Sweet Olive." She made a noise that sounded feminine and condescending at the same time. "How soon can you drop it?"

"You know I don't talk about my cases. Especially this one. Especially to you."

"You're not going to make a dime off of this. The consensus after the party was that Sweet Olive doesn't have a clue how to handle J&S or Bienville Oil."

"Thanks for the feedback."

"I wish you'd reconsider Daddy's offer." Valerie reached toward him for another hug, and he leaned in and patted her arm. The interaction resembled an awkward move at a school dance from their junior high days.

"You'd make an excellent partner."

He watched as she glided toward the street. Valerie was a beautiful woman with her long hair and shapely figure. She looked like the southern royalty she was. She turned and spoke in a voice that echoed through the garage.

"Let me know if you find out anything interesting about Ms. Camille Gardner."

Everything about Camille interested him — her surprise appearance in Samford, her oil-and-gas know-how, that old Chevy, just like the one his father drove, and the way her eyes sparkled when she talked.

He turned up an Eric Clapton song and headed for lunch, readying himself for more questions.

Marsh had promised to stop by his mother and stepfather's house for a late lunch, but office voice mail and his encounter with Valerie knocked his appetite down a notch. One of his biggest clients already needed placating over his Sweet Olive work, and his e-mail inbox overflowed with work that demanded attention.

He sat in his car for a moment, surveying the two-story classical brick house where he lived during his teen years. Even then it didn't feel like home.

Summer yard decorations had been replaced with full autumn regalia — bales of hay, pumpkins, even a scarecrow, all artfully arranged. Bronze mums filled a little wooden wagon, probably an expensive antique. He shook his head. How much had the landscape designer charged for that?

His stepfather opened the door before the knocker hardly landed on the wood door, a flicker of disappointment in his eyes.

"Hi, Doc." Marsh gave him a half hug. "Did I miss the food?"

Roger Aillet, one of the state's preeminent ophthalmologists, smiled. "You know your mother never has lunch on the table this soon. She keeps hoping your brother will show up."

"He'll get here sooner or later."

His stepfather nodded. "We don't see as much of him as we'd like." Marsh laid his keys on a silver tray that sat on an ornate walnut table inside the door.

"Is that Marshall or Thomas?" his mother called from the back of the house.

"It's me, Mom."

Doc lowered his voice to a conspiratorial whisper. "I stashed snacks in the den, and the game's on. Come on in when you can."

Marsh smiled and strolled toward the kitchen. His mother wore the beige suit she'd had on at church, covered with a frilly apron that was as impractical as his mother's meal preparation. The only sign that Minnette Aillet was cooking was the brocade house slippers she had changed into — her kitchen shoes.

An array of take-out dishes from the Samford Club and a casserole the housekeeper had cooked earlier — he'd recognize that squash anywhere — were lined up on the granite countertop. Lunch assembly was underway.

"I'm running a little behind." She moved forward to give him a peck on the cheek, and her hand moved to his shirt collar. Her mouth turned down. "I wish you'd keep your tie on."

Marsh came to his mother's house for Sunday lunch at least twice a month, and each time she said the same things: Lunch would take awhile. He should have worn his tie. Thomas — never T. J. — was wasting his life as a carpenter, and Marsh should move to a bigger house.

He grabbed the lapel of his suit coat and gave her the smile that usually softened her. "I did leave my jacket on."

She shook her head. "You youngsters are more casual than we used to be. I can scarcely get Thomas into a tie."

Marsh risked her wrath by nibbling on a celery stalk from a vegetable tray. "His church is more laid-back than ours."

"Hmm," his mother grumbled. "I still don't see why he left First Church." She paused. "And how can a *handyman* business be that difficult?"

Marsh's temper rose, despite the talking-to he'd given himself on the drive over. "T. J.'s in high demand."

"He could have been a doctor, like his father."

"The world needs carpenters too." He shot her the grin he'd used in T. J.'s defense for years. "People love T. J."

"He'll never make anything of himself." She looked at Marsh, her gaze lingering for a split second on his open collar. "At least you went into law — and you're here for your stepfather, even if his own son isn't."

Marsh reached for a carrot and rubbed his shoulder.

"Have you hurt yourself?" She walked over to the counter where he stood. "Do you need your stepfather to look at your arm?"

"I pulled a muscle working in the yard yesterday. I'm fine."

"I don't know why you refuse to hire a yardman. Those Mexicans are very reliable."

"Mother . . ." Her condescension troubled him, but he hated to get into yet another argument.

"You could use the help." She opened the silverware drawer. "Especially when you move into a bigger house."

Marsh reached for another carrot, plotting his exit. Before he could vacate the room, his mother moved on. "Did Val tell you we're planning a party to celebrate your state commission post?"

He chewed slowly. "That's in the early stages, and I asked you not to talk about it."

Her hand fluttered. "We can't throw something together at the last minute. By the time the governor makes the announcement, we'll have the invitations ready to print. I've already got a calligrapher lined up."

"Calligrapher?" A dull ache throbbed at his temples.

"Don't worry, Marshall. It'll look elegant."

"No invitations, no calligrapher. If an announcement is made, we can discuss it."

"Maybe by then you'll have washed your hands of that silly Sweet Olive mess. Who in the world is that woman J&S sent in?"

Marsh bit his cheek to keep from groaning. "You know I can't talk about my case."

"It's not like it's a secret after that show she put on at the Richmonds' last night."

His resolve shattered. "What show?"

"She marched in there like she owned the place. I'm just thankful Claire was out of town. She would have been mortified."

Valerie's mother stayed at the Richmond beach house when she wasn't at the family condo in Colorado. His mother pretended like Claire and Slattery still lived together, and Val commented on her rarely.

"Ms. Gardner comes in acting all warm and friendly. Why would they send someone like her to Samford?"

"I suspect they want to finish up the Sweet Olive leases." He glanced at his watch, and his mother held up her hand.

"Don't rush me. You know as well as I do that your father will be sitting on that porch whenever you get there."

She was right. Bud Cameron would be in the porch swing, whittling or visiting with a friend. He would tell Marsh to change out of his "monkey suit" and regale him with stories about the neighbors, some amusing, some sad. Not one word would be critical. Marsh looked over at his mother, setting crystal water glasses on the countertop.

"I'm going to see Doc," he said and hurried from the room.

CHAPTER 7

The aluminum door creaked as Ginny opened it, a rusty noise like fingers on a chalkboard. A dog, smaller than the one in the yard, sauntered in from another room, tongue out, tail wagging. He nudged his head between Camille and Ginny.

"Aunt Ginny, come see what I drew," a childish voice called from across the room, and a "me too, me too" joined in.

"Camille, meet North Louisiana's future Picassos."

"I . . . I didn't realize you were in the middle of a class," Camille stammered.

Ginny made a dismissive noise. "This is my niece and nephew. They're used to interruptions. We're quite popular lately."

"I could make an appointment for another time. I don't want to bother —"

"We'll look at their drawings," Ginny cut in, "and you can tell me what you've got on your mind."

Before they could reach the little art table, however, Ginny's cell phone, clipped to her pocket, rang. She glanced at the number while a classical tune blared. "This'll only take a minute."

Camille stood in the middle of the room, surrounded by art. The two children, both with curly red hair, painted at easels next to a small, splattered table. A wall full of drawings was displayed behind them, and a shelf of misshapen pottery sat on a bookcase in the corner.

To the side was an array of carvings, glasswork, and figures that looked like they were made from fancy gourds.

"Do you like my picture?" the girl of about six asked.

Squatting, Camille nodded. "Those look like the trees across the road."

"That's what they are!" the girl exclaimed, her missing front teeth obvious in her big grin. "How'd you guess?"

"You drew those angles perfectly." Camille smiled. Her own brief stint as an art teacher pierced her heart.

"That's what Aunt Ginny said." She twisted her head to look into Camille's eyes. "What's your name?"

"This is Miss Camille," Ginny said, hanging up the phone.

"My name's Kylie," the girl said.

"Look at my picture." A boy of about four held out his drawing, his eyes downcast. His hair curled into a sweet sphere around his head.

"That's my brother, Randy," Kylie said. "He's shy."

Camille sat on the floor beside him. "I'm shy too."

Ginny raised her eyebrows as she put the phone on a small table cluttered with art books and paintbrushes. "They don't usually take to visitors. I guess they know you appreciate fine art." She gave Camille a small smile.

"They're gifted." Camille forced herself to stand and back away from the table, although the setting made her want to sit down and draw something. "You are a fantastic teacher."

"I can't take credit for any of this." Ginny put her hand on the boy's shoulder. "Folks say there's something in the water out here."

"Whatever causes it, keep it up."

"We're doing our best," Ginny replied, her voice losing some of its warmth.

"All of this work is . . . I'm at a loss to describe it." Camille gestured at a display of primitive oil paintings on a massive piece of Peg-Board, similar to one in her dorm room

81

in college.

"They're beautiful, aren't they?" Ginny said. "That's why my house looks like a gallery."

Camille picked up a small basket made of woven pine needles. "This is one of my dreams — a house filled with original art."

Ginny's eyes widened and Camille walked over to a muted painting of a Louisiana swamp, murmuring her praise.

"My brother did that, only a few weeks before he died. He saw nature differently than most Louisiana men. Todd said we shouldn't expect everyone to see the world the same way."

"That's why I love art," Camille said. "There's more going on beneath the surface."

"Sort of like your oil-and-gas business, I suppose."

"They're nothing alike." Camille's voice was abrupt.

"We're blessed with more than our share of fine artists out here," Ginny said. "And apparently we have a lot of gas too."

"All of this was done by local artists?"

Ginny looked like a parent bragging on a child. "Neighbors on a one-mile stretch of road created all of this."

Camille raised her eyebrows.

"Paintings. Pottery. Carving. Weaving. Sculptures." Ginny gestured to a series of stands Camille had not seen. "We fire that raku in the backyard."

The black clay showed through the colors in vases and geometric sculptures, and Camille spent a few seconds looking at each piece.

"Go ahead. Pick them up."

"I'm afraid I might break something."

Ginny tsk-tsked. "You're not the kind of person to break things."

Camille picked up a rectangular vase. "This is beautiful."

The classical tune blasted out of Ginny's phone again, and she motioned for Camille to follow her into the kitchen.

Camille set the vase down, giving it one last gentle touch.

"No news," Ginny said into the phone. "I plan to send out a group e-mail tomorrow."

A voice sounded angry on the other end.

"Feel free," Ginny said. "The children are here this afternoon, so I'm going to have to cut you off." More loud words erupted. "Let me know. I've got to go." Ginny frowned before laying the phone on the table. "I vowed I wouldn't do business on the Sabbath, but it is hard to shut people up."

Moving a stack of papers out of a chair,

she motioned for Camille to take a seat. "The neighbors call this my command center. It's a mess." Her voice held amusement instead of embarrassment.

Sinking gracefully into a chair that resembled something from a 1950s diner, Ginny glanced at the phone, buzzing again, but didn't answer it. She moved a pile of file folders and a yellow legal tablet to the side of the Formica table.

Camille could not keep from glancing at the papers.

"Perhaps we —" Camille was interrupted by the children squabbling in the other room, and Ginny gave a loud sigh and headed back into the living room.

Camille watched her disappear before straining to read the paperwork. Three or four names were listed under a heading that said *INTERESTED.* On the right side of the sheet was a list of a few more names, individuals and couples, some scratched through.

Ginny's phone squirmed as it simultaneously rang and buzzed. The caller's name flashed. *Marshall Cameron.* Camille apparently wasn't the only one working Sunday.

"I thought I turned that thing off." Ginny strolled back into the kitchen with an oversized tabby cat under one arm and

Randy under the other.

How she opened the back door, Camille wasn't sure, but she dropped the cat outside, accompanied by a dog's barking, and sat at the table, the child in her lap.

The phone dinged again, and a text message popped up.

Camille looked out the kitchen window at the whirligigs. She was beginning to see where Ginny got her inspiration for art in motion.

"Where were we?" Ginny pushed the hair off her face with a harried shove.

"I think you'll be pleased with the new J&S offer. Could we set up a meeting for tomorrow?"

"I don't want to waste your time, Camille. We don't want a bunch of gas wells messing up our community. J&S will get our mineral rights, drain our water supply, and tear up our land. We'll be stuck with what's left."

"Once the wells are drilled, you'll hardly notice they're there," Camille said. "And the money can help families, schools, churches. Will you at least meet to explore possibilities?"

"I teach school. Children come afterward for Kids' Art Club. I can't meet until later — or on Saturdays. And I have to tell you again — we're not signing over our land."

"We don't want the land. J&S wants to lease the mineral rights. You'll receive a payment up front and retain use of your property."

Ginny was silent. A clock shaped like a cat, tail moving, ticked so loudly that Camille felt like she could hear her new job slipping away. "Will you at least consider it?"

Exhaling, Ginny leaned over the table. "You seem like a nice person, but you don't know anything about Sweet Olive, do you?"

She spoke the words *Sweet Olive* not with reverence, as Camille half expected, but with pure affection.

Camille considered for a second and shook her head. "Not much."

CHAPTER 8

The purple-and-gold golf cart was draped with Mardi Gras beads and fringe.

From her spot in the front seat, Camille threw a rare longing look at her truck.

Ginny twisted her hair up in a clip and turned toward Camille. "You good to go?"

"I think so." Seeking something to hang on to, Camille brushed against a feather boa and clamped her fingers around the cart's metal frame.

Ginny gave a big, loud laugh as she looked at Camille. "Don't be scared. I've only taken this thing into the ditch once."

"That's reassuring," Camille said, her voice sober.

"What's the problem? I thought you'd want to see the place you've come to woo."

Camille nodded. "That's a generous offer . . . but I didn't mean to barge in on your afternoon."

Ginny raised her eyebrows as she turned

the key. "Why else would you have come out here without calling?"

"You're right, of course. I just rarely find myself in this situation. Most landowners are more interested in the amount of the check than in showing me around."

"Sweet Olive isn't like most places." Ginny turned from the conversation to call to the children, putting on rubber boots under the carport.

"So I gather," Camille said dryly.

"I'm not going to consider negotiating until you know more about this place you want to destroy."

Camille, captivated by this enchanting home for the past few minutes, drew in her breath. "That's not true. J&S will enhance Sweet Olive. There'll be more jobs and land bonuses. It will make this a better place to live — not destroy it."

Ginny peered through her giant black glasses. "You're making promises based on information that has more holes in it than my overalls. You don't know what's important to us."

The children raced toward the cart, the dogs barking alongside them.

"I'll make you a deal, Camille. Spend time with us and see what you think. If you still believe drilling is the right thing, I guarantee the artists will hear you out."

"But that's not how this business is done. We have deadlines, schedules, plans to make."

"Then I'll tell you the same thing I told that guy from Bienville. We won't sign."

Camille's mind raced.

"This may be all business to you," Ginny continued, "but I promised my father, on his deathbed after a stroke, that I would protect the family land. And I will."

Camille wanted this to be business — only business. But to Ginny, it was as personal as it got.

Truth was, it was personal to Camille too.

"If you're sure . . ." She fastened her seat belt. "At least if you throw me out at top speed, it can't be *too* bad."

Ginny gave the hoot of a laugh that Camille had already come to listen for. "We usually take a Sunday afternoon drive. The children enjoy looking at the art. Everyone buckled up?"

"Yes, ma'am." Kylie and Randy practically sang their answer from their rear perch.

Camille clutched the edge of her seat as Ginny pushed on the accelerator. The souped-up cart lurched onto the bumpy road, leaving the people on the whirligigs hard at work in the background.

"Yay," Kylie squealed, as though they were on a ride at a theme park. "Can we see the funny flowers? They're my favorite."

"Absolutely," Ginny said.

"And the trees with clothes on?" Kylie added.

"If you insist." Ginny glanced back. "What about you, Randy? You haven't told us your favorite."

Camille shifted to see the little boy, who had closed his eyes and screwed up his face.

"He likes the bottles," Kylie said solemnly.

"No, I don't." His eyes flew open.

"Yes, you do," Kylie said.

"Don't either."

"I can't wait to see it all," Camille interjected. "I love art."

"So do I," Kylie said.

"Me too," Randy added, his voice louder.

The children launched into loud chatter on topics from their favorite color to a new video game. Randy pulled one of Kylie's red curls, and she screamed and pinched him.

"Kids, settle down, or I'm going to make you walk home," Ginny scolded.

"They sure are cute," Camille said as the commotion grew calmer.

"And loud."

"I wish I had your patience."

90

Ginny snorted. "I've pretty much got God on speed dial." She gripped the wheel tighter as they hit a bump. "I fantasize about a clean, quiet house where someone else does the laundry."

She bobbed her head toward the rear. "They stay with me most nights." Her voice lowered. "The house was too quiet anyway, and their mom has had a few challenges since my brother was killed." Her words wobbled.

Camille considered her next question carefully. "Had you lived . . . alone . . . a long time?"

"My husband passed away five years ago," Ginny said matter-of-factly. "We'd just celebrated our twentieth wedding anniversary."

Camille's face must have showed her surprise.

"We got married the week after we graduated from high school. We were young and stupid and in love. By the time Dennis died, we were older, fatter, and not much wiser — but we were still in love."

Unable to think of a response, Camille remained silent, the children still chattering between themselves.

"He encouraged me to take up art when we realized we weren't going to have a passel of kids after all. Wasn't meant to be." Her voice had gotten even softer, its southern accent sounding like a sad song.

"Was your husband ill?"

Ginny's foot jerked off the accelerator and the little cart stopped. "Dennis was killed in an oil-field accident. He fell off a rig into a tank, and they didn't have a rescue crew on duty. He died on the way to the hospital."

"I lost a family member in a similar accident." Camille could not resist touching her knee. "I'm so sorry for your tragedy."

The gesture seemed to rouse Ginny from her memories, and the cart lurched ahead. "That's in the past. Right now I'm trying to help us all move forward." Then she drove on.

The cart reminded Camille of a bumper car at a carnival, and the kids' voices made a playful soundtrack, at odds with the melancholy Ginny's story had produced in Camille's heart. For years she had pushed down any thoughts of her father, the sweet memories mangled by bitterness and anger.

She drifted back to that last summer and was jolted when, after only a few yards, Ginny slowed almost to a halt and made a sweeping motion with her arm. "Well? Is it what you expected?"

Camille felt as if she was still in a dream.

The afternoon sun glowed on the lawns. Lime-green birdhouses lined the fence. The September sky was bright blue, and golden-rod filled the ditch. Red sumac dotted a small grove of trees, and a few leaves drifted to the ground. Round bales of hay lined the ditch adjacent to the fence, and a horse stuck its head over the wire, as though watching them.

Ahead, trees lined both sides of the road, creating a vivid green tunnel, leading to a church.

"It looks like a painting," Camille said.

They surged forward, swerving around a pothole. "Hold on," Ginny said, looking over her shoulder.

Camille hadn't expected the twinge of excitement at the tour-guide exuberance in Ginny's voice, nor the delight from the backseat as the cart zipped along and topped a small hill.

"My house is the starting point of Artists' Row." Ginny nodded. "It runs from here all the way up to Samford, almost to the intersection of Trumpet and Vine."

Camille clutched her seat.

On the left was a small pecan orchard, the backdrop for the tiny church. A sign said "Sweet Olive Community Church. All welcome." Peeling white boards contrasted with the colorful jumble of houses on both sides of the road. A whirligig depicting a manger scene was planted by the edge of the gravel parking lot.

"My grandfather made that one," Ginny said, following Camille's gaze. "I refurbished it a couple of years back."

The row of homes was unlike anything Camille had ever seen — old frame structures with tin roofs, similar in small size and design. Each had a front screened porch, and a few had added-on rooms sticking out to the side or rear.

The big yards, at least an acre each, were neat, though grass was sparse. Most had withered gardens. Perhaps they'd been fruitful in summer but played out by now

The difference in each house, though, was the color — and the contents of their yards, adorned with whimsical accumulations of art. The first house was electric blue with yellow shutters, the next, purple with pink trim. Down the road, she saw sunflower yellow and teal blue.

"We're subtle," Ginny said with a grin. "And maybe slightly competitive."

After going almost the length of two football fields, she pulled off the road and turned the key. The whir of the golf cart silenced, leaving only the cawing of three crows flying by. "Voilà. Louisiana's outdoor folk-art exhibit." Ginny chewed on her bottom lip. "It's sort of gone down the last couple of years, but it means a lot to us."

Camille tried to absorb the sight.

Yarn covered everything in the first yard, and she wondered for a moment what the artist's car looked like.

"We call that Afghan-istan," Ginny said. "Everyone in Sweet Olive donated their old sweaters, afghans, you name it to cover the yard. Lillie Lavender and her knitters also make prayer blankets for soldiers all over the world."

"Does that stay out all year?"

"Lillie insists the weather adds character," Ginny said, her head bobbing. Patches of afghans covered tree trunks. A flowerpot was swathed in a cardigan. Even the mailbox was covered.

"Lillie also does watercolors. She paints Louisiana life the way she sees it." Ginny chuckled. "Ever since an armadillo had babies in her backyard, she puts a tiny one in every picture."

"I'd love to see those," Camille said.

"She visits her kids on Sunday afternoons." Ginny pointed down the road. "We can come back another day, though."

"Miss Camille, Miss Camille," Kylie interrupted. "Do you see the flowers?"

A garden of metal flowers stuck up from the ground in the next yard — abstract designs with startling color combinations. A huge bouquet of bold tulips, daisies, and zinnias with a butterfly or two dominated the space.

"That's Evelyn Martinez's work," Ginny said. "You'll have to ask her to tell you about it." Ginny steered the cart ahead, as though giving a VIP tour of the Smithsonian. "Evelyn's studio is a delightful place to pass an afternoon."

The studio would probably be as different from Allison's gallery as Camille's truck was from Valerie's BMW. But Camille's desire to get on with her life in Houston made the visit seem unlikely.

A flock of birds made out of farm implements inhabited the next yard. Figures fashioned from old car mufflers stood across the road — a tin man who looked like he'd stepped right out of *The Wizard of Oz,* a fireman, and a football player.

"We've got primitive painters in that next house — elderly twin sisters. They're a mess." Ginny chuckled.

Across the road, Camille spotted two more ponds, these slightly fuller than the ones she had passed earlier, right where the surveyor's map indicated. Large welded insects graced the adjacent yard.

"Those bugs scare me," Randy said, his lip sticking out.

"Oh, honey, they're just pretend. They're sweet bugs." Ginny eased the cart forward. "Here's Randy's favorite."

Camille inhaled. "May we please get out? Just for a minute?"

Ginny looked pleased. "What do you think, kids? Do we have time?"

"Yay," they yelled, and Camille thought she even saw a brief smile on Randy's face. An orchard of bottle trees, bright glass stuck on limb after limb, grew on the lawn.

"The artist blows all of his own glass," Ginny said. "One of his pieces is in the mayor's house in Samford."

"They're incredible." Camille looked at the unique shape and color of each bottle. "Look at that pale green."

"That's one of his seasons. The mint green and pink illustrate the newness of spring."

Camille once again found herself giddy. One tree was made of clear bottles that glittered like icicles and another was a deep green.

"That's 'Louisiana Summer,' " Ginny said. "It's my favorite." She looked around. "I suspect he hasn't had time to do the fall

97

one yet. He's a busy guy."

"I like the purple." Randy took his aunt's hand.

Watching the quiet boy absorb the art, Camille felt like she was on holy ground. Something special went on around here. When she had been Randy's age, her father was gone more often than not. But when he returned, he would draw with her for hours, teasing her about how much better her artwork was than his.

Camille soaked up the entire scene along the short stretch of road — porch swings and yard chairs and hummingbird feeders by the dozens. Towels flapped from the occasional clothesline, reminding her of the whirligigs.

"Now you see why we don't want gas wells nearby," Ginny said. "They'll take away any charm we might have. Art's about all we've got in Sweet Olive."

Before Camille could address the sinking feeling in her heart, Kylie ran toward the house. "There's Lawrence!" she shrieked, practically flying across the yard.

A tall man rounded the corner of the teal-and-brown house. As he drew closer, Camille saw the tuxedoed waiter from the night before. Shirtless, he had a bandanna over his shaggy black hair and a tattoo of a

Celtic cross on his light brown forearm. His jeans were tight, and his feet were bare.

"Hey, Lawrence," Ginny called. "We're giving Camille the tour."

"Hey." He smiled down at Kylie, who was only a step or two away from him. "Let me grab a shirt."

"My," Camille said.

"Yep," Ginny said, her gaze following Lawrence. "Nice art, nice artist."

"But what was, I mean, the party . . ." Camille stopped and thought. "Lawrence?"

"Lawrence Martinez. Some people in town call him Larry. He works a couple of jobs."

"He does this?" Camille didn't try to hide her awe.

"He does art on the side — for now." Ginny shrugged. "Pretty amazing, isn't it? His father immigrated here from Mexico and married a local girl. He brought a different kind of art to Sweet Olive."

They settled in a wooden glider in the yard as they waited. The slats in the back and sides were shaped like bottles, and Camille ran her hands across the varnished wood. Sunlight shot through the glass bottles, making rainbows. The children chased the patterns on the ground and danced around the trees.

Lawrence emerged from the house wearing a black T-shirt that pulled across his broad shoulders. He dragged a yellow bayou chair up next to the glider. With the black shirt and yellow chair, he gave Camille the impression of a good-looking bumblebee.

He looked at her. "Sorta figured you'd come around." His tone was polite, but not friendly.

"Your work's beautiful." Camille pointed to the displays.

Lawrence surveyed the yard, a thoughtful look on his face. "Thanks," he said after a second. "I've got a ways to go, but I'm improving . . . I hope."

"Camille's out here to learn about our art," Ginny said.

Lawrence twisted his head around, his eyes perplexed. "I thought she wanted to convince us to sign away our mineral rights."

"That too," Ginny said.

"Darn," he said with a crooked grin. "And she's so cute." He stood abruptly and leaned in to the side of the swing, his hands on the metal bar. "I suppose Ginny explained to you that we don't do business with people who presume to know what's best for us."

"Something like that." Camille's face was still warm from the "cute" comment.

"Camille knows we're not inclined to sign," Ginny said.

His gaze locked with hers and he raised an eyebrow. "And yet you're still here."

"The money could do so much," Camille said. "I won't go back to Texas until I know you understand its potential impact."

"That's more encouraging than what we've been hearing," Lawrence said.

"I'm authorized to increase the earlier offers and to provide community help, that sort of thing." These people deserved candor.

He frowned. "Sweet Olive means more to us than a new car or a vacation to the beach."

"I can see why you're fighting for this place," Camille said. "But you can trust me."

His gaze was steady. "Folks think you tricked us. They hold that against you."

"I didn't trick anyone. I'm here to help you." Her frustration with the way the landowners had been treated mounted.

"Your company tried to lease our land for much less than it was worth," Ginny said. "And much of that was done by people on the phone in the Samford office. They didn't even bother to come out here."

"I wasn't —"

"Camille, you've got a job to do," Lawrence interrupted. "But J&S doesn't care about us, our land, our water, or our traditions. They've let it be known that they only care about drilling."

Camille couldn't deny his words held truth.

Ginny sat up straighter. "It actually turned out to be a blessing — the way your company treated people."

"That's one I haven't heard before," Camille said.

"We realized we didn't want certain things to change. We don't want to be at the mercy of a big company."

Camille cleared her throat. "J&S takes a risk too. It costs a lot to get to the gas — and there's no guarantee what we'll find." Conversations like this were easier in a sterile conference room.

Lawrence looked as her intently. "You don't seem like the kind of person to do us wrong, but we aren't interested. Marsh can probably explain it better."

"He has a lot to gain from this too. He's an attorney, for heaven's sake."

"He's doing this job pro bono," Lawrence said.

Camille fingered the chain on the swing to hide her surprise. "No one does something for free."

"Sure they do," Lawrence said. "Neighbors help each other out. Marsh is a good friend, laid-back most of the time but wound tight when it counts."

The landowners' emotions were hard enough to deal with. Add a lawyer with a personal interest and . . . "I must have caught him on one of the wound-tight days." Camille brushed away the memory of him working in his yard.

"He looks out for the people he cares for," Lawrence said.

"Do you have children?" Ginny asked abruptly.

Camille shook her head.

"Our dream is that Sweet Olive children will want to come home to raise their families, that they'll become artists the way their parents and grandparents were."

"That they can put down roots here," Lawrence said, "make a life the way my father did for us."

The comment stung. "These leases can help pay for those dreams." Camille nodded to where Kylie and Randy played. "Don't you want security for them?"

Ginny's look was sober, eyes unblinking behind her glasses. "I want only good things for them. But I want them to trust God to provide, not obsess about money in the bank."

"Have you thought that maybe God provided this opportunity?" Camille couldn't hold back her agitation, and her voice got a little louder.

"We've talked about that a lot." Lawrence nodded. "We've sought God's guidance every step of the way. That's why we convinced Marsh to become involved."

"I pray about that each day." Ginny clasped her hands together as she looked at Kylie and Randy.

"The money's tempting. We'd be lying if we said otherwise." Lawrence gave a snort of laughter. "Art sure doesn't pay the bills."

Ginny's look grew more solemn. "How's Evelyn?"

"A rock," he said, before looking at Camille. "My mother was diagnosed with cancer three weeks ago. We're in the tests and decision phase."

"I'm sorry." Camille touched his hand.

"Circumstances like Evelyn's make our decisions harder," Ginny said. "Everyone could use the money." She took off her glasses and worked on a smudge with the sleeve of her T-shirt. "That's why it's imperative that you get to know us — and we get to know you."

They sat for a moment, only the sound of the children breaking the silence.

Camille stroked the smooth wood of the swing's arm. "I'll make this work," she said, speaking as much to herself as to them.

CHAPTER 9

Dinnertime was approaching by the time they left Lawrence's house, Camille clutching a blown-glass amber vase shot with strands of deep blue.

She tried to pay for it, but Lawrence insisted it was her welcome gift. "I look forward to visiting again — and not talking business." Lawrence winked as Ginny turned the key in the golf cart's ignition.

"We'll have you over for supper one night." Ginny seemed to notice Camille's blink of surprise. "Would that be okay?"

Camille tilted her head. "To be candid, landowners don't usually invite me over to eat."

"We're not like all those other landowners you've met." His mouth eased into a crooked grin.

"That thought had crossed my mind." Camille returned his smile as she climbed aboard the crazy little cart.

When they pulled out of the yard, Lawrence stood next to a bottle tree done totally in shades of violet and tossed an easy wave.

"Bye!" Kylie called out. Randy was silent.

Ginny gestured with one hand, the other on the steering wheel, as she headed away from his house.

"This work is amazing," Camille said.

"And there's more." Ginny revved the little engine. "Some people think Sweet Olive's dying, but there's a lot of life here. I'm unwilling to believe that the best is behind us."

As they approached a curve, bright houses on either side of the road, Randy spoke from the backseat. "Aunt Ginny, I want to go home."

She looked in the rearview mirror, and Camille turned. The boy was pale and had tears in his eyes.

"You're right, buddy. We'd better head back." Ginny kicked up a cloud of dust as she did a U-turn. "Camille will have to come back to see the others."

"Yay!" Kylie said. "She needs to see the wood man."

"I like the wood man." Randy's voice was a whisper. "I miss my daddy."

Ginny pulled the cart over and hopped out in a fluid movement. "I know you do, baby." She pulled him into a hug.

Kylie sat quietly, twisting a piece of clover she had pulled from Lawrence's yard.

"You come here too, sweet girl," Ginny said, drawing them together. "Group hug!"

"What about Miss Camille?" Randy asked, his bottom lip still trembling.

Camille, who prided herself on never crying, felt her eyes grow moist as she put her arms around the trio.

By the time the golf cart rolled into Ginny's yard, Randy's cheeks were pink, and he was giggling. Ginny studied him with a pensive look as the children scampered toward the house.

"I could wring his mother's neck," she said with a sad shake of her head. "All Janice wants is money. She bought a big car thinking she was going to get a settlement. Then she practically moved in with her boyfriend." She looked at the children hopping off the porch again and again. "She'd sell our land if she could."

Ginny threw a hasty look at Camille. "That probably ranks at the top of the list of things I'm not supposed to tell you."

"You have a list?"

"Longer than my arm," Ginny said. "Marsh e-mailed it to me after we convinced him to take our case."

While Camille knew she should worm information out of Ginny, it was hard to summon a strategic thought, so she nodded wordlessly.

Kylie skipped to the door and gave the cowbell a ring, and Randy petted the dog. They waved and called good-bye to Camille before disappearing into the house.

Ginny looked from the children to Camille. "Why don't you come meet with the Sweet Olive landowners this week at the library? You were willing to look at our world today, and we owe you the courtesy of doing likewise."

"You truly love Sweet Olive, don't you?"

Ginny gave a dramatic groan. "Why else would I be mixed up in this lease foolishness?"

"I've always wanted roots like this," Camille said.

"Where do you call home?"

"My mother's in Amarillo, but we moved a lot when I was a child."

Ginny's face creased. "That must have been hard."

"We never really got to know our neighbors. Your community is . . . indescribable." She headed toward the truck.

"I'd have pegged you for more of an SUV

woman," Ginny said, walking beside her.

"I'll race you in that golf cart sometime. I might actually outrun you."

As she chugged out of the driveway, Camille saw the small green classic convertible zooming toward her, the top down and Marsh Cameron at the wheel. His brown hair was windblown, and he wore a chambray shirt, the sleeves rolled up.

An eighties dance tune blared from his radio.

She shifted gears and slowed, rolling her window down. Marsh slowed to a stop, turned down the music, and peered at her over his sunglasses. "I should have known you wouldn't waste any time. You haven't been harassing my clients, have you?"

Ahhh, broad shoulders. Narrow mind.

While his attitude wasn't unexpected, she was disappointed by it. Somewhere deep inside she had wanted Marsh to prove her wrong.

"Good afternoon to you too."

"I don't want you bothering them," he said, but his tone was calmer. "They're good people — people not used to dealing with corporate types."

"And this astute observation from a corporate lawyer," she said. "I'll consider the source."

He removed his sunglasses, his blue eyes vivid in his tanned face. "You're quick. I'll give you that."

"I'm not so sure about you. Attorneys usually want to wine and dine me — soften me up for the big deal. You act like you'd rather run me out of town with a torch and an ax."

"Sweet Olive's different."

"So I noticed," she said and eased off the clutch. "Enjoy your visit." She proudly glided off without a hitch.

CHAPTER 10

The automatic doors to the office building, Samford's answer to a skyscraper, slid open, and a security guard jumped to his feet when Camille entered.

"Good morning, Miss Gardner. Welcome."

Camille hesitated, and he held up a photograph of her. "I've been waiting for you," he said. "Let me call your assistant to show you to your office."

"That's not necessary. I can find my way."

The guard looked either pained or annoyed; Camille wasn't sure which. "I'm sorry, ma'am. All unbadged persons must be escorted."

"But you already know who I am. I work for J&S Production. Where did you get that picture, anyway?"

"From the Houston office." He picked up the phone. "You'll need a new ID for full access to J&S offices and other parts of the building."

While Camille waited for her assistant to appear, she checked again for messages, angry that there had been no further word from Scott. Then she studied a list of tenants written in small white letters on a black background.

"Pretty impressive, isn't it?" the guard asked as he hung up. "Some of the best companies in Samford have offices here."

She pondered the list, noticing names of several of the people she had met at Saturday's party. Slattery Richmond & Associates, Attorneys-at-Law, had larger lettering. Marshall Cameron, Attorney-at-Law, was listed under another firm, which she had read was headquartered in Baton Rouge. Marsh's office was two floors above hers.

She had been looking forward to taking Marsh down a notch — until she visited Ginny.

The arrival of the elevator interrupted her thoughts, and Camille brushed a microscopic piece of fuzz off her newest suit, still wrinkled from the suitcase, and held her shoulders straight, a practiced smile on her lips.

The smile disappeared when Valerie Richmond rounded the corner, wearing the exact suit Camille had chosen for her corporate job. Only Valerie's was at least one size smaller. Maybe two.

"Valerie!" Camille said a bit louder than intended. "What a surprise. I was just noticing your dad's firm is in this building."

She didn't seem the least surprised to see Camille, but her lips thinned at the mention of her father. "Daddy moved here after he talked J&S into buying this building. He likes to keep an eye on me."

"That must be easy with you working so close," Camille joked.

Valerie pointed to the guard's desk. "You'll need to sign in until we get your badge."

"If you don't mind." The guard held up a notebook with a place for her signature and the time. "Then Miss Richmond can take you on up."

"Miss Richmond?" Camille looked at the guard and then at Valerie, completely baffled. "I don't want to hold you up, Valerie. I'll wait for my assistant."

The guard cocked his head as though facing a lunatic. "Miss Richmond *is* your assistant."

The resigned look on Valerie's face confirmed his statement. "Sign in, and we'll get on with this."

"You work for J&S?" Camille's mind whirled back through Saturday's party,

114

searching for clues she had missed. She added a new reason to strangle Uncle Scott to her list.

"Who'd you think I worked for?" Valerie gave her hair a flip with her hand, her nails still perfect, and headed for the elevator.

"Your father." Camille pointed to his name on the sign as Valerie punched the button for the sixth floor.

"That didn't work out, so J&S bailed me out."

Camille fought to keep her face impassive.

"My father and Scott Stephens go way back. Mr. Stephens hired me to set up a small office here when the Cypress shale field was discovered. I do a little of everything." Valerie stepped into the elevator. "Or at least I did until Saturday night."

"So you've been involved in the Sweet Olive deal?"

Valerie hesitated. "To a degree."

The elevator stopped, and Camille automatically stepped out. "This is five," Valerie said. "The J&S office is on six." She sounded like a teenager telling her mother she hated broccoli.

"Oh, of course." Camille brushed against the closing door as she stepped back in.

"You've got something on your skirt."

Camille looked down to see a black mark. "Not a big deal. I'm much more interested in the paperwork you and I have to review — and how we came to upset the Sweet Olive artists so thoroughly."

Valerie picked at her fingernail, her first hint of nervousness.

The elevator slowed and jerked slightly. Valerie stepped out first, swinging her arm around. "The Samford headquarters of J&S Production. It's probably not as fancy as you're used to in Houston."

"It'll do." Camille moved in front of Valerie onto the stylish carpet. The wall in front of the elevator was painted with the J&S logo with two lines underneath: Samford Office, Camille Gardner, Manager.

She jerked her head back. "Who did that?" she asked, but Valerie had walked toward the glass doors into the suite of offices and either didn't hear or pretended not to. How long had Uncle Scott been plotting this? Probably about as long as she had been begging him for the Houston job.

Rubbing at her skirt, Camille glided into the office, sidestepping Valerie. Her assistant — how was that even possible? — was right on her heels when Camille stopped in the reception area.

"Your office is down that hall," Valerie said

in a hushed voice. Camille couldn't tell if she was subdued or putting on airs. "We catch our own phones."

"I don't plan to be in the office much," Camille said. "Once you brief me on the Sweet Olive files, I'll be out in the field."

Valerie started shaking her head as soon as Camille spoke. "I don't know much about those people," she said, again in a low voice.

"You certainly seemed to know Ginny Guidry Saturday evening."

Valerie rolled her eyes. "Who doesn't know that publicity hog? If she wasn't in love with the spotlight, J&S would have settled this by now . . . and you wouldn't be stuck in Samford."

Camille pursed her lips. "I've seen plenty of 'publicity hogs,' as you so elegantly put it. Ginny Guidry doesn't strike me as one."

"She plays up that 'poor me' act. Things aren't always what they seem."

"Perhaps you're right." What would Scott say if she fired Valerie on the spot?

"However, you clearly have years more experience than I do."

"Clearly," Camille said dryly.

"While you're here," Valerie cut her gaze behind her, "business leaders will expect to meet with you."

"No problem. I've met with people around the country." Perhaps getting to know the power brokers would give her a bargaining edge when Marsh Cameron came to call — and she knew he would.

"Since I didn't know you were coming," Valerie continued, "I have an appointment at the bank this morning and a lunch with the Downtown Development Council later this week."

"E-mail details about the luncheon," Camille said. "Let's plan to attend together."

"Together?" Valerie's voice sounded as though Camille had suggested they dance through downtown naked.

Camille nodded. "As you said, I need to get acquainted with the players."

Valerie seemed to deflate for a moment, but gave a secretive smile. "You won't have any trouble getting to know them," she practically purred and turned and walked away.

Camille followed down the wide hall, lined with old photographs of oil and gas wells. "Nice touch. Where did these come from?"

"I found them in the archives at LSU in Shreveport." Valerie gave a careless shrug.

"I forget sometimes how gritty those early days were," Camille said as she studied the photos.

"They're still plenty gritty if you ask me." Valerie sauntered into a small office, speaking over her shoulder. "Your office is down there."

Glass enclosed the corner office, except for a dazzling mosaic of white tile behind the desk. Camille's gaze went from the striking design straight ahead to the business district of Samford as she walked slowly to the window. Although the city was small, the architecture was an intriguing blend of old and modern.

Shifting slightly, she saw a massive conference table to her left.

With at least half a dozen men in coats and ties rising to their feet.

"Good morning, Camille," Slattery Richmond said with a smile. Marsh stood next to him and nodded, his face stern, bearing little resemblance to the man in the convertible.

"Good morning," she stammered.

"Here's the file on the meeting." Valerie breezed into the room.

"But . . ." Camille's voice trailed off as she watched the men sizing her up, Valerie's triumphant grin solidly in place.

Camille reached for the folder. She would not flinch — but she'd throw a Texas-sized fit in private.

"I hope I didn't keep you gentlemen waiting too long. I had a few snags getting through security. Airports could be so fortunate as to have our entrance guard on their team." The men gave a knowing chuckle and their attitude appeared to warm.

Catching Valerie's eye, Camille motioned toward the door. "Thank you, Valerie. That'll be all."

Camille was ashamed at how much she enjoyed watching the woman's face when she dismissed her. Valerie wouldn't get away with stunts like this one, nor would she keep Camille from meeting her goals.

"Doesn't Val need to be part of this?" Marsh asked. "She usually sits in on our discussions."

Camille waved her hand. "Not to worry. I'll catch up in no time."

Valerie's mouth turned white around her perfect pink lipstick. "I look forward to visiting with y'all at the luncheon later this week," she drawled, posing near the doorway. "Daddy, don't forget to remind them you're looking for a foursome for the golf tournament." She took one slow step toward the door. "Marsh, after that game last week, you're off the list."

The men settled into the chairs, their

laughter mixed with Valerie's giggle as she walked out in her spotless suit. Camille stood at the head of the table, hoping it shielded her smudge.

Marsh placed his hands on the table, leaning over slightly. He wore a gray suit, his striped tie and blue eyes the only spots of color. "Perhaps the senator could get us started."

Slattery looked around the table before he rose to his feet, smiling. "Our area's relationship with J&S has been exceptional. We want to make sure we're all on the same page."

Several of the heads around the table nodded at what sounded like a canned speech. "The development of the newly discovered shale fields is monumental to our economy," Slattery said. "We want to remove any roadblocks."

Camille felt a flare of anticipation and leaned forward. "We're in perfect agreement. That's precisely why I'm in Samford."

Marsh shot to his feet, shaking his head. "My clients aren't roadblocks."

"I didn't mean to suggest they were, Mr. Cameron," she said.

"To clarify," Marsh looked pointedly around the table, "these men represent the broad business interests of Cypress Parish.

They're not here to speak for Sweet Olive."

The smile left Slattery's face. "Don't be a troublemaker, Cameron. We're only getting acquainted. What could be the harm in that?"

"No harm in a friendly visit." His gaze met Camille's. "But there's a fine line between harmless chitchat and digging for information."

Camille couldn't hold back a slight smile. "I think we all understand the difference between business and being neighborly."

"If you think I'll be railroaded because I came into this case late, you're mistaken." Marsh put his hands on his hips, his stance making the seated men look like toddlers.

Camille held the file folder in front of her like a shield. "We pay generously for leases," she said, once more looking at her file. "And we've contributed to nearly two dozen local causes, including our donation two days ago."

"You can't put a price tag on water or history," Marsh said.

"I thought that's what you were just attempting to do," she said.

"As I said, my clients aren't prepared to discuss their case."

"So they told me." She knew she didn't imagine the look of surprise that flashed across Marsh's face before he slowly returned to his chair.

"If the discussion veers off-limits, I'll leave immediately."

"Should that be necessary, I'll show you to the door." Camille turned her smile to its highest voltage.

Slattery's face had taken on a mottled look, and he wiped his brow with a monogrammed white handkerchief. "Sniping won't get us where we need to go. Everyone in the state — and I mean from the governor on — wants to know how J&S sees this project unfolding. Marsh, that will benefit everyone in this room, including you."

"Point well taken, Senator." Marsh looked at Camille. "Please don't let me hold things up."

Camille plunged ahead, realizing she hadn't enjoyed one day of her Houston job this much. "The discovery of the Cypress shale field is monumental. We anticipate removing an immense amount of valuable energy from right underneath North Louisiana's feet."

She sounded like a television commercial, but her audience appeared to listen.

"This gas is trapped in shale," she said, "and requires great expense and effort to extract." The process was complex, and she doubted that most of Cypress Parish had any idea how gas was produced — or cared. "Shale is —"

"With all due respect," Marsh said, "we don't need a lesson in oil-and-gas production."

Shoving her irritation aside, Camille put both of her hands flat on the table, mimicking Marsh's earlier posture. "Of course you don't. I'm used to dealing with newcomers to the process."

She pretended to look at the folder while she collected her thoughts. "We plan to pay the landowners generously for their mineral rights — the use of the underground gas and, in a few instances, surface water. We'll move forward as soon as we strike a deal with landowners, starting with those in Sweet Olive."

"What about other parts of Samford?" the man from the Chamber asked. "Will you be drilling there as well?"

"I certainly hope so," she said so quickly that it drew a small round of laughter. "We want to start with Sweet Olive because we believe it has the most potential."

"What if the production doesn't meet your expectations?" a banker asked.

"That's not likely," she said. "Your area has been blessed with abundant gas."

"Bienville Oil said the same thing," the banker continued. "But they curtailed production when prices went down."

"Some companies use that as a negotiation tactic, but J&S doesn't."

"That's a bunch of baloney," Marsh said.

"Baloney?" He was definitely going to be more combative than she had hoped.

"These are honest country folk, not big-city wheelers and dealers," he went on. "They know some of the people in Samford aren't getting the royalties they were promised."

"I can't speak for Bienville Oil."

"But you know most oil companies look for ways to cut their royalties once they have a deal."

An uncomfortable silence fell over the room. At Saturday's party, this group of men had appeared congenial, friends even. Today they seemed more like a pack of dogs fighting over the same piece of meat.

Slattery looked like a parent whose children had gotten unruly in church. "You'll have your opportunity to make your case, Marsh, but today isn't the time." He pushed his chair back farther from the table. "If you could excuse us for a moment, Camille . . ."

Before she could digest being asked to

leave her own office, the glass door opened and Valerie stepped in, carrying a tray of mugs and a coffee carafe. "I hate to interrupt," she drawled, "but I needed an extra shot of caffeine and thought y'all might too."

The look of relief on Slattery's face was unmistakable. "Thank you," he said as Valerie handed him a mug, the J&S logo on the side. She served it with a smile as big as a billboard.

Marsh towered, rigid, for a moment and then accepted a cup and sat back down.

"You raised her right, Slattery," one of the older men said and slurped the drink.

Camille said nothing, eager to see how the meeting would unfold.

"I'll be back after my appointment, Camille," Valerie said. "You have my cell number if anything else comes up."

Watching Valerie waltz out of the room, Camille realized she was the only one who hadn't gotten a cup of coffee.

"Now, where were we?" Slattery asked.

This promised to be a long couple of weeks.

CHAPTER 11

Marsh turned into Ginny's driveway Tuesday evening, thankful he had sunglasses on.

The house reminded him of a tie-dyed T-shirt he'd worn to a frat party one Halloween. He supposed he should be used to the place by now.

His gaze flew to the pickup, and he thought for a moment that his father was there. Marsh had asked Ginny for a private meeting, but his dad would add wisdom to the discussion.

These Sweet Olive people might be "salt of the earth," as his brother T. J. called them, but they didn't have an ounce of business sense.

Then Marsh looked at the truck more closely, and his energy — along with his blood pressure — surged.

He yanked open the screen. Refusing to use the ridiculous cowbell, he raised his hand to knock. The door flew open before he connected, and he had to catch his balance to keep from falling.

"Marsh!" Camille, flowers painted on each cheek, took a quick step back.

"What in the — ?" His voice blasted out as he stared at her, his prepared lecture lost at the sight of her.

Her faded jeans were splattered with paint, and she wore a baggy white T-shirt that resembled something his father wore on a carpentry job. Her short tawny hair looked like she had just rolled out of bed.

"What are you doing here?" he asked, lowering his volume.

"Helping with an art class." She put her hands on her hips and thrust her chin out. With scuffed cowboy boots, she looked like a gunslinger about to whip out her weapons — except for the face paint.

"Whose idea was this?" He narrowed his eyes for effect.

She smiled. "Ginny's."

"I bet it was." He looked past her. "Where is she, anyway?"

Camille's face twisted in amusement. "Do you think I buried her in the backyard?"

Her tone annoyed him further. "I find it peculiar that an oil-and-gas landman decided to help with an art class at my client's house."

She shrugged, a small grin coming to her mouth. "It is a little weird, isn't it? But then Ginny's not an ordinary landowner."

"It doesn't matter what kind of landowner she is." He looked in her eyes, trying to summon his courtroom intimidation stare. "You shouldn't be here."

Camille raised her eyebrows. "Don't worry. I won't ask her to finger paint away her mineral rights."

"Very funny." So much for his intimidation stare.

Ginny emerged from a nearby room, drying her hands on a towel. "Hel-lo," she sang out as he glared at Camille. Ginny had on one of those long skirt-things she wore everywhere. A scarf was knotted around her neck, and a large silk flower perched in her hair. "Come on in, Marsh."

"Your new doorman took me by surprise." He tried for a lighter tone.

"Wasn't it nice of Camille to help with the children?" Ginny beamed. "Evelyn couldn't make it, and I wanted Camille to get to know our community."

Marsh sighed. "That's not wise."

"She has natural artistic ability."

"I think he's saying you shouldn't trust me," Camille said.

"Marsh, you've been acting like I don't

have good sense."

"I'm sure he doesn't mean it like that." Camille patted Ginny's shoulder.

"You're defending me?"

"Of course not." That amused look popped up again.

"That's what it sounded like." Marsh looked from woman to woman. "J&S wants to break up the Sweet Olive group. They're ruthless when it comes to breaking up coalitions."

Ginny gave a huff of laughter. "It's probably a stretch to call the Artists' Guild a coalition, and anyone can see that Camille isn't ruthless."

"I can be," Camille said, but the words sounded more like a confession than a warning.

"This is a serious matter." Marsh frowned.

"Is this some sort of lawyer lecture?" Ginny asked. "Camille knows I'm not going to give up my land. We're learning to understand each other. I needed her help today."

Over Ginny's shoulder, five children had stopped drawing and were staring, their eyes open wide. Their faces were decorated with ladybugs, spiders, stars, and clouds.

"Perhaps we could continue in the kitchen," Marsh said in a quiet voice. "Can you join us, Camille?"

"As soon as I get the children settled."

Marsh watched Camille stroll to the art table, her scuffed cowboy boots tapping the floor. The peewee artists clamored for her attention, as though she'd returned from a long journey.

The oldest girl, about six or seven, was loudly explaining a picture of a tree and the other children jabbered about their work. Camille paused to offer a word of encouragement to each.

"Want to join the class?" Ginny said from a few feet in front of him.

He shook his head. "What is she up to?"

"Trying to find her way is my guess."

He resisted the urge to roll his eyes and stepped close to Ginny. "Some of your group are talking about giving in," he whispered. "You may wind up with little or nothing if that happens."

"You and I see things differently. Camille's a nice person. She'll give us a fair deal."

"How can you say that? You only met her three days ago."

"Haven't you ever just *known*?"

"This is business," he said. "Not art camp."

"Marsh, I know you're doing this as a favor to your father." Ginny steered him into the kitchen. "Maybe we made a mistake in twisting your arm to take our case." She held up her hands, smeared with paint. "No hard feelings."

He winced at her words and felt something rub against his leg. A small terrier was de-hairing itself on his navy slacks. Stooping to pick up the dog, he collected his thoughts. His father and the row of old friends had much at stake, and he had committed to help them.

While he might not be much use with a hammer, like T. J., or with glass, like Lawrence, he knew the law. He wanted a chance to work more with everyday folks, people whose lives could be changed by the right champion at the right moment. *Wouldn't Mother love to hear that?*

Camille came to the kitchen door and looked from him to the dog in his lap. "Are you ready for me?"

"Excellent timing," Marsh said. "I think Ginny was about to fire me."

"I was not firing you," Ginny protested, orange nails tapping on the kitchen table. "I want to make sure you know what you've gotten yourself into."

Camille looked from one to the other.

"He's not an artist, so he doesn't quite understand," Ginny said.

"How can you say that? I was born a few miles from here." That tidbit seemed to take Camille by surprise.

Ginny smiled. "Marsh's father, Bud, is an excellent woodworker. There's nothing that man can't carve."

Marsh set the dog down on the floor and brushed at his pants. How had they wound up talking about his personal life? "Camille, I represent one of the most unique artists' groups in the country." He paused. "I consider that a blessing."

Ginny reached over and patted his hand, as though he were one of the young students.

Leaning forward with her elbows on the table, Camille murmured in agreement. "Do you think it's possible to move this deal forward?"

In an instant, she transformed from perky art tutor to serious businesswoman. That he found easier to handle. Her affectionate work with the students and the way she looked in those jeans wreaked havoc with his resolve.

"I'll draft a list of Sweet Olive questions and get them to you within the next week," he said. "You submit your answers, and the Sweet Olive group will vote on the direction to take."

The words were hardly out of his mouth before Camille shook her head. "I — we — don't have that kind of time. And this is a rare opportunity —"

Ginny adjusted her big black glasses. "We've waited this long, Camille. We'd rather do it right than do it in a rush."

Camille's face had gotten pale underneath the paint. "There's a lot at stake here," she said.

From across the table, Ginny nodded. "We depend on each other — and we have to work together."

"Maybe you should tell her your Artists' Guild's motto," Marsh said.

"It's a passage from Ecclesiastes," Ginny said. " 'Two are better than one, because they have a good reward for their toil. For if they fall, one will lift up his fellow . . . A threefold cord is not quickly broken.' "

Ginny's voice sounded like a Louisiana melody as she reverently recited the Scripture. Marsh couldn't tell what Camille was thinking — and his own thoughts were scrambled. Camille's background — outlined online and confirmed by his colleagues in Texas, Oklahoma, and a half-dozen other states — was exemplary. She discussed oil and gas with confidence, more informed than any of the men who had ambushed her in her office Monday.

But Marsh had learned to read people from his very wise father, and Sweet Olive seemed to bring out a pained look in her whiskey-colored eyes.

He hadn't figured out what was different about this case, but he would.

CHAPTER 12

An officer in an orange vest directed the creeping line of vehicles toward a detour and frowned as Camille pulled onto the shoulder, hoping she wasn't going to be late for the Thursday luncheon.

She met his eyes just as she pounded on the steering wheel.

She lowered her window and smiled. "Sorry," she said, twisting her lips. "I'm from out of town, and I really don't know my way around the area."

"Move along, ma'am. We've got a hazardous spill here. Follow the other cars."

"If I can scoot around there, it'd be a tremendous help." She hoped her voice had the proper cajoling tone.

"Ma'am, I'm working my third industrial accident in a month. If you don't move your vehicle immediately, I'll ticket you."

The driver of an SUV behind Camille honked, and other cars sounded accompanying beeps.

She swallowed hard and eased off the clutch. Her heart sounded louder in her ears than the honking behind her.

Edging along the road, she saw a tanker truck on its side, fluid covering the pavement. She couldn't see the logo on its side but suspected it belonged to Bienville Oil, whose safety record was one of the worst. Blowing a loud whistle, an officer motioned into the air. He blew the whistle again, three sharp bursts.

Camille fell in behind the backed-up line of cars and squirmed, adjusting the radio, side-vent window, and rearview mirror. She fiddled with her phone. A small detour, even one in this neighborhood, was nothing to be concerned about.

She had outgrown those childish fears.

Haven't I?

"Keep going," she yelled at the car in front of her when the light turned yellow. But the driver stopped.

Despite her reluctance, she twisted her neck and peered at the two-story duplex on the corner. A bus bench sat across from the house, next to a pay phone stand, the telephone removed. The front yard contained more dirt and litter than grass. The periwinkle-blue paint had peeled, and the screen door hung at an angle.

The tap of another horn jolted her, and she turned onto Vine Avenue, traffic backed up. She was now squarely in front of the house at Trumpet and Vine. A large wooden Realtor's sign announced the house was available.

"Zoned for Business," the small sign underneath said. She recognized the broker's name — Ross Broussard, one of the men who had sat in on that awful Monday morning meeting.

When the traffic started moving again, Camille threw another look at the house, grateful to drive away. This intersection on this edge of Samford looked worse than she remembered.

Her mother had liked the house, thought it felt homey, but to Camille it represented one more time her father had let them down.

And called to mind the day Uncle Scott had taken over her life.

Camille was clammy by the time she stood at the luncheon sign-in table, resigned to more stalling, but Slattery strode forward immediately.

"This is Camille Gardner from J&S," he said to the woman checking off names. "I'll show her to the head table."

"Certainly, Senator." She threw a smile at Camille and nodded, before turning back to the line of mostly men who waited to sign in.

"I'm not at the head table," Camille said as they stepped away. "I should have waited my turn like everyone else."

"Of course you're at the head table. All of our speakers sit up there."

"But I'm not a —" Sweat poured off of her. "Are you telling me I'm on the program?"

He gave a small frown. "Only briefly. You'll lead into the keynote."

Camille swallowed. Her mind felt like the one time she had tried ice-skating. Her thoughts slid around, and she feared she might land on her rear. "I don't speak before large groups."

Slattery's response sounded like a growl. "All you have to do is say hello." He looked at her as though she were a preschooler who didn't want to go down the tall slide.

With his hand on her back, he guided her to a corner near the front, effectively blocking her from other guests. "You're underwriting this event." He pointed to the discreet J&S Production sign attached to a lectern at the head table. "You're also a club member. Working for J&S has plenty of perks."

"I don't like public speaking." Camille restrained a nervous laugh. "And I'm supposed to offer perks, not take advantage of them."

"I get it." He nodded slowly. "You don't want to throw your weight around until the right time. That's a smart strategy."

"It's not a strategy." A pulse pounded in her head. "It's good manners."

Slattery's eyes narrowed, and he nodded again. "We need someone with charm to clear this mess up."

Marsh stepped into the outdated club and greeted the headwaiter. An army of helpers lined up behind him with trays of food.

"You're right on time, Marsh. They just started their salads."

"Thanks, Lawrence." Marsh lowered his voice. "I hope to have an update for you soon."

"Mama's cancer may change things."

"It'll work out." Marsh halted as Slattery stood to open the meeting. Camille sat to the left at the head table. She laid her fork down and shifted to watch as Slattery lounged against the lectern.

Looking for an open seat, Marsh saw

Valerie wave him to a chair next to her. He headed for the table, his mood lowering after Lawrence's mention of Evelyn's health.

Slattery, never missing a beat in his good-old-boy opening remarks, acknowledged Marsh subtly as he worked his way to the table. Marsh tilted his chin up in return and allowed his gaze to drift over to Camille, who tapped her fingers lightly on the white tablecloth.

He slid into the chair next to Valerie, and she gave him a big smile. He turned his chair to face the head table, and Val shifted her chair so their knees nearly touched. "I'm glad you're here," she whispered. "My dear father is long-winded today. He wants to impress Camille."

"Shh," Marsh said softly. "You know he hates it when we whisper." Marsh focused his eyes on the head table, staring at the woman who had drawn him to the meeting despite his overloaded schedule.

Slattery was in the midst of an enthusiastic litany of Camille's qualifications, including her degree, with honors, "in geology and — get this — a double major in art."

Her double major in science and art from SMU had come up in her background check, but he had dismissed it as unimportant. Hearing Slattery's introduction called to mind Camille's cheerful volunteer work at Ginny's. Maybe art was the key to getting the right deal for Sweet Olive.

When Camille stood, she seemed nervous, running her hand through her hair, leaving one strand sticking up. She adjusted the microphone, looked across the full room — and offered a super-sized smile.

Camille was one of those women whose face was transformed by a smile. While Valerie was glamorous, Camille was enchanting — and the smile made her glow.

Marsh felt certain he wasn't the only man in the room who hoped her look might be directed at him.

"Thank you, Slattery." She glanced at him before surveying the others at the head table. "I'm certain I shouldn't be up front with all these distinguished folks, but I'm delighted to be in North Louisiana."

"I bet she is," Valerie said in Marsh's ear.

Camille seemed to gaze right at him at that moment, and her smile faltered for a split second. She paused and gripped the lectern.

"I'm not a public speaker, so you may notice I'm perspiring," she said, drawing a few chuckles. "I didn't expect the honor of speaking today, so I'll keep it brief." She glanced out toward Marsh and Valerie again. "But I appreciate the chance to say thank you for what you've done to make Samford stronger."

"She's more polished than I realized," Valerie murmured.

Marsh ignored Val, watching the way Camille's eyes darted around the room, as though seeking a friendly face.

"I especially thank Valerie Richmond, who many of you know." A smattering of applause went through the club.

"Unbelievable," Valerie said through clenched teeth. "Doesn't she know I hate her for taking my job?"

Marsh sighed. "Val, people are looking at you. Smile, and be quiet."

"You're right, as always." She put her hand on his shoulder.

Marsh moved his chair away from the table a couple of feet for a better view of the podium.

An out-of-town marketing consultant followed Camille's brief comments, giving a PowerPoint presentation on how North Louisiana could improve its image. Marsh wasn't all that interested in image, but he did hold on to the idea that Samford could be more than it was.

For that to happen, companies like J&S would have to learn they couldn't always get their way.

When the meeting ended, he walked to the front, Valerie at his side. A mass of attendees surged forward, reaching the head table to welcome Camille and slip her their business cards.

Ross Broussard, his oldest friend, made his way across the room, looking like a golf pro instead of a real estate genius. He gave Valerie a quick hug and shook hands with Marsh. "Late night?" he asked as Marsh rubbed his eyes.

"Way too late."

"Tell us more." Ross grinned. "A new romance?"

Val frowned.

"Hardly. I worked until three this morning trying to unravel archaic statutes."

"If you'd gone to law school in Louisiana instead of at *Hahvod,*" Ross mocked, "maybe you'd have it figured out by now."

"Not this one," Marsh said. The choices in this case were murkier than the water in the Red River.

The law he had studied — and practiced so successfully these past nine years — had been law of the intellect. This case involved the heart.

Landowners needed the money.

But that money carried a high price for

the row of neighbors he held in such regard. They wanted an art colony in Sweet Olive, not an oil field.

"Did you doze off on us?" Ross asked.

"You poor man." Val wrapped her arm around his waist, as though holding him up. "You're asleep on your feet."

"Val," he said, edging away.

"Your competition gave a good speech," Ross said.

"My competition?" Valerie raised an arched eyebrow.

"He was talking to me," Marsh said dryly. "Camille seems to know what she's talking about."

"Good thing because she'll need that and more when she heads out to Sweet Olive," Valerie said. "They'll eat her alive."

"Didn't happen," Marsh said. "She's been out there a couple of times — that I know about."

Valerie flipped her long, blond hair back from her shoulder, irritation etched on her face. "Daddy says you're as hardheaded as the rest of Sweet Olive. She hasn't caused them to go with Bienville Oil, has she?"

Marsh looked across the room where the Bienville Oil manager had been trying to catch his eye. "No comment," he said. "How's the real estate business, Ross?"

As his friend laughed, Marsh shifted his gaze to Camille, whose outward nervousness had vanished. She laughed occasionally and mentioned her delight with the Sweet Olive community. She didn't refer to Samford, except in polite generalities. Although she wasn't talkative, she leaned in to listen to each person who approached.

Valerie had gotten it right — sort of. Camille *was* polished. But it went deeper than that. She radiated an affection for the artists. She seemed right at home, which troubled him.

Camille's heart was still pounding from the impromptu speech, and she tried to concentrate on the civic leaders welcoming her to Louisiana.

But even with their kind words and hearty handshakes, Camille couldn't keep her eyes from veering to Marsh. She told herself it was because she needed to know what he was up to, but she also enjoyed the assured way he moved through the room. In his tailored suit, he looked as though he had been born for the private club.

Leaving Valerie's side, he stopped to greet a variety of people but seemed to be looking for someone and stayed in conversations only a moment or two. His longest chat was with a middle-aged man in a sport coat and golf shirt.

Marsh was animated as they spoke and pulled out a card, wrote something on it, and passed it to him before walking to the side of the room where Lawrence cleared a messy table.

As Marsh approached, Lawrence wiped his hands on the edge of the tablecloth he had just removed and stepped into a corner by a row of windows.

Camille's position on the platform gave her a good view of the two, but she regretted that she couldn't hear their conversation. Marsh pulled another piece of paper out of his jacket pocket, wrote on it, and handed it over. They shook hands and exchanged smiles before Marsh strode toward the elevator.

Disappointed that he hadn't shown her the courtesy of a hello, Camille shifted her attention to Valerie, smiling and talking to nearly everyone who strolled by — until her father approached. Walking away with Slattery, she paused for a brief look at Lawrence, and her father nudged her.

The clatter of dishes being cleared from the round tables rang through the room. Camille drew a deep breath and faced the last of the well-wishers, the man in the sport coat who she had seen talking with Marsh.

"Welcome to the best oil state in the country, Miss Gardner," the man said, his voice scratchy, like a heavy smoker's. "I'm an old friend of your uncle's."

Camille had wondered how long it would be before someone made the connection between her and Scott, half expecting it every time she encountered Marsh.

"I hope you won't hold that against me," she said with a silly little laugh.

The man's smile didn't work its way up to his eyes, but his yellow teeth flashed at the quip. "Scott and Slattery and I worked together in the oil field one summer during college. I'm Jason Dinkins."

Camille studied him for a moment, trying to figure out how much he knew about those early days. "It's nice to meet you, Jason. I'm sure Scott will be tickled to hear I ran into you."

"I doubt that. I'm the field manager for Bienville Oil." He waited a beat, as though to ensure the words sank in. "I'm sure I'll see you out in Sweet Olive."

CHAPTER 13

As Camille looked around at the gold-and-green flocked wallpaper, old light fixtures, and heavy molding, the weight of the elite club pushed at her, and she imagined the index card in her purse pulling her down further.

She shoved open the heavy door of the restroom and stepped into a sitting room, the kind of spot where heroines in romance novels went to swoon. The air smelled of potpourri, and the bamboo design on the wallpaper matched the rattan settee.

She propped her hands against the marble vanity and stared at her pale face in the mirror. Jason Dinkins's approach was perplexing since Scott's notes indicated Bienville Oil was losing interest in Cypress Parish. Despite being waylaid by an unplanned speech and Dinkins, though, she was surprised at how much she enjoyed the enthusiastic greetings. She regretted, for the blink of an eye, that she wouldn't be in Samford long enough to become friends with them, a pattern she was all too used to.

She flopped down on the little couch and fingered the silky fabric on the cushion. She thought it was a pattern from an Impressionistic painting and wondered why people did things like that. The art on the wall was a poor quality print that looked like it had been ordered from a supply catalogue.

Camille pulled the card from her purse and looked at the ink-written notes on the front and back. She reread the notes. Front and back. And again.

Although she didn't know why she bothered.

In the past five days, she had memorized each word. She could flush the card down one of the nearby toilets and still recite the names when she lay in her bed unable to sleep.

With a deep sigh, she put the card between two fingers on each hand and turned it over and over, as though practicing a card trick. She chewed her bottom lip, postponing the meeting she needed to have.

On the three-by-five-inch index card was the list of names Uncle Scott had given her. On the front were the men she was to impress. On the back were families she was to court.

Scott had described the list as "vital landowners in the race for gas production in Cypress Parish," and she attempted to think of them as the number of acres they had to offer. But in a matter of days the numbers had morphed into real people, individuals more interested in art than gas.

On that list were Ginny's deceased brother, people she hadn't met such as B. B. Cameron, who she assumed was Marsh's father, and the Martinezes, the reason she was sitting here at this moment. She put her head in her hands, the card flat against her forehead.

The door of the restroom flew open, bumping against the counter. Camille wasn't sure who was more startled — the elderly cleaning man or her. "Oh, miss, sorry," he mumbled, backing out the door.

"Wait! Sir!" she called. He stopped, his mop bucket holding the door ajar.

"I was leaving." She brushed her skirt. She looked at the card again for courage. "Do you know where I might find Lawrence Martinez?"

The worker looked surprised.

"I'm a new club member," she said. "I need to ask him a question."

The look turned from suspicious to deferential. "He's in the hall."

"Thank you," Camille said, and the door clunked shut as the man backed away. Sticking the card back in her handbag, she gave herself one more look in the mirror and stepped out.

Lawrence stood a few feet outside the restroom, handsome even in a waiter's uniform. He turned as soon as Camille appeared, the janitor disappearing into the men's bathroom.

"You get around." His face lacked the flirtatiousness of their Sunday afternoon meeting.

Camille twisted her mouth. "So do you."

"Art's not exactly the most lucrative career." He finally revealed his crooked smile.

"About that. I wondered if you have a few minutes . . ." Her voice trailed off.

"Only a sec." He pointed to a pile of dirty dishes. "As you can see, I'm busy."

"I'd like to ask you about the community needs you support."

The amusement on his face was obvious. "Camille, you need to take that question up with someone else. My worthwhile causes are keeping my bills paid."

"Please." She touched his sleeve as he turned to walk away. "I want to ask you again to consider leasing the Martinez mineral rights. I think you'll like what we're offering."

"As I said Sunday, you seem like a nice person. But I will not have some oil company hurt my mother."

"I . . . I'd never hurt your mother."

"She's not in good health."

"I'm so sorry. I truly am." Camille felt a lump in her throat and hoped she wouldn't cry.

"Right before her diagnosis, J&S offered her a fraction of what her land's worth. How'd you feel if someone did that to your mother?"

"I'd be furious. That was wrong."

"Mama doesn't think leasing the land is the right way to go." He swiped at a table with a white cloth, but the action didn't cover the doubt in his voice.

"Perhaps I could talk with her. We could visit, like you, Ginny, and I did. No pressure."

"Like we told you, we don't want to give up our property."

She rushed on. "Your homes won't be affected, and surely you could use the money." She tried not to look at the tables waiting to be cleared.

"I've thought about this endlessly. Our

land won't be worth a dime if J&S ruins the water or kills the livestock."

"We won't do that." Camille knew she was speaking too fast.

Lawrence studied her, his dark eyes anguished. "We're part of the Artists' Guild. We've always stuck together." He motioned to the tables. "Lots of chocolate mousse dishes to clear. You'd better discuss this with Marsh."

She stepped toward the stairwell.

"Camille," he said in that baritone voice. "If we were to sign, we'd get the money right away?"

"I'll write the bonus check the day you sign. Royalties will be paid as the well produces, which could be within a few months." She debated prodding him again but settled on a smile. "You'll call me if you have other questions?"

He nodded.

Camille pushed open the door to the stairs but turned back. "I apologize for anyone who troubled your mother in any way."

The sun beat down on her as Camille walked to the parking garage, her feet burning in the blasted heels. They weren't one bit more comfortable today. As she walked, she thought of Lawrence cleaning out pudding cups. She had been unable to push to close the deal, even though he was waffling.

She tried to force her thoughts away from the purple-and-gold golf cart and the tour of Sweet Olive. She despised the idea of hurting Ginny and the two children — or any of the artists who had created such a place.

Looking up at the nearby buildings, she soaked up the personality of downtown Samford. Mostly old, it had personality with a small southern-city feel. Downtown Houston felt like business to her, while Samford seemed like a college campus.

As she studied her surroundings, a town bus slid by, painted in bright colors with a public art logo. She stood in the shade of an office building to examine the bus, its mishmash of geometric shapes making her smile.

What an ideal project for J&S community funds — and an assignment for Valerie, who spent too much time surprising Camille. As the bus pulled away from the curb, three waiters from the Samford Club walked out and yelled. The bus stopped and the door opened with a whooshing sound.

Lawrence, behind the trio, waved to the driver and headed toward the parking garage, rubbing his neck.

Camille shook her head. His mother was

sitting on six figures' worth of mineral rights, and he was working two jobs.

Usually people like that grabbed the money first thing.

By the beginning of the next week, Camille's nerves were as frayed as the upholstery in the old truck.

Scott called daily and sent dozens of texts and e-mails, demanding to know when he would have signatures. Allison phoned twice, marginally placated by the assurance that this was a short-term project. Valerie evaded Camille on a daily basis, calling with vague reasons for frequent absences from the office.

Even Camille's mother, always cheerful, had begun to fret. "You deserve a home and a family," she said on the phone one evening, Camille at her desk deciphering convoluted mineral records.

"I'd settle for a dinner that wasn't takeout."

"Honey, you don't sound like yourself."

"What if they don't sign, Mama?"

"Things work out for the best."

"I'm not sure what is right." Camille flipped through a file as she spoke. "For the first time in my career, I almost wish they'd turn us down flat."

"Is that what's best for them?"

"Possibly."

"Have you told Scott?" Her mother's voice was calmer than it had been when their conversation started.

"Of course not. He's looking for an excuse to snatch that Houston job from me. If Sweet Olive signs, he'll say I need to stay in the field. If they reject our offers, he'll want to punish me." She ran her fingers through her hair.

"What's the latest from the landowners?"

"That's part of the challenge," Camille said. "I've had one brief e-mail from their lawyer since the beginning of last week."

"How about that lovely woman with the art classes?"

Camille laughed. "That's the only bright spot. She invited me out to visit at the first of next week."

"I thought you were volunteering with her students."

"I quit going."

"Oh, honey . . ."

"I got attached to them so fast."

"Sweetie, it's good to get close to people."

"But I'm leaving."

"Then enjoy them while you're there. At least you'll have happy memories to take with you."

Camille forced a chuckle. "You're so soft-hearted. I love you."

"I don't want to see you make the mistakes I made when I was your age," her mother said, her voice quieter. "You need a place to call home."

"I know, Mama. I know."

Unsure what was going on, Marsh wore a tie and brought copies of a revised contract to the meeting Ginny had called with Camille.

Ginny had refused to give details over the phone, but his father said he knew of no settlement. Lawrence, probably at one of his jobs, hadn't returned a call.

Marsh had learned as a law clerk in New Orleans that when it came to legal matters in Louisiana, anything could happen. Add to that the state's unique blend of European law, and contracts like this could be free-for-alls.

But despite his legal training, he predicted Sweet Olive artists would never sign away their mineral rights. The beauty of their Louisiana land, earned through hard work and family tradition, would not be sacrificed for oil company cash.

Even the delightful Camille Gardner wouldn't change that.

Marsh pulled into Ginny's drive, looking up at a barnyard whirligig swirling around. As he looked to the side, he noticed Camille had climbed out of her truck and was watching it too.

"An American original," she said. "I want to see one of those in the American Folk Art Museum in New York City one of these days."

"That'd be something." He glanced at his watch. "But first let's see what the artistic genius has on her mind tonight."

Camille, wearing a dress and a pair of high heels, carried a leather briefcase, but her business attire was softened by the lithe way she moved.

Walking onto the porch, she picked up the cowbell and gave it a shake, prompting the usual cacophany of dog barking and the excited rise of children's chatter.

"Have your clients made a decision?" she asked as they waited.

"I probably shouldn't admit this, but your guess is as good as mine. For some quaint reason, they don't always keep their lawyer in the loop." He smiled, hoping it sounded more like a joke than it was.

"They probably don't want to bother you since you're generous with your time."

He leaned closer, looking for sarcasm but

saw none. "I suppose."

Camille ran her hand through her hair at his scrutiny and shook the bell again.

When Ginny answered, she had her cell phone to one ear. Motioning them in, she made an "okay" sign with her fingers. "Yes," she said. "That's right. Absolutely. Perfect."

Shooing them toward the kitchen — with Camille detouring past the children's art table — Ginny dug around in one of her folders, a mass of paper flying. "I know it's in here somewhere." She put the phone down. "I am so excited."

Camille met Marsh's gaze. He shrugged.

"Here it is." Ginny held up a piece of paper that Marsh assumed contained the group's decision. He reached for it, marveling that the case was coming to a head this easily.

Then his brow furrowed. "This is a flier for a festival at the park."

"What?" Camille reached for it.

"Not just *a* festival, *the* festival for local artists." Ginny's collection of bracelets banged together as she clapped. "Camille, you're invited to be our honorary judge." She clapped again, with more jangling of jewelry. "Won't that be perfect?"

Marsh could not keep from putting his head in his hands for a second or two. "You called us out here to talk about this?" He looked over at Camille. "So much for your theory about my time."

Camille looked as though she was trying to hold back a smile.

"This is not frivolous." Ginny looked at them suspiciously. "It will be the optimum chance for local people to get to know Camille and for Camille to see a representation of our best art."

"But I'm not an artist," Camille protested.

"I can't believe I didn't think of it sooner." Ginny dismissed Camille's comment with a wave of her hand. "You have an art education and appreciate art. Bienville Oil and J&S always have a big presence at this event, so it makes perfect sense."

"J&S is part of this?" Camille's brow crinkled.

"They throw money around like crazy for community events," Marsh said.

"They're sponsoring a tent and paying for a clown," Ginny added.

"That's appropriate," Marsh murmured.

That earned him glares from both Ginny and Camille.

"I would love to see everyone's work," Camille said, her face softening.

"Outstanding!" Ginny said with another clap. "Marsh, I'm going to need you to give

Camille a lift Saturday, and I'll meet y'all there."

"I can drive myself. I'll probably do some work beforehand."

"Marsh will be happy to pick you up. His father is entering a sculpture, and he'll want his son there. Right, Marsh?" Ginny's hair, looped on top of her head like an out-of-control waterfall, bounced as she cut a grin at him.

He looked at Camille, her eyes duskier this evening. They gleamed with what looked like mischief, but he couldn't tell if she was trying to keep from laughing or waiting for him to come up with an excuse.

"Sounds great," he said, unable to hold back his own smile. "What time should I pick you up?" His inner rationalizations were as lame as a weak witness in the jury box.

Despite his determination otherwise, this case was personal.

CHAPTER 14

Camille met Marsh in the parking garage on Saturday morning, hard-pressed to remember this was a business event.

Leaning against the jaunty car in a baseball cap, Marsh looked as casual as he had during their first encounter. His khaki shorts showed off muscular tanned legs, and she wondered what sport took him outside so much. The car's top was down. A U2 song played at high volume.

"Did you get a lot of work done?" He leaned in to adjust the radio volume as he spoke.

She shrugged. "My mother called to chitchat, and I wound up talking to a friend in Houston." Allison had called to tell her a volunteer — with a master's in art — had signed on for Saturdays until Camille's "situation" was resolved.

"Do you get used to traveling all the time, or does it feel like your life's on hold?"

With the music playing in the dim garage, she felt disoriented for a moment, almost like she was on a date. "Some of both, I suppose. I plan to settle in Houston."

"So that's home?"

"Not yet, but it will be soon." If she said that out loud, maybe it would come true.

"I would have pegged you as more of a small-town woman."

"We'll see. I've never lived in one place long enough to know." She opened the door and crawled in. "Don't you think we'd better go?"

Marsh turned and pulled a cap out of the backseat. "You're probably going to need this."

An odd zap of jealousy flowed through her as she looked at the pink cap with a golf resort logo, but she put it on, pulling the bill down until it shielded her eyes.

As they reached the garage exit, Valerie turned into the other lane, lowering her window to insert her passkey. Her head jerked as she saw them approaching. "My, my. Don't you two look cozy? Nice hat, Camille."

"Hey, Val," Marsh said.

"I didn't know you were coming in today," Camille said.

Valerie's gaze went from Marsh to Camille, unsmiling. "Looks like the new boss won't be looking over my shoulder."

"Val . . ." Marsh's voice sounded as it had at the party the first night.

"I left a couple of file requests on your desk." The words gave Camille a perverse measure of satisfaction. "If you can have them to me by Monday, that would be great."

Valerie's eyes narrowed, and Camille detected a hint of a grin on Marsh's face. "We're off to Sweet Olive," she added. "Big art show today."

"I thought that —" Valerie stopped mid-sentence, and a smirk crossed her face. She slowly raised her window, blowing a kiss just before it closed. "Y'all have fun."

Marsh reached up to grab his sunglasses from the visor. "You two seem to be getting along well." This time his grin was full blown.

"You really didn't have to pick me up." She frowned

"You mentioned that. At Ginny's, twice by e-mail and on my office voice mail." He straightened his cap. "Ginny's right — this is a good way for you to learn more about us."

Camille removed the hat and stuffed it in the glove box, silent while Marsh maneuvered through Samford. When they passed Trumpet and Vine, she ran her fingers through her hair.

With the beautiful blue sky and a slight shift in the light, the duplex looked almost . . . homey.

"You interested in that place?" Marsh's joking voice interrupted her thoughts. "My friend Ross is the broker, and he'd love to unload it." He gestured at the intersection. "This corner isn't the best place to sell a piece of property. Even that church is on the market."

"The area seems to have potential." Camille kept her voice steady.

"Local developers have been saying that for years, but it would take a miracle."

They drove through North Samford, silent except for the radio, approaching the area where Bienville Oil had drilled two new wells.

Marsh's tiny car scraped bottom on the rutted road. "Potholes," he said. "Sorry."

They jostled their way down the parish highway, swerving every few yards. The Saturday traffic included a stream of work trucks, few of which belonged to J&S. The car made a loud thunk, audible even over the music, and Marsh made a face. "Oil-and-gas equipment has wrecked these roads.

It's one reason Sweet Olive doesn't want wells."

She turned toward him. "Louisiana didn't have bad roads before the shale was discovered?"

"Not like this."

"We should have brought my truck."

He raised an eyebrow. "I like my car. Don't let a few potholes spoil your day."

"I'm not letting anything ruin my day. Ginny says this festival shows a lot about Sweet Olive."

"I need to warn you —"

"Warn me?"

"This isn't the kind of art show you're used to," Marsh said, his mouth turned up in a small grin. "The wine-and-cheese crowd won't be around today."

She studied him as the wind whipped her hair. "I can't tell if you're really a snob or just act like one."

"I'm not a snob! I just don't want you to be disappointed."

"What we'll see today would interest collectors anywhere."

"You're expecting too much."

She shook her head. "A gallery should represent these artists." She thought of Allison. "Their work's unusual — especially Ginny's whirligigs, Lawrence's glass . . ."

She laughed. "All of it, actually." She tilted her head. "Which one of your father's carvings will be on display?"

"He was still trying to decide last time we chatted," Marsh said, as they pulled in to the park area. He positioned them in a line of cars.

She leaned forward. "Are you close?"

He pointed. "There it is, right there."

She shook her head with a cough. "Are you and your father close?"

"He's the best. I can't imagine where I'd be without him." Marsh turned the radio down. "How about you and your father?"

"He sounds like the opposite of your dad. He died when I was fifteen."

Marsh surprised her by taking off his sunglasses and looking into her eyes. "I'm sorry."

"Don't be." Camille could barely think of her father, much less talk about him. "My mom makes up for it. She's my rock."

His mouth twisted. "My mother's not the nurturing type. She's sort of a cross between Emily Post and Margaret Thatcher."

"You don't get along?"

He put his sunglasses back on. "Good question. We disagree on a lot of things."

"That's too bad. Hardly a day goes by that I don't talk to my mom." The words felt like a confession. "She thinks she made mistakes when I was a kid, but she was doing her best." The thought resonated in her heart. Camille felt a sense of relief that had eluded her for years.

"My mother never made a mistake," he said with a grim laugh. "She calls me once a week on her way to get her hair done. And before you ask, yes, she gets her hair done every Thursday afternoon. Funerals have actually been scheduled around that appointment."

Camille giggled, the sound catching her off guard. "Do you call her?"

"Not as much as I should." He eased the car into a shorter line, the parking spaces a few yards away. "You're probably a pro at this, but I'm not quite sure how it works."

She squinted.

"Have you judged a lot of shows?" he asked after a moment.

"Sweet Olive's my first," she said. "And I'm only an honorary judge."

"You actually sound excited about this."

"I'm thrilled. I want to help Sweet Olive artists connect with a gallery." She squirmed. "Would you mind if I got out? I'll meet you in the area where the winners are announced."

169

"Sounds like a plan." He glanced at his watch.

"I need to warn you . . ." She could not hold back her grin as she mimicked his earlier words. "I plan to look at every single piece."

"Do your best. I'm in no hurry."

Leaving the car, Camille wanted to skip across the grass toward the festival site. Balloons and streamers hung from the pavilion, under the Cypress Parish Park sign. A cheerleading squad pranced around adjacent to the driveway with posters advertising corn dogs and lemonade. Their voices were hoarse as they screamed.

Camille caught a hint of the unusual fragrance, the one from Ginny's yard, as she made her way to a big tent pitched on a baseball field.

She spotted Ginny near home plate. Wearing a flowing skirt and a gauzy peasant blouse, her hair was hidden under a floppy pink hat that shielded her face. A row of five or six bangle bracelets lined her left arm.

Camille smiled. "Isn't this the most perfect day? There's even a breeze."

Ginny responded by dipping her head, the hat flying off to reveal her messy topknot. "Camille." She snatched the hat before it could hit the ground. "I need to tell you something."

"I know, I know." Camille patted her arm. "It's fine, really."

"You know?"

"Marsh told me," Camille said.

"He knew?"

"It's no big deal."

Ginny's nose crinkled. "I thought you'd be crushed."

"Don't be ridiculous. I know this isn't a big-city show, but unlike some people" — she cast her gaze around until she saw Marsh chatting with Jason Dinkins across the baseball field — "I'm not a snob."

"I broke my word. I promised if you gave us a chance, we'd give you a chance."

The sun felt suddenly hotter, and Camille wiped her forehead. "And you are. Being an honorary judge is a big deal for an art lover like me."

Ginny drew in a deep breath and exhaled. "The artists are boycotting the show."

"Boycotting? The show?"

"What's *boycott* mean, Aunt Ginny?" Randy approached with a hot dog in one hand and a balloon in the other. His red hair glowed in the fall sunshine. Kylie was behind him with a corn dog, smiling with an orange mustache.

"It's like when you take your toys home

because you don't want to play with one of your friends anymore," Ginny said, then looked to Camille. "More or less." Ginny took off her glasses and rubbed her eyes. "They're a bunch of stubborn coots."

"I'm not following you," Camille said, her face frozen.

"Apparently they're not following me either."

"But what — ?" Camille ran her fingers through her hair.

"The anti-drilling crowd said it would be disloyal to the heritage of Sweet Olive if they showed their work. The pro-drilling crowd said they want to remain neutral."

Camille threw her hands up. "Ginny, you're going to have to spell this out for me."

"They're mad at me, mad at you, and trying to stay on Bienville's good side." She shook her head as Camille gasped. "I'm doing my best to keep the art and gas separate, but most folks didn't think you should be a judge."

"If I'd only known — they must be devastated."

Ginny's face crinkled. "You're worried about them?"

"They've worked on their exhibits for months."

"You had every right to judge. You're way more qualified than most."

"They deserve to show their art," Camille said.

Marsh wandered toward them. He had a relaxed look on his face and stopped to shake hands, hug babies, and chat, looking like a candidate for office. "Where's this soon-to-be-world-famous art?" he asked as he drew near.

No one spoke for a second, and then Randy piped up. "They don't want to play today."

"O-kay," Marsh drawled. Sunglasses shaded his eyes, making his expression hard to read.

"A misunderstanding," Camille said.

"The artists pulled out of the show," Ginny said. "You may be wasting your time on us. We can't get Sweet Olive to agree on anything."

"Is my father around?" Marsh's brow furrowed.

"He's working the hot dog stand, but he didn't bring his work either." Ginny's tone was sorrowful. "Lawrence is here too, but he pulled his glass pieces a few minutes ago. Said it didn't seem right to go against the group — even if he does like Camille."

Camille scuffed the ground with her

boots. "I'm going to look at the children's booth."

"May I go, Miss Camille?" Kylie scurried from across the packed playground and grinned as she spoke, showing her missing front teeth.

"Me too," Randy said. He had seemed glued to Ginny's side until this moment.

Camille summoned a smile and, after a nod from Ginny, took the children's hands. "Lead on. Which drawings did you two decide to enter?"

"I painted the funny flowers," Kylie said. "They make me happy."

"The dog picture, the one that's your favorite," Randy said shyly.

As they wandered toward the funeral home tent housing the exhibit, she saw a sign with a giant X over the words *mineral leases,* and a woman wearing a T-shirt that said "Water Wells, Not Gas Wells."

She squeezed Kylie's and Randy's hands and hoped they didn't notice.

A few yards from where they strolled, Lawrence sat alone at a picnic table, looking at a newspaper. Pretending she hadn't seen him, she veered to the left, but Kylie spotted him too.

"Hi, Lawrence," she said, her voice high with delight. "Lawrence!" At the sound of his name, he turned and smiled, the children climbing up on the bench next to him as he started to stand. Wearing a pair of cargo shorts and a black T-shirt, he folded up the arts section of the *New York Times* as they approached. With a pair of aviator sunglasses and no cap, he would have been at home on the cover of *Vanity Fair.*

"Well, if it isn't the best artists in Cypress Parish. I saw your entries."

"Where's your bottles?" Randy asked, looking around.

Lawrence made a small clicking sound. "I left them at home today."

"Aww, man." Kylie glanced up. "Are you mad at Miss Camille?"

"Of course not."

"Aunt Ginny said people took their art home because they couldn't get along with each other," Kylie said.

"That's not nice." Randy stuck his lip out in a pout.

"You're right." Lawrence produced a few dollar bills from his shorts pocket. "But it's a grown-up thing." He offered them the money. "Would you guys like a snow cone?"

"Please, Miss Camille," the two children pleaded together.

Camille looked over at the stand. "Stay where we can see you," she said, and the children dashed off.

He patted the bench. "Have a seat."

She sat as far to the end as she could without falling off. "How's your mother?" she asked, after a moment.

Lawrence drew back. "That wasn't the question I expected."

Camille's mouth twisted. "I should have known better than to come today. No matter how hard Ginny tries, the landowners aren't likely to be my friends."

"I don't know," he said with his crooked grin. "You're one of the most interesting things to happen to Sweet Olive in years — and a lot better looking than Jason Dinkins."

"Right." She snorted. "That's why you yanked your glassware out of the exhibit."

"I didn't know what to do, so I went along with the crowd." He grimaced. "That makes me sound like a junior high wimp."

"You could have let me know. I would have stayed away."

"I considered calling, but after our visit at the Samford Club, it didn't seem like a good idea." He put his hands behind his head and stretched his legs out. "The Sweet Olive artists vowed to stay together, to decide together what was best for Sweet Olive."

"And my putting a blue ribbon on a piece

of art threatened that?"

"I've been Mr. Adamant about not sign-ing. With Mama sick, though, I'm afraid I'm going to be the first to cave."

"Is your mother worse?"

"We're waiting for more tests."

"I'm not good at waiting," Camille said. "Would it be okay if I asked my mama to pray for your mom?"

"She'd do that?"

"She's always got me praying for people from Maine to Miami." Camille was unable to hold back her smile. "She'd be delighted to add your mother to the list."

Watching Kylie and Randy playing in the distance, Camille put her hand on Law-rence's arm. "Take it a step at a time. Don't worry about anything but getting your mother well."

He threw her the same surprised look he'd had when she sat down. "Why aren't you swooping in, telling me how the gas money will solve all our troubles?"

"I probably would have a week ago, but seeing all this . . ." Camille's voice trailed off as she gestured at the kids squealing, a clown making animals out of balloons, and the line at the corn dog stand. "Your deci-sions go beyond the J&S money."

"I thought you had a deadline."

Camille shrugged. "You have to do what works best for you."

"And your boss accepts that?"

She stood, the sun suddenly unbearably hot. "I'd better get Kylie and Randy."

Lawrence rose slowly to his feet and wrapped her in a hug. "Thanks for listening, despite what we did to you today."

Camille, at odds with Lawrence and his friends, felt a strange sense of belonging.

CHAPTER 15

Marsh was restless and ready to leave.

The absence of the artists might actually strengthen his bargaining power in the long run, but he couldn't forget the hurt look on Camille's face.

He had been ridiculously pleased when Ginny asked him to give Camille a lift to the festival and had gotten such a kick out of her excitement at being asked to judge the exhibits.

Scanning the crowd, he tried to convince himself that his interest was all in the name of business. The better he and Camille got along, the more likely he was to strike the best deal.

This could turn out to be a career-making case for him — even change the way deals were handled throughout the state. He could be known as the lawyer who helped the little community fight big oil. If the state appointment came through, he might help unravel Louisiana's arcane mineral laws.

But the most fascinating thing about the skirmish at the moment was standing across the dusty baseball field, talking to a client.

"She's something, isn't she?" Ginny asked from behind him.

Marsh adjusted his cap. "It's turned into a hot day, hasn't it?" he asked.

Ginny rolled her eyes as she stepped to his side. "Camille's special."

"At least one of your artists seems to think so."

"Lawrence's got better sense than some of them," she said.

"Will he fold?"

"I hope he'll vote with the group," she said. "Sweet Olive's under his skin."

Marsh watched as Lawrence stepped closer to Camille. "Apparently that's not all that's under his skin."

"Interesting." Ginny put her hands on her hips. "Come to think of it, they do have a lot in common."

"Such as being on opposite sides of a major issue?"

"Camille's coming around," she said. "She's aware of our concerns."

"The deal you want — no gas wells in Sweet Olive — is not going to work for her," Marsh said.

"You'll come up with something. You're too much like your father not to."

Marsh adjusted his Ray-Bans. "He probably wouldn't like hearing that, but I take it as a compliment."

"I hate it when you do that," Ginny said.

"Do what?"

"Act like a smart-alecky lawyer."

"I am a smart-alecky lawyer."

Her lips, outlined as always in bright red lipstick, turned up slightly. "You can play that role pretty well, but you don't fool a one of us who grew up in Sweet Olive."

He put his finger to his lips and grinned. "Keep those opinions to yourself or we'll lose."

She shook her head, the brim of her hat swaying. "I don't want a penny," she said. "I want the kind of spirit Sweet Olive had when my grandfather started making windmills."

"Isn't that what all the artists want?"

"Some days," she said. "Until their roofs leak or they can't pay their car insurance. Do you know how hard it is to walk away from money?"

"I most certainly do."

Camille didn't speak as they walked to the car, a cute pair of tortoise-frame glasses perched on her sunburned nose.

"This is unusual," he said. "You're actually quiet for a change."

"Not much to talk about after today's incident." She ran her fingers through her already-mussed hair.

"You and my client certainly seemed to have a lot to talk about."

"You're spying on me now?"

"Merely observant."

"Turns out Lawrence and I have a lot in common," she said. Marsh felt another flash of irritation.

"You should have figured that out earlier, and he might not have boycotted the art show," Marsh said as they reached the car. He slammed his door, started the car, and reached for the radio.

Her hand stopped him. "Is that really necessary?"

"I like music. Loud music."

"I *meant* is it really necessary for you to goad me?" Camille said, her hand still on his.

Looking at her closely, he noticed tight lines around her mouth, the same mouth that had been so lively that morning.

"Can we please go?" she added.

He looked down at her hand, and she jerked it back as though it were on fire. "I'm not myself," she said. "It's been a rough day."

Marsh pulled out of the lot, heading in the opposite direction from which they'd arrived.

"I want to go home," she said, her voice soft.

"Let's take the scenic route. It's only a few minutes longer, and it always makes me feel better."

She slumped down in the seat without answering.

He fished for benign conversation, hating her dejection. "I didn't know you wore glasses."

"There's a lot you don't know about me."

"Then tell me something. Who knows? Maybe you and I have something in common."

She remained slouched down. "Of course we do. Both of us work for companies that like to win." Now she looked at him. "Sometimes that means people get hurt."

"Camille, I'm sorry about today."

She sat up straighter and clasped her fingers in her lap. "I'm sure you were delighted. Isn't that the solidarity you've been aiming for?"

"Perhaps," he admitted.

"There you have it. You won this round."

"I disagree with how they handled it."

Her eyes widened.

"And I'm not divulging secrets because I intend to tell them the same thing."

She exhaled, once more combing her fingers through her hair. He had seen many more sophisticated women — even dated some — but Camille conveyed . . . He shoved the thought aside. "May I offer you a piece of advice?"

"Do I have a choice?"

"You're a good listener. And you seem to like Sweet Olive."

"I do."

"But you won't get very far throwing money at people who aren't motivated by money."

"Eventually people will want the money," she snapped. "And you'll make more if they lease than if they don't."

"In Sweet Olive, the money's not the point."

"You know how this works." Urgency flowed through her voice. "J&S doesn't have to have Sweet Olive's permission to drill. There are wells all over Cypress Parish, and we can put more nearby. Then it might be years before your clients received a payment."

While he considered her words, she

jumped back in. "Your clients need to sign — and sooner rather than later."

"Why the rush? That gas has been down there for centuries."

She adjusted her body in the seat so she was almost sitting sideways. "This business is volatile. The offers are high now. And J&S employs hundreds of people in Louisiana."

"And?"

"Our country needs the fuel. Rumor has it you have political aspirations, and you could get clout from a deal."

"We're a patriotic bunch, but something tells me you're not doing this for Uncle Sam."

She made a small noise.

"More likely for the good of Slattery Richmond," he said. "He's been trying to encroach on Sweet Olive since I was in high school."

"Marsh, help me understand this. I've done deals with the richest and poorest, and I've never seen anything like this. No one . . . and I mean no one . . . turns down money."

"Folks in Sweet Olive decided years ago to live simply. That goes back to my grandparents and great-grandparents." He waved his arm at the pine woods adjacent to the road. "As silly as it may sound to someone like you, if Sweet Olive fades away, the world won't be the same."

Camille gave an awkward laugh. "We want their mineral rights, not their souls."

"Art is what they were called to do. That is part of their souls."

"Aren't you a corporate attorney?"

"Most of the time," Marsh said.

"Then why are you handling this?"

"Because I never say no to my dad."

CHAPTER 16

When Camille stepped into the blessedly cool office tower, the guard greeted her as though she had worked in the building for decades rather than two weeks and chided her for not having had her ID photo taken.

"Miss Richmond told me she scheduled that." He shook his head as he had done every day since she arrived. "Security is of utmost importance to tenants."

She bit her cheek to keep from smiling. She would be surprised if as much as a pack of chewing gum ever went missing around here. But he seemed so distressed that she let him take her photo and slip the badge around her neck.

Scarcely had she made it upstairs before Valerie surfaced, a scowl on her face. "I don't know what you're looking for in those records." She sunk into an upholstered office chair, her floral scent wafting across Camille's desk. "Everything's fine."

"We need to find people willing to sign leases, or we both stand to lose our jobs."

"You're not going to lose your job," Valerie retorted. "You practically have an oil-and-gas halo."

"I'm not putting up with this anymore." Camille stood. "The landowners in Sweet Olive haven't caused half the headaches you have. If things don't change immediately, I'll have you fired." Just saying the words made her feel better.

Valerie crossed her arms, uncrossed them, and gripped the arms of the chair, her knuckles white. She reminded Camille of a coworker in Houston who had just quit smoking.

"It'll be you against the powerful Senator Slattery Richmond. I wonder who Mr. Stephens will side with?" Her eyes opened with the innocence of Shirley Temple as her voice trailed off.

Camille moved back around her desk, torn between fury and amazement. "If you were as good at your job as you are with your attitude, *Mr. Stephens* would probably side with you. But as of today, he's depending on the person he always depends on — me."

"Louisiana's mineral laws are so confusing that even Daddy can barely keep them straight — and he's the best oil-and-gas lawyer in the business." Valerie's tongue darted out to touch her pearly lips. "Scott Stephens knows I'm important."

Valerie leaned closer. "You had just been given a cushy corporate job when you got booted to Samford," she said. "I was close to getting this office, and they sent you in. I doubt either of us is very happy about that."

"This is business, not corporate espionage," Camille said. "The next time you sabotage me, I contact Scott."

"That's a good idea. You can remind him about that interview you gave to a network reporter — on camera. Great job, Camille — if you wanted to raise questions about our image."

She slid her perfect coral nails back and forth on the desk, the noise matching the grinding of Camille's teeth. "You were demoted — and you know those Sweet Olive yokels stand between you and your fancy job. You're no different from me."

"You seem to have it all figured out," Camille said. "So maybe you can enlighten me on why I have this office and you don't."

"My interim work as the head of this office was outstanding. How was I to know they'd think I was cheating them? I offered more money than they've ever had. Then Marsh went all soft and took the case."

"I don't even know why J&S let you go out in the field." Camille was half thinking out loud but couldn't deny she wanted to prod Valerie.

"I know the well-to-do landowners in North Samford — and was . . . friends . . . with the Martinezes. If you ask me, they should take the J&S money and bulldoze every one of those tacky houses."

"That would be terrible," Camille said. "There's quite possibly not another place like that in the South . . . maybe in the entire country."

"That's what Larry says, but it would give them a new start, bring them into the modern world. They could even send some of the money to all those relatives they still have south of the border."

Camille raised her eyebrows. "Are you talking about Lawrence Martinez?"

"He was Larry when we were engaged, and I'm not going to call him anything else." Valerie stood. "Do you have more to say, or am I free to go?"

The Samford Club grill was packed for South by Southwest Night, a contrast to its staid lunch personality. Scott believed in making business friends over dinner, and Camille was reluctantly employing that technique on Valerie.

After today's blowup, she figured she had to try something.

The place was so noisy that Camille strained to hear Valerie across the table and watched with amazement the action at the adjacent bar.

She passed on the offer of "the best margarita you've ever had," although the idea of numbing this meeting with Valerie was tempting.

Valerie ordered a beer but changed her mind after Camille declined alcohol. "I'll have a Diet Pepsi with a real lime, extra ice," Valerie said. "And we need chips and hot sauce."

As the server walked away, Valerie leaned in, as though they were having a girls' night out. "I hope you didn't take our talk this morning personally."

Camille, who had spent the rest of the day wondering if everyone in Samford knew about her botched TV interview, stared into Valerie's eyes. "Everything that J&S does is personal to me."

"Would you really complain about me to Mr. Stephens?" Valerie asked.

"In a heartbeat. But I don't need to."

Valerie gave a smug smile before Camille continued. "He depends on me to take care of problems like you."

Drawing back, Valerie's heavily made-up eyes opened wide. "You *are* good," she said, and Camille thought she stopped just short of a thumbs-up sign. "So you work closely with him?"

"Certainly." Camille kept her face passive, as though reading from her résumé. "I interned at drilling sites and started as a landman right out of college. I'm returning to Houston as soon as I wrap up this assignment. To keep you from asking, I'm thirty."

Valerie gave Camille a rare smile, her perfect teeth gleaming. "I'd rather tell you my weight than my age, but I'm ahead of you by a couple of years."

She positioned her elbows on the table, her eyes slits. "You've traveled a lot, while I've been stuck in Samford." Valerie wrinkled her nose. "My parents live in the same house my grandparents lived in. I lived there until last year."

"You're certainly plugged in here."

"When your father's Slattery Richmond, you're born plugged in." She leaned forward. "What kind of work does your father do?"

"He died a long time ago." Camille swallowed.

"Was he in the oil-and-gas business?"

"Yes," she said, the short answer difficult to utter. But sometime in the last few days, she had decided she was not going to ignore her past anymore. Bad memories bound her every bit as much as Uncle Scott's machinations.

"A friend of Mr. Stephens?" Valerie pressed.

Camille broke a chip in half and then fourths. "Something like that."

Valerie lowered her voice. "Did they have a falling out?"

Wiping her forehead, Camille toyed with her fork. "This hot sauce doesn't seem to agree with me."

"We're eating greasy chips on an empty stomach." Valerie cast her gaze around the room and waved a waiter over. "We need to order."

Camille looked up and met Lawrence's eyes. "Valerie, please," she said, embarrassment flooding through her.

"Larry's used to my impatience. Aren't you?"

"Lay off, Val," Lawrence said.

"You'll have to speak louder. We can't hear you over that mariachi music."

"Valerie!" Camille snapped and then looked up at Lawrence. "We're not in that big a hurry. How's your mother feeling?"

Valerie's gaze narrowed. "What's wrong with Evelyn?"

"I'm sorry." Camille put her hand over her mouth as her gaze met Lawrence's. "I didn't realize it was confidential."

Camille was fairly certain murderers had gentler looks than the one that passed across Valerie's face.

"We've only told a few people, but it's no secret," Lawrence said. "My mother has been diagnosed with cancer, Val. Now, what would you ladies like for dinner?"

As he walked off with their orders, Valerie made a huffing noise but her eyes followed him. "He could quit these silly jobs if he'd sign the land deal. He and his mother have twenty acres right in the middle of Sweet Olive. His mother toughened up when she married a foreigner, and she's still a stubborn old biddy."

Camille looked back at Lawrence, delivering a tray of food to an adjacent table.

"We can still get Larry," Valerie said in a whispered voice, barely audible over the recorded music. "If his mother's got cancer, they need the money."

Camille gasped. "Why would you say such a thing?"

Valerie shrugged. "They're hung up on

'community history.' " She put air quotes around the words. "And they don't want a gas well right by their house. And he's punishing me for breaking up with him. We need leverage."

Camille picked up a chip and dipped it in the red salsa. "Doesn't Lawrence work for your father?"

"Weird, huh?" Valerie said. "Larry and I were engaged for two years, and most people — my father included — pretend it never happened. I was the spoiled girl who dated the pool boy to get the other guy's attention. Unfortunately, I still haven't talked Marsh into marrying me."

"You and Marsh —" The words flew out of Camille's mouth almost as soon as they hit her brain.

"Power couple, right? Maybe one of these days . . ."

Camille stared, wondering if she could feign illness and leave. Or if Valerie kept talking, maybe she wouldn't even have to pretend. Her stomach roiled.

Valerie broke a chip in half. "You actually got a degree in art?" Her tone suggested an interest in art was somewhere along the lines of an infectious disease.

Camille thought of the students at Ginny's house and wished she were crowded around the little art table.

"Daddy would have had a fit if I'd studied anything but business." Valerie held her hand up and gestured for Lawrence. "I believe I'll have one of those margaritas after all. How about you, Camille?"

"I'll pass," she said and tried to sneak a look at the time on her phone.

"You're just like Marsh. Don't you have any fun?"

Marsh stepped through the door of the club and walked toward the noise in the rear. Even though it was past the dinner hour, the little room was packed, and a few people stood on the fringes, drinks in hand.

While Marsh scanned the bar, Ross greeted diners, a gregarious charmer through and through. "May I help you, Mr. Broussard?" the hostess asked. She was an attractive college-aged woman in a miniskirt that would have had Marsh's mother clucking under her breath.

"Val's car's out front, so she's here somewhere," Ross muttered.

"Mr. Broussard? Hel-lo," the hostess said. "May I help you locate someone?" Her flirtatious smile flitted to Marsh and then lingered on Ross.

That had been the response to the two

since eighth grade when Ross scored the winning touchdown in a district football championship. He had turned that personality into Samford's most prestigious commercial real estate business.

"Do you know where our friend Valerie's seated?" Marsh asked.

"Valerie . . ." She looked down at the diagram of tables. "She's around the corner there, near the back."

Ross had already plunged into the crowded room. He smiled and spoke to almost everyone in his path, many greeting him by name.

"Thanks." Marsh gave a quick follow-up smile and wondered why he'd let Ross talk him into this. He'd planned to do paperwork in his office at home and call it a day but had been looking for an excuse to close the J&S folder when Ross had called. A little baseball would have sufficed.

Marsh spotted Val, her table half hidden by an aqua post that held a temporary sombrero. Leaning over the table talking, she looked a bit frayed, her face tight, her hair actually slightly out of place.

"Valerie's with someone." Marsh took a couple of steps toward the table. The moment he saw her companion, he knew for sure he should have passed on this evening.

Ross increased his speed.

"Hey, guys," Val said, and her voice suggested she was not on her first drink of the evening. She stood to give each a brief hug. "Camille, you've met our star Realtor, Ross Broussard, haven't you?"

"We met at the fund-raiser," Ross said, "and I've sat in on a couple of business meetings."

Camille gave him a cordial smile but seemed to be eyeing the door.

Val patted the chair next to her. "Why don't y'all join us?"

"That'd be great," Ross said.

"We're getting a table," Marsh said at the same time.

"It'll take forever." Val pulled him toward a chair. "Sit here." She smoothed her hair.

Camille picked up her purse. "I'm not much of a night owl, and I need to finish up a couple of things before I call it a day."

"Has Val been teaching you the ins and outs of oil and gas in North Louisiana?" Ross asked. "She's a pro in this area, you know."

Marsh watched Camille, whose thoughts played across her face. Without saying anything, she placed her purse back on the floor and nodded.

"Camille's quite taken with Sweet Olive's . . ." Valerie twisted her head to look at Lawrence, approaching their table ". . . art."

"It's a neat little community," Camille said.

What kind of corporate dragon used the word *neat*? Marsh rose to shake Lawrence's hand.

"Did you . . . ?" Lawrence stopped, looked to Camille then back at Marsh, who gave a quick shake of his head.

"This is complicated," he said in a low voice.

"Are you here for a business meeting or a beer?" Val said.

"Give me a second," Marsh snapped.

"You don't have to get testy." She threw him the look that had charmed men across Louisiana for years.

"Lawrence, I'll get with you later."

"Now, how about that drink?" Val drawled.

Camille picked up her purse again. "Valerie, sign this to the J&S account. I enjoyed our . . . visit."

Ross shot to his feet. "Are you sure you can't stay?"

Marsh stood more slowly.

"It's been a long day." Camille turned her smile on Lawrence. "Let me know if there's anything I can do for you."

He nodded.

Marsh cleared his throat.

Camille looked him in the eye and walked toward the elevator.

CHAPTER 17

Camille had not planned to drive by the duplex at the corner of Trumpet and Vine, but her discussion with Valerie had opened a vault of memories — and Camille couldn't seem to close it.

She'd spent fifteen years learning how to blot this place from her mind, her mother's weeping, her uncle's preaching.

Easing off the clutch, she surveyed the corner. "What am I doing?"

The convenience store on one corner was closed, although she couldn't tell if it was shut for good or just for the evening. The church on the other corner had a For Sale sign in front of it. A locked gate blocked the park across from the duplex, the grass tall and ragged by streetlight.

She pulled into the duplex, the rutted driveway making her appreciate the work-horse of a truck.

As she stared at the house, she remembered her mother and the woman who had lived there sitting on the porch, shelling peas. Her mother had been smiling, looking at Camille sprawled on the steps.

"She's my one and only best girl," her mama had said.

The old woman had smiled in return. "You two have a special bond."

Camille pictured the old-fashioned apron the woman wore with deep pockets attached to the front. As though on rewind, she climbed out of the truck and walked up on the porch.

Dead oak leaves had blown into the porch's corner, and she nudged them with her foot, the fetid smell transporting her to another rundown house in Wichita Falls, Texas, where her father had abandoned them her entire years of second and third grade.

The traffic light at the corner glowed, but the eeriness didn't frighten her. She'd been independent for a long time, had visited oil fields far more off-putting than this.

"Hello?" she called out. No one replied, and Camille knocked on the door and gave it a small shove. If the door was unlocked, she would walk through it, although she wasn't sure why.

She and her mother had shared a rollaway

bed that the old woman pulled out of a closet. The sheets had smelled clean. The door didn't budge tonight, though, and Camille walked back to the truck. Still she didn't drive off, staring at the house, angry at Scott for forcing her to come back to Louisiana.

She punched his number into the phone, but the call went to voice mail, and she left another irritated message before calling her mother.

"The house is still here," Camille said after a moment of their regular nighttime chitchat.

"How does it look?"

"Worse for the wear."

"Aren't we all?" her mother teased.

"Speak for yourself."

They laughed, and then a long silence fell between them, broken only by the wail of a siren down Vine.

"Your father would have come back for us." Her mother's voice was so soft it was barely audible. "He always did."

Camille picked at a loose thread in the seat's upholstery. "I guess we'll never know."

Her phone beeped and Scott's name popped up.

"Wish me luck, Mama. I've got to go."

■ ■ ■ ■

The street in front of the Samford Club was almost empty when Camille returned. Her palms sweated and her mouth was dry as she cautiously pulled in to a parking place.

Her phone still lay on the floor where she had thrown it after Uncle Scott's call.

Realizing she couldn't see the door from this vantage point, she pulled out and wrangled the vehicle into a spot nearer the door, scraping the curb with her tire. She gave a shaky laugh and checked the time on her phone.

According to a discreet placard she'd seen on the elevator, the club closed at eleven o'clock on weeknights.

She had no idea, of course, if Lawrence worked till closing time, but at least she wasn't sitting in her hotel room waiting for something to happen. She wanted her new life. And Lawrence had told her he was afraid he would be the one to cave.

The sight of a waiter and a young waitress interrupted her thoughts, and she patted her hair and stepped out of the truck. A neon sign illuminated a few feet of pavement, but the street was dim, and she could barely make out Lawrence leaving the building.

Standing unnoticed in the shadows, Camille listened to the three talking, their Spanish words mixed with laughter. A few yards from where she stood, Lawrence turned and headed for the parking garage.

"Excuse me." She walked faster and raised her voice. "Excuse me! Lawrence?"

He peered into the darkness. "Camille? Is something wrong?"

She hurried forward. "I didn't mean to startle you. I'm sorry for the way things went at dinner," she said in a rush.

"I'm a waiter," he said, his crooked smile appearing. "I'm used to pushy customers." His smile disappeared. "Why are you here?"

"I thought you might be reconsidering the offer." She looked over at the heavy wooden door of the club. "It would make life easier."

He frowned and shook his head with the jerky rhythm of a lawn sprinkler. "Camille, I'm beat. Do you want me to walk you to your truck?"

"No. I'm sorry. I just . . ."

"You're in the same mess I am," he said with a strained laugh. "For some crazy reason, God sent us a landman who likes us — and likes art. But if you're going to get out of Samford, you need to drill." He sighed. "My mother's illness is rough. The treatment is more expensive than I realized."

She heard the ugly sound of defeat in his voice and despised herself for helping put it there. "I shouldn't have come," she said.

"That's the same thing you said that day at the festival. Are you playing us?"

"No!" A knot formed in her stomach, and she regretted eating the spicy salsa. "I had a call from my boss tonight." She paused. "He's not pleased with how this is going."

"Good."

"Not good." She drew in a breath of the humid air. "He'd fire me for telling you this, but his tactics are about to change. He wants me to cut the land bonuses, scare people."

She ran her hands through her hair. "I don't want to push you, but I wanted you to know. If you *are* going to sign, you need to do it fast or you could lose thousands."

The sound of music thumped out of a passing car, and Camille looked up.

A carload of teenagers whizzed by, yelling out the window.

But Lawrence's eyes were focused on Camille. "Why would you risk your job to tell me this?"

She hesitated. "My mother's a cancer

survivor. I know how expensive treatment is."

"Is she well now?"

"In perfect health — other than worrying herself sick that I haven't settled down." Camille thought for a second and continued. "Our family had some rocky times years ago, and she frets."

"That's what mothers do."

"Thanks to my uncle, everything turned out fine. He rescued us." Now that she had decided to open up her past, she couldn't seem to keep her mouth shut.

"That's the kind of man I want to be for my mother." Lawrence gave a halfhearted laugh. "I should have chosen a better career for starters. Maybe then we wouldn't be so desperate for this money."

She stood, waiting. In the past, she had done it because Scott had taught her to. Tonight she did it because she knew Lawrence was struggling to do the right thing.

Lawrence leaned forward. "How much?"

She quoted a higher price than Scott had approved. He would be so thrilled to get a well going that he wouldn't quibble over a few thousand dollars extra. "That's per acre."

She forced herself to plow forward. "Lawrence, you'll probably have to decide immediately. I'll give you as much warning as I can, but this can change in an instant."

He jingled change in his pockets. "What about the others? Our neighbors?"

"They're free to negotiate their own deals. But it'll be up to Marsh to help them get the best deal."

"When would we get the money?"

"If you sign the paperwork I have in my truck, you'll have the check tomorrow."

"Tomorrow?"

"I'll deliver the check myself."

"Where will the well be?"

"If everything goes as planned, we can put it out of sight, away from the main road."

"And if not?"

"I'll do my best to protect your view," she pledged.

"And Mama keeps the land?" he reiterated. "She can live there as long as she wants?"

"Absolutely."

He sighed, an uncertain sound of surrender. "She needs the money," he said, almost as though talking to himself.

"Deal?" She extended her hand, forcing a smile.

"Deal." He took her hand and held it for a moment.

When Camille got back to her hotel room, she flung herself onto the bed and cried.

CHAPTER 18

Marsh inhaled the morning air as he headed out for his daily jog. These minutes before sunrise were his favorite of the day, not yet overheated, dark and quiet. A few houses on his route had lights on, but most of his neighbors had yet to stir.

Setting off through the neighborhood, he sorted out his day, considering the files on his desk. Sweet Olive work required skills as lawyer and counselor, son and friend. He had originally favored a quick deal. But after extensive late-night research and visits with his father and Ginny, he knew a more deliberate approach was called for.

Marsh had scoffed at their original request — keep the oil companies out of Sweet Olive. He had figured the best they could hope for was a hefty price per acre and assurances about noise, traffic, and their water supply.

Until Camille had come along. She might

be the miracle Sweet Olive had prayed for.

Turning down the street where his mother lived, he wiped the sweat from his face with the hem of his T-shirt.

If he could navigate this Sweet Olive maze, maybe he would walk away from the big retainers and direct-deposit salary and explore going out on his own again. He could restructure his schedule. He might get another dog.

He picked up his pace, glancing at his watch. He had shaved two minutes off his run, pretty good considering he had stayed out later than intended with Ross and Valerie.

Marsh stumbled on the sidewalk where a large root protruded, but he didn't slow down. His best ideas came when he pushed himself, and he was in dire need of ideas today.

Camille Gardner's arrival had stirred everyone, including him, up. He expected to know exactly how to deal with her, but she was unlike the businesswomen he usually encountered.

"I certainly didn't expect to see you two sitting here all chummy," he had said to Valerie when Camille departed the evening before.

Valerie smiled and sipped on her margarita, blotting the sweating glass with a napkin. "You don't know everything," she teased but didn't volunteer more.

Marsh didn't say anything and glanced at his watch.

"Do you really have something better to do?"

"I'd like to catch the end of the Rangers game," he said.

"You're acting like an old man," Ross said. "Baseball's about as exciting as counting the chips in this basket."

"That's because you lack the intellect to follow it," Marsh said, the familiar argument relaxing him. "A man who can't tell the National League from the American League is not to be trusted."

Valerie leaned back in her chair as though watching a show. "This is more like it," she murmured and signaled for another drink. "Finally, a conversation that doesn't revolve around land deals."

"Who's driving you home?" Lawrence asked her when he approached the table.

"You sound like Camille. That woman is so self-righteous she would hardly take a wedge of lemon in her water."

Enticing was more the word that entered Marsh's mind when he thought of Camille, but he shook the thought off. "No drinking and driving. It's our pact."

"It's only my third," she said. "I had dinner, and I've been here for hours."

"You know the drill, Val," Ross said. "We're not fooling around about this."

"All riiiight. One of you can drop me off, and I'll pick up my car in the morning."

Lawrence gave her an angry look and rubbed the back of his neck as he walked away.

As Marsh jogged, he realized he didn't have time for his planned six-mile route. Since he was nearby, he might as well bum a cup of coffee from Valerie and arrange to pick her up before work.

As he turned onto the boulevard, the first streaks of sunlight inched their way up in the east. Oaks arched over the median, and majestic old homes lined one side of the street.

Val's place sat on the other side, among a collection of recent New Orleans–style townhomes. Marsh bent to pick up her newspaper, slipped it out of its plastic bag, and read the headlines as he strolled to the front door.

A sound caught his ear and he glanced up, expecting to see one of the familiar early morning runners. He prepared to nod and speak — but froze.

Camille Gardner had great legs.

She missed a step when she saw him, recovered, and ran on past. Checking her watch, she slowed and turned back, jogging slowly over to where he stood.

"I didn't realize you were a runner." He might as well have been a college student bumping into a cute girl on campus.

"Depends on what day it is," Camille said. "You too?"

"I took up track in high school and decided I liked it."

"I've never met anyone who actually likes running." The look on her face was curious. "Did you move?"

Marsh didn't quite follow her at first and then looked down at the newspaper and over at the front door of Valerie's house. "Oh," he said, "this is Val's place."

"I see. Well, tell Valerie 'hi.' "

Before he could answer, she had resumed her run, faster than before.

Annoyed with Valerie, Marsh knew he had only himself to blame.

Camille had gotten up that morning feeling as though she'd been sick with the flu. Her muscles ached, and her head was stuffy. She'd never been a drinker — her father had cured her of any interest in alcohol —

but she thought this must be what a bad hangover felt like.

Seeing Marsh at Valerie's house had made her feel worse.

She rebuked Valerie in her mind, telling herself she was concerned about a J&S employee sleeping with the enemy. But, as she ran, she acknowledged that she was more than a little disappointed. She somehow had expected better of Marsh.

Checking the time, she cut across a side street and found herself on Trumpet Avenue.

She turned and headed for the familiar house.

Sweating by the time she got there, she dashed into the ramshackle convenience store on the northeast corner, now open, and bought a bottle of water. Then she jogged across the street and sat on the front porch.

While she resented Scott for his controlling nature, she'd been in his debt since she was fifteen. He'd saved her and — more important — her mother.

She considered how he would handle Sweet Olive, how he'd barge in on Ginny and issue an ultimatum, visit Sweet Olive residents and imply their community association was ruining their future, and whirl through downtown Samford, pounding on desks and reminding the business community how much they owed him.

Camille sipped the water, her muscles tight.

For Scott, jobs like Sweet Olive were plain. Make J&S look good. Tie up a few loose ends.

He liked mud and machines, wildcatting and drilling. His vision for the gas deep in the shale of North Louisiana was all about the prize — and nothing about the people.

But to Camille, the past few days had been a new look into the untidy world of emotion and money.

This she knew: With the Martinezes committed, the rest of Sweet Olive would come around in a few days. That kind of money turned heads.

She felt no pleasure.

Her run back to the hotel was five minutes faster than her earlier pace, and she sprinted through the back door to the lobby. A man was talking to the desk clerk, his tone querulous. He turned as she drew closer.

"There you are!" Slattery said. "I wanted to stop by on my way to the office to congratulate you."

She adjusted her glasses, buying a moment.

"I heard you struck a deal last night. That should get everyone else moving."

In small towns, word of oil money often spread as quickly as a major illness on the prayer chain at her mother's church, but this was definitely a record. "That deal has nothing to do with you." She didn't blink as she spoke.

Slattery looked smug. "Every deal in Cypress Parish has something to do with me. I'd encourage you to remember that."

CHAPTER 19

Marsh rushed out of a long meeting to get to a court hearing — only for it to be postponed again.

He had missed four calls from keyed-up clients and a vague message from Lawrence.

Add to that the clumsy jogging encounter with Camille, and this day was officially off to a rotten start.

He bolted for the elevator at the office building, flashing his badge to the overzealous guard. The elevator stopped on the sixth floor, the doors sliding open to reveal Ross, who grinned when he spotted Marsh.

"What are you doing here?" Marsh grumbled, catching a glimpse of Camille at the J&S office door. Her brow was furrowed, and she didn't seem to notice him.

"Trying to interest Camille in some real estate," Ross said.

"Why would she want real estate in Samford? She's only here for a few weeks."

Ross shrugged. "She had a question about a property."

"What property?"

"You know I can't tell you that," Ross said. "But I must say, she seems like a nice person."

"Don't forget who she works for," he snapped.

"Not a chance of that. A lot of my deals are on hold until we get this gas mess straightened out. Everyone's nervous about where the wells are going — and about the impact on drinking water."

From the corner of the elevator, Marsh examined his friend. Ross wore a sport coat and no tie, a contrast to Marsh's tailored suit and sedate tie. Ross spent so much time on the golf course that his hair looked like it had been highlighted.

Noticing that made Marsh feel ridiculous.

"That land's going to be just fine," Marsh said, weighing his words. "You know Ginny's group. They're not yielding when it comes to the future of Sweet Olive."

"You might want to tell Lawrence that." The elevator halted and Ross stepped off first.

"What's that supposed to mean?" Marsh said to his back.

■ ■ ■ ■

Camille listened to her voice messages, most requesting meetings now that she was "settled in."

Scott had sent her an e-mail congratulating her on the Martinezes but saying he hoped for more signatures. He added a P.S.: "Slattery Richmond is an important part of our business there, and, thus, so is Valerie."

The thought of the first Sweet Olive contract made her queasy, and after reading the note, she threw her pen across the room and then got up to retrieve it, embarrassed. This was not the time for a tantrum.

She picked up her oversized mug, a piece of green pottery she had bought from an artist in the Ozarks during a tough Arkansas land deal. It was the one piece of art that traveled with her, the rest boxed up in the spare room at her mother's.

She touched the cup, savoring the feel of the glaze, imagining the artist plopping a lump of clay on the wheel. *Things take shape in unexpected ways.* She chuckled at the thought — her one attempt at pottery had resulted in a lopsided vase her mother had pretended to love.

Mug in hand, she wandered out of her office and stuck her head in Valerie's office, wondering how she would react to the Martinez contract, a deal she had been unable to close with a man she had once planned to marry.

But Valerie hadn't made it in after her fiesta last night, and Camille turned to leave. And then took a step back into the office. What would a brief look hurt? A narrow window showcased the parking garage, and a cardboard box sat open on the desk. Had Valerie been packing or unpacking?

She caught a whiff of a man's cologne and thought it was Slattery's. She wondered when he had come by the office, shivering slightly at his curious appearance at the hotel that morning.

Ross Broussard's unscheduled visit, in response to a brief e-mail she had sent, had been a nice distraction. His upbeat manner steered her thoughts from Lawrence and momentarily erased the memory of the mortifying morning encounter with Marsh.

She had asked vague questions about Samford property, mentioning several signs she had seen in town.

"Are you looking for a home or an investment?" Ross asked.

"Nothing, really. I'm probably wasting your time," she said. "But I appreciate the information."

Now she stared at Valerie's white desk, adorned by two items. One was a leather date book open to this week, a red ribbon marking the page. The other was a crystal clock with a tiny engraved brass plate: *To V: For old time's sake. M.*

She studied Valerie's appointment book. Most of the notations seemed personal, from a mani-pedi to having her teeth cleaned. One said, "S.O. folo." Another from two days before said, "Dinkins? Deal?"

Why would Valerie have an appointment with the field manager of Bienville Oil?

A laptop was closed on a nearby table, and Camille approached it cautiously before forcing herself to move to a trio of framed snapshots perched on a large bookcase. One of the photos was of Valerie, Marsh, Ross, and another woman at the beach.

A second showed a group, including Marsh, on skis with a snow-covered mountain in the background. A professionally done portrait of a fluffy white dog in front of a red barn rounded out the grouping. An engraved plate said, *Cotton Grove III.*

Camille wandered over to the window, her thoughts jumping around like a pack of monkeys as she examined the view. The river lay to the west and the courthouse across the street, very scenic. If she was going to be here longer, she would search for a painting of downtown Samford.

"So you not only stalk my clients, but you look through your employee's office?" Marsh's angry voice said.

She whirled, dismayed to find him standing within a few feet.

He reached into his suit jacket and pulled out a folded sheaf of paper. "Lawrence asked me to give you these. You omitted the water clause — among other things. Turns out it wasn't quite the deal he expected."

Camille frowned but didn't take the contract — or the check, clipped to the top. "That's not true. I proofed it myself, and he signed it. I hand-delivered the money first thing." Her mind whirled faster than one of Ginny's whirligigs in a windstorm. "He took the check."

"He agreed under duress," Marsh said. "We're declaring it null and void." He waved the check under her nose.

She jammed her hands into her skirt pockets. "We can sue to enforce the contract."

"Try." His jaw was set.

"Every landowner has to make the decision that bests suits him or her."

"Is that how you get to sleep at night? You

hounded my client after work. I thought you cared about the artists, that you saw them as people and not numbers." He gave a disgusted snort. "I thought you were different."

"Apparently I'm not." Camille walked past him, her head held high. Valerie had printed the contract a few days earlier, and it wouldn't take much computer work to see exactly what she had chosen to delete.

Marsh was furious as he followed Camille.

"This is unacceptable," he barked. "It's unethical." In addition to professional fury, he felt personally deflated.

She slipped behind her desk but remained standing. "Why can't you let these people do what they need to do?" she said quietly.

He took a step back. "I'm not the one stopping them."

"They're confused. I get that. But you and I both know that wells will be drilled in the vicinity, whether they sign or not."

She eased onto her desk chair. "J&S was generous with the Martinezes. We'll be just as generous with the others. It's the best offer they're going to get."

"Camille, most of these people are hanging on by a financial thread. But their legacy is a big deal to them."

She drew in a slow breath and exhaled it just as slowly. He waited for her to speak, but she remained silent, staring at him.

"This is home to them," he said. "It's special."

"It *is* special," she said in that quiet way of hers. "Very special."

"Gas wells will ruin the charm."

She stood and walked to the window, her silhouette lovely in the shifting light. "Maybe I shouldn't have approached Lawrence. I don't know."

"My clients want you to know that J&S won't get anywhere if you keep rushing things."

"You know how this business works," she said, combing her fingers through her hair. "We lose money every day we don't produce."

"You lost a lot of trust with that stunt you pulled with Lawrence. You might want to reconsider the community meeting."

"There's no way I would back out on that," she said.

Ginny answered the phone on the first ring. "I defended you. I told people it couldn't be true." Camille heard tears in her voice. "I'm a fool."

"You're the least foolish person I know,"

Camille said, her own voice shaky.

"Not only did you sign the Martinezes behind our back, but you tried to cheat them out of their water."

"But I didn't."

"So you're telling me Marsh is a liar?" Ginny demanded.

"It was a mistake."

"You told me you'd work with me."

"I am," Camille said.

"Your idea of working together is not the same as mine. You promised you would get to know us before you took it further."

"It's complicated."

"I'm tired of all this," Ginny said. "I've half a mind to call off tonight's meeting and let everyone do what they want."

A dog barked in the background, and Camille could hear the children chattering. "Please don't do that. You're fighting for what you believe in. It's totally different from the way most of the world operates. Don't quit."

"That doesn't even make sense." Ginny's voice was irritated. "You're on the other side of this argument, in case you forgot."

"I feel like I've been on a roller coaster since I got here, and most of the time I'm upside down. I don't make sense to myself, either. Not to mention to my boss."

"This has got to be worked out and worked out soon," Ginny said.

"I couldn't agree more."

"Half of my friends think I've already ruined Sweet Olive, and the other half think I'm taking money out of their pockets. How would you feel if this were your neighborhood?"

Camille grew quiet. "I think I'd be more confused than you are," she said finally. "I didn't grow up here — but I love what you're trying to do. You've got the kind of roots I've longed for my whole life."

"Then why did you betray me?" The question was soft, so different from Ginny's usual boisterous style.

"I was trying to help Evelyn," she said. "Give me a chance to answer questions tonight."

"People are plenty hot about all of this. You're probably not going to like what you hear."

"I probably deserve it." Camille hung up the phone with a heavy heart.

CHAPTER 20

Camille stormed into Valerie's office, her head throbbing. "You deliberately altered a legal document. Do you know how serious that is?"

"The paper jammed when I printed the document. How was I to know a section had been omitted?" She somehow managed to assume a hurt expression. "Haven't you ever made an error?"

Camille ground her teeth so hard that her jaw ached.

"Oh, I forgot. You're the perfect Camille Gardner."

"This may wind up in court."

"It was a mistake." Valerie hissed the words, loud and slow.

"The section was deleted before it was printed. I checked the computer file. Do you think I'm an idiot?"

Veins popped out on Valerie's temples, her blond hair pulled back into a French twist.

"Take your conspiracy theories to Mr. Stephens." She flung a file at Camille. "And while you're at it, tell him about all the time we're wasting looking at ancient records."

Camille bent to pick up the folder. "I'll need a signed statement of how the error occurred. We'll run it by the corporate attorney before it goes in the file."

"Fine. But with that and the other *homework* you've given me, I'll be late for the community meeting."

"Make it quick." Camille scanned the file as she walked to the door. "I'll see you there."

Camille pulled into the library five minutes before the meeting and let out a small *yes.* Only two pickups — including one almost identical to hers — were in the lot, alleviating her fear that every resident of Cypress Parish would show up.

She climbed the steps and stopped, that same light scent from Ginny's house tickling her nose. Looking around, she pushed on the heavy old door.

A man in khaki work pants and a white Western shirt stepped forward to hold the door for her, a questioning look in his deep blue eyes. "May I help you?" A guy in his midtwenties paused from on a ladder, giving her a nod and a smile. His brown hair was cut short, and he wore jeans and work boots.

The smile Camille had forced onto her face disappeared as her gaze flew around the construction site. "I'm here for the Sweet Olive meeting."

The older of the two tilted his head, rubbing his trim salt-and-pepper beard. "You're that J&S gal, aren't you?"

"That's me. Camille Gardner."

The guy on the ladder increased his smile as he descended the rungs. "You must not have gotten the word that the meeting's been moved to the school." The younger man's voice was quiet and not as southern as expected. "We're remodeling this week, so the library's closed."

"The school?" Camille looked at the clock on her phone. "The meeting's about to start."

"You're only a hop, skip, and a jump away," the older one said. "Just head south on the highway there, take a left at the blinking light, and you'll see it on your right, about three miles."

Her heart pounding, she murmured a thanks and stepped quickly to the door.

"I suspect you'll run into my brother there." The parting words came from the younger man, who moved with grace to open the door for her. "He's a big-shot attorney, and I'm proud of him for helping out." His voice held a teasing note. "It never hurts to have a person used to dealing with bureaucracy and such."

"I'm sorry. I didn't catch your names."

"T. J. Aillet." The younger man's dark brown eyes twinkled as he shook her hand. His grip was firm, his palm calloused.

"And I'm Bud Cameron, Marsh's daddy." The other man's voice had a country twang. "You got his attention with that Martinez deal." He winked.

Camille looked from one to the other, attempting to hide her curiosity. Other than their work clothes, the two looked nothing alike.

T. J. laughed. "I'm Marsh's half brother."

She shook her head. "I'm sorry, but —"

"It confuses everyone," Bud said. "Marsh's mother remarried."

"My father is Marsh's stepfather. We're sort of an unusual family."

They followed her a couple of steps into the parking lot. "Nice truck," Bud said.

T. J.'s parting smile was warm. "Good luck tonight."

Camille wished she'd listened more closely to Bud's directions, but she'd been much more interested in the fact that everyone seemed to know everyone else's business — and that Marsh's dad and half brother were some sort of country carpenters. And they worked together?

Marsh's mother was a social diva if ever there was one. That didn't fit with the men Camille had just met. Grinding gears, she groused at the truck and tried to remember what Bud had said. Was she looking for a stop sign or a light? A right turn or a left?

With relief, she glimpsed a green highway sign directing her to North Cypress Parish High School. She hadn't asked *which* school but hoped it was that one.

Expecting a quaint old country school, she was surprised by a modern brick building with a large metal gymnasium. The parking lot near the road had seven or eight pickups and SUVs in it, enough to convince her she was in the right spot. She was oddly comforted to see a variety of J&S trucks, from pickups to flatbeds to tankers.

Uncle Scott had definitely made his presence known here, and maybe that would make her role tonight easier.

When she pulled in, she saw the parking area around the back overflowing. Some people had pulled up on the grass, seeking the shade of a trio of scrawny live oaks. According to the thermometer taped to her dashboard, the temperature was still in the high eighties.

Her cell phone buzzed, and she glanced down to see a text from Ginny: YOU RUN-NING LATE?

Parking out front, she grabbed her file folder and jogged to the end of the building, texting as she went: HERE.

The door opened before she could reach it, and Ginny stepped out, her face flushed and her brow wrinkled. "We were about to give up on you." Her tone was annoyed.

"I went to the wrong place. The library."

Ginny's expression shifted. "Valerie said she left a note on your office door."

"She's here?" Camille trailed Ginny into the steamy, noisy gym. Sure enough, Valerie had her arms outstretched, greeting people in the packed bleachers, like a candidate for office.

Jason Dinkins, wearing khakis and a golf shirt, appeared to be working the crowd from the other end of the bleachers.

"Valerie did you a favor. She's been listening to landowners the past ten minutes. She's staying one step ahead, I'll give her that." Ginny looked back at the door. "I have to tell you, Camille, we're all stunned by what you did. The water. The land. All of it. I expected better."

"It was a mistake —" Camille's voice was rough with emotion.

"I can't talk about this now," Ginny said, brushing her aside. "We're starting late as it is."

Camille stepped aside and steeled herself. Every resident of Sweet Olive and their relatives must have shown up, along with the other residents of Cypress Parish, and they all seemed to be in animated conversation.

The people milling around wore everything from cutoff shorts to overalls without shirts — but no one except Camille had on a suit, not even Marsh, standing to the side in an animated conversation with a man in an LSU cap. Marsh looked at ease in a pair of pressed khakis and a yellow long-sleeved oxford-cloth shirt. Valerie had changed into a pair of dressy jeans and a short-sleeve pale orange blouse.

Three microphones stood on the edge of the shiny wood floor, with four folding chairs. Elementary-age boys were having a jumping contest on two of the chairs, and a handful of younger children played tag beyond the chairs. A lone girl dribbled a basketball, the bouncing noise sounding like a drumbeat.

A toddler cried, barely audible in the

cavernous room. Most people smiled and shook hands, as though at a high school football game, while a few looked dour.

Someone had propped a poster that said, "Don't give away our water" at the end of the bleachers. Another poster said, "All things work for good."

Standing at the end of the bleachers, Camille started toward Valerie, now talking to a group of people in matching red church T-shirts, a drawing of praying hands next to an oil rig accompanied by the words, "Pray for wisdom."

As she debated what to do, Lawrence strode forward, wearing a pair of olive cargo pants and yet another black T-shirt, once more looking like a big-city artist.

He shook his head slowly. "I refuse to believe you deliberately left the water clause out of the contract, but a company as big as J&S should not do business that way."

"It was a clerical error," she said, "but I should have caught it. I can easily correct the contract. I'll bring it to you . . . tonight, if you want."

He shook his head. "Not going to happen."

"So you've changed your mind?"

He looked directly at her. "It was unfair to bail on the rest of the group. And my mother wasn't very happy with me."

"How could she not be happy with that check?" Camille's brow creased.

"The older artists are like family. She doesn't believe that's the direction God is leading us." He looked down at his black high-top tennis shoes. "I owe you an apology, though. I was an idiot to sign that contract, but I know it puts you in a bind."

"It's just as well. Something about it didn't feel right."

"You're a good woman, Camille." He motioned toward the crowd. "Are you sure you're ready for the circus?"

"I'm ready to run away and join one." Camille looked around. A tall man shook his finger in the face of the man seated near him, and the woman next to him stood, hands on her hips.

An older woman sat in the front row talking to a thin African American woman, knitting. Marsh's father, still in his painting clothes, had appeared and Valerie stood next to him.

Lawrence nodded toward the door. "I think the spectacle just got bigger."

A young man carrying a large video camera walked in, accompanied by a perky brunette holding a microphone and lights.

"You made it!" Ginny exclaimed, scurrying from behind the information/sign-up table. She looked over at Camille. "We can't wait to tell you our story. Camille, these folks are working on a documentary on the local gas boom. I'm sure they'd love to hear your tactics."

Camille's head began to pound. Her other interview had infuriated investors; a documentary film could run them off altogether — not to mention how Scott would react.

Ginny let out a shrill whistle. "Take your seats," she yelled, "and we'll get started."

To Camille's amazement, the room grew quiet. Several adults rounded up the children, and even the baby quit crying.

Ginny tapped the microphone, and Val took a seat in the front row, shooting Camille a quick nod and glancing away.

Marsh gave Camille a curt hello, and a local pastor, also wearing a red T-shirt, rose to give the invocation. His prayer was poetic, full of Scripture and a plea for God's help "as Your servants gather to decide what You would have them do."

A resounding "Amen" filled the room, and Ginny took the mike again, sounding like a mix between a revival preacher and a stern principal. "You were given a copy of our key concerns when you came in. I drew those from the surveys you mailed back."

Her comments were like the opening bell at a horse race, with everyone talking at once. "I didn't get a sheet," three or four people yelled, as though in a shouting contest. "Where does it say what the going rate per acre is?" someone else called out.

"Where does it explain how those chemicals kill your hogs?" a little man in overalls shouted. "Replanting trees is not a concern," a red-faced man in his thirties yelled. Camille recognized him as the guy who had been talking with Marsh a few minutes earlier.

"One at a time," Ginny said, tapping the mike. "Come to a microphone and ask your questions one at a time. Raise your hands if you need an information sheet."

The questions came loudly to Camille and Jason Dinkins, who assured residents Bienville Oil could serve them better because he had grown up in North Louisiana.

Some attendees focused on potential damage to roads, while others asked environmental questions. "I've read that drilling can cause earthquakes," an older woman in the Sweet Olive group said. A few people laughed while others widened their eyes.

Jason jumped to his feet. "That's one of those rumors started by the liberal media,

Miss Lillie. You don't need to worry about it."

The crowd applauded, and the woman sat back down.

Camille rose with reluctance and put a microphone to her mouth. "To clarify, ma'am, we all know it takes a lot to shift Mother Earth, but no one knows for sure. The handful of recent small quakes in the U.S. are still being studied."

"Hmm," Marsh said under his breath, his comment among the hum that ran through the crowd.

Jason grabbed a mike, sweat pouring down his face. "With all due respect, Camille . . ." He threw her a poisonous stare. "There is no known correlation between drilling and earthquakes."

"No *known* correlation, but I would be less than candid if I didn't tell folks that J&S continues to study this impact from its Houston office." Projects like that were among the reasons she wanted the executive job.

"Thank you for your honesty," Ginny said, her red lips curving into a smile that had been missing all evening. "Now let's move on."

A handful of people complained about "oil-field trash" that the wells brought in, and Camille cringed. More than a few in the audience were in J&S and Bienville uniforms.

A thin woman of about sixty-five stood, smiling when Lawrence assisted her. "Good evening. I'm Evelyn Martinez — or, as I'm apparently now known, the old lady who turned down the money."

The crowd laughed.

"I've prayed hard about this, and I believe we are to take good care of our land. A big payout now won't mean anything if we don't have water to drink."

A few people applauded.

"If I may?" Camille looked at Ginny as she reached for the microphone. "I'm Camille Gardner, Mrs. Martinez. I don't think we've met."

"Get on with it," the red-faced man in the LSU cap yelled.

"I don't know how this is all going to work out." Camille looked over at Jason Dinkins. "But I promise I've made my last secret deal. I will abide by the wishes of Sweet Olive, whatever those turn out to be."

"This has gone on long enough," the LSU-cap guy called out. "I think we should sign."

"Don't do it! We signed, and we're not getting half what J&S promised in our part of the parish," a woman yelled.

"At least you got something, pal," the other man retorted.

"They need us more than we need them," someone else shouted.

"We need each other," Camille murmured — and wished she had taken an aspirin before she left the office.

CHAPTER 21

Marsh felt as though he were watching an Olympic Ping-Pong match.

Slattery Richmond, looking every inch the senator, slid into the meeting late with his usual air of importance and stood to the side, his eyes sweeping the room.

Marsh acknowledged him with a slight nod and then looked over at his father, seated in the front row, paint splattered on his pants. Just the sight of Slattery and Bud in the same room made Marsh thankful again that he came from Sweet Olive stock and not that clique his mother so adored.

Bud Cameron was an original, a guy's guy, who went to church and loved his neighbor and took brouhahas like this in stride. When he and Marsh's mother had divorced, Marsh had said and done plenty of dumb things — but his father had loved him through them.

Even while not putting up with Marsh's

teenaged stupidity, his dad told him he would always have a home in Sweet Olive.

With Slattery approaching the microphone, Marsh caught his father's eye and winked.

"My family has lived in Cypress Parish for more than one-hundred years," Slattery said. "My granddaddy would have my hide if we let anyone hurt any of you."

Marsh had to bite back a groan. Slattery would sell his grandfather if he thought he could make a buck. One of his subsidiaries had bought half of the mineral rights in Cypress Parish for a tenth of what they were worth — and brokered them to Bienville Oil for a hefty profit.

The rash of drilling that followed — everywhere except in Sweet Olive and near Slattery's high-end Cotton Grove development — had changed the area forever.

Marsh had been taken aback when Ross informed him about Lawrence's offer from Camille. He hadn't pegged her as bold enough to go downtown at midnight for a land deal and worried about what other foolhardy stunts she might try.

He'd been pleased at the size of her offer but furious that she'd bypassed the artists' association — and him. He thought they had come to a truce of sorts.

While he wouldn't admit it to Camille, Marsh did not even feel 100 percent sure that he had done the right thing in calling off the deal, but an angry Evelyn had been adamant that the Martinez land — above- or belowground — was not for sale.

And now Dinkins was showing up everywhere, acting as though he had an infusion of cash, waiting for the right person to take it.

What a day . . .

If there was anything worse than fighting one oil company for property rights, it was getting caught in the middle of two. If the artists splintered between J&S and Bienville Oil, the entire community could become an industrial wilderness.

Listening to Camille's polite answers to questions tonight, he wondered why she had gotten so tangled up in this fiasco. In his experience, landmen generally didn't tutor art classes and track waiters down on the job.

While Valerie sat in the front row and seemed disdainful, Camille looked engaged — almost as though she were explaining herself to a group of friends.

"Marsh?" Ginny's voice interrupted his thoughts. After two-and-a-half hours of bickering, he'd lost track of the conversation.

Camille made a quiet sound next to him, drawing his attention. "He wants to know why you're moving so slowly," she said under her breath, reaching for the microphone.

"If I may jump in — J&S has had conversations with both Mr. Cameron and Ms. Guidry within the past few days," Camille said, "but they've expressed the need for consensus in your group. They understand that strands together are stronger."

Marsh heard his father's chuckle across the gym floor. He ran his fingers through his hair.

"Miss Gardner's correct," Marsh said. "Each of you has the right to act individually, but you'll get a better deal if you stick together." Marsh could tell he wasn't the only one losing interest in the meeting. Half of the people talked among themselves, and a few women were picking up their purses.

"I know a few of you are ready to get on home," he said, "but I'll stay and answer individual questions for anyone who has them."

"That's an excellent idea." Ginny stood in a whirl of long skirt.

"I don't think we should leave till we've

decided who we're going to sign with," Drew Cross, who apparently never left home without his LSU cap, said. His face had gotten redder as the room had gotten warmer.

"I agree," a thin, flushed woman shouted. Both Ginny and Camille started at the words, and he looked closer. Janice Procell, Ginny's sister-in-law, sat next to Drew, her two children playing on the floor nearby.

"Let Marsh review the offers and make a recommendation," Evelyn said. "He has the best interests of the community at heart."

"With all due respect," Cross said, "that's a crock."

Lawrence jumped to his feet, and Marsh groaned. He drew in a breath and looked at Jason Dinkins, wondering if he'd help break up the fight that was about to occur.

But before Lawrence could make his way down the bleachers, Marsh heard the clatter of a chair turning over. Camille had jumped to her feet and marched up to the edge of the bleachers, right in front of Drew.

The room was quieter than a cathedral Marsh had visited in Seattle once on vacation. Even Lawrence stopped.

"Mrs. Martinez does not deserve to be spoken to like that," Camille said in a loud, clear voice. "I am willing to stay here all night and talk about your land, but I will not tolerate that kind of disrespectful behavior."

"Just who do you think you are?" Drew asked, but he did move back an inch or two. "You haven't been in town for ten minutes, and you think you can tell us what to do?"

Marsh frowned and took a step forward.

"I may not be from around here, but my mother taught me manners." Camille turned slightly. "I apologize for the tone of tonight's meeting. I didn't expect it to be so . . . ugly."

Marsh had to concentrate to keep a poker face as Evelyn, aided by Lawrence, made her way down to Camille and gave her a hug, the crowd dispersing like a spilled carton of milk.

"Call me Evelyn, honey, and quit fretting. It'll all work out, Camille."

Lawrence reached over to hug Camille.

Ginny tapped the mike two or three times to get the crowd's attention. "I think we've accomplished all we can tonight. Send me an e-mail with your feedback."

Marsh rose, a crick in his neck, noting that Camille was still chatting with Lawrence, smiling more than he'd seen her do in the nearly four weeks she'd been in Samford. The sight brought a weight to his gut, and he wished, not for the first time, that something other than oil and gas had caused their paths to cross.

Valerie was talking to Slattery but eyed Camille and Lawrence.

Marsh's head hurt. Maybe he should stay with nice, quiet business law, where people wore suits and ties and he rarely had to wrestle a chair from a child in a jumping contest.

But he looked over at Camille and knew he'd stick with the case. Her smile drew him in as no woman's ever had, and the sadness that flickered through her beautiful eyes tugged at his heart. Perhaps by the time he unraveled the mineral leases, he would have discovered what brought that look to her face.

His father emerged as the crowd eased up. "You have time for a quick question, son?"

Marsh started, his eyes fixed on Camille.

"You look worn out."

"What a zoo." Marsh wiped his forehead. "My world revolves around gas leases."

"And a perky landman?"

"Tell me you're not matchmaking." Marsh cut his eyes at his father but couldn't resist another glance at Camille.

His father followed his gaze. "I liked the way she jumped in to help Evelyn tonight."

"There's something special about Ca-mille . . ." Marsh couldn't seem to keep his eyes off of her as she chatted with the motley assortment of citizens, smiling and nodding. "She cares about people, even though I could wring her neck over that Martinez deal."

His father laid his hand on his shoulder. "Why don't you ask her to dinner? Try to work this out personally?"

"Don't go there, Dad."

"What could it hurt?'

He gave his father a quick hug. "I'd better get back to work."

He took a couple of steps before turning around. "Dad, have I mentioned lately how much I love you?"

Camille had been intrigued by the way Marsh handled the meeting. He must be quite a presence in a courtroom.

She lost sight of him, though, as the crowd swirled around.

"You gave that Cross boy what for all right," Evelyn said. Her raven hair was thin-ning and gray at the temples. Her dark eyes flashed. "He ought to be ashamed of him-self."

"It's hard," Camille said, "when money's involved. Everyone gets nervous."

"I'm not nervous. I came into this world with nothing, and I'll leave with nothing." She pointed her finger at Camille. "I like that you stood up for me, but I don't like what you talked Lawrence into."

"Mama," Lawrence said, but then stopped and directed a small smile toward Camille.

She smiled back.

Two or three people nearby stepped closer.

"We should never worry about money," Evelyn said. "It's not what God wants for us."

Lawrence mouthed "I'm sorry," grinning his crooked smile as he and his mother walked away.

"Man oh man," Marsh's voice said behind her. "Nothing like a little greed to get people stirred up."

Camille stepped out of the shadows next to the truck.

He gave an embarrassed laugh. "I thought for a second you were my father."

"That's a first."

"My dad has a truck just like that."

"I saw it," she said. "Poor guy."

"Poor guy? He loves classics." Marsh nodded toward the MGB. "He fixed this up for me when I graduated from college."

"That car looks like one of those Hot

Wheels that boys play with . . . But it does have a good radio."

"So what'd you think of the show tonight?"

"Not a night I want to repeat." She took a step toward him. "I feel awful about what I did to Lawrence. I owe you and the artists an apology."

Even in the twilight of the parking lot, she recognized the surprise in his vivid blue eyes. "Thank you." He raised his eyebrows. "I must add that I've never returned a check that size before."

"My mother told me I should be ashamed of myself," she said.

He drew back. "You told your mother about that?"

"I tell her everything," she said with a smile and then cut her eyes away. "Well, I didn't tell her I hung around downtown at midnight." She pointed toward the gym. "It was a zoo in there, but the artists are such good people."

"The best." He nodded.

She studied him, chewing on her bottom lip. "I'm glad they have you on their side." And with that, she climbed in the truck.

CHAPTER 22

The red-faced LSU-cap man from the town meeting was waiting for Camille in the parking garage the next afternoon.

"You might want to be careful," he said, adjusting his hat. "Downtown can be dangerous."

Camille looked around, but the garage was empty. Even the attendant was missing from his little shed.

The man — she remembered his name was Drew Cross — reached into his pocket and pulled out a container of snuff, took a pinch, and stuck it between his lip and teeth. He shuffled his feet and put his hands in his pockets. Camille looked over his shoulder, hoping to see anyone.

"Is this a bad time?" He followed her gaze. "For what?"

He looked around and pitched his voice low. "I've got four acres, and I want to sign."

She took a step back.

"I don't want my neighbors to know until it's a done deal. They'll try to talk me out of it."

"I'm —" *Stunned? Surprised? Sad?* "Are you sure?" she finally said.

He looked confused. "Are you trying to trick me?"

"I . . . I want you to be sure before we do all the paperwork."

"I'm tired of waiting for a bunch of old people to get a sign from God or something."

His behavior, much as it had the previous night, reminded Camille of one of the wild hogs that rampaged around Uncle Scott's ranch. From his questions, though, she suspected he had good business sense.

"What about the Artists' Guild?" she asked. "I've been instructed to work through their attorney." She gave a little smile, intended to charm him.

"I've had it with them. This is my land, my life. I'm not holding out any longer." He stepped closer. "A couple of the younger artists want to talk to you too. Will you pay me extra if I talk others into leaving the group?"

She moved back, slightly nauseated by the question. "I can't do that."

Drew gave his head a quick shake. "You

are one peculiar woman. You've been pushing us to sign, and Janice said you were trying to meet a deadline."

She let out her breath. "I am."

"Then give me my money."

"This is complex," she said, glad Uncle Scott wasn't able to hear this. "I don't want a repeat of the Martinez situation. J&S lost a lot of time and effort on that."

"If you don't come through, I'm going to Bienville Oil. And some of the others are too."

"Don't do that," she said, keeping her voice calm. "We'll work this out."

"Is this a good place to meet?"

"Wouldn't my office be better?" Camille looked at the few cars still parked nearby.

"I'm not a fan of office buildings. They give me claustrophobia."

"Maybe a restaurant? I'd be happy to buy lunch or supper."

"We want this to be private," he said, as though she'd suggested they discuss the matter on stage.

"J&S shares this garage with several businesses," she said patiently. "Marsh Cameron, among others, parks here."

"You call me then. You have my number." He tipped his cap and started to walk away before turning back. "Janice loves them kids. She's a good mother, no matter what Ginny says."

Camille froze. "They're sweet children."

He turned to walk away again, and this time Camille called out. "Drew, there's one more thing."

His eyes narrowed in suspicion.

"Are you an artist?"

"Everybody in Sweet Olive's an artist."

"What medium do you work in?" she asked, her voice eager.

Drew wore a puzzled look. "I'm not right sure what you're talking about."

"Do you paint or carve or do some other kind of art?" she asked.

"My people make things out of old mufflers, and I make metal bugs."

"The bugs! Those are great, very entertaining."

"Entertaining?" He lifted his cap and scratched his head. "I reckon they are."

He was almost to the side exit of the garage when he nodded at someone and slowed his steps.

Camille saw Valerie, standing on the other side of her car, the BMW that had been a gift from her parents when she turned thirty.

Standing still, Camille tried to hear what they said, but echoes of the garage mingled with street noise prevented it. Drew smiled and nodded, then reached out to take a piece of paper — a business card, maybe? — from Valerie.

Scooting behind a nearby SUV, Camille fished her cell phone out of her purse. Holding it up over the edge of the hood, she snapped a picture as Valerie and Drew shook hands. The camera looked like a periscope in an old submarine movie, and her lips curled in amusement.

One way or the other, she'd convince Valerie to work with her. With Slattery somehow involved in Uncle Scott's deal, firing the annoying Miss Richmond was not an option. But Camille was not going to let her hurt the artists, whatever it took.

Chapter 23

Since the incident with Lawrence, Ginny had remained distant, which hurt more than Camille could have imagined.

Only through Camille's persistence had she persuaded Ginny to meet with her at the reference department of the Cypress Public Library on a Saturday afternoon.

Carrying her usual stack of notebooks, Ginny entered in a pair of balloon pants and a tunic that resembled Joseph's coat of many colors. She slammed her things on the table. "I can't stay long. Evelyn's keeping the kids."

Camille tried to disguise the pain that ran through her at the abrupt words. "What are they working on?"

"Etchings with waxed paper." She dug in her bag. "Kylie asked me to bring you this."

The drawing of a row of bright houses caused Camille to swallow hard. "I miss them . . ."

"They keep asking when you're coming back."

"I never meant to hurt them — or you."

"Then why did you?"

Camille had prepared a long list of answers: The J&S offer was fair, and the money could be put to good use. Businesses had schedules to meet. The landowners would lose out if they didn't sign soon.

But she didn't speak. She sat there breathing in and out, regaining control of her emotions.

"I was wrong," she said finally.

Ginny twisted her hair into a bun and used a yellow pencil to secure it, her eyes intense. The library was tranquil around them, the occasional patron perusing the nearby card catalogue. The room had the pleasant smell of old books.

Camille continued in a quiet voice. "I thought J&S was going to lower its offer, and I wanted Evelyn to have that money if she needed it . . . I kept thinking about my own mother and how I would do anything to help her."

She held up her hand when Ginny started to interrupt. "Hear me out, please . . . I've never had neighbors before. I want what you have."

Ginny gave one of her big laughs, the

sound reverberating through the library. A patron or two looked curious. "You want what *I* have?" She swung her arm through the air and knocked half the stack onto the floor. Ginny looked down at the papers and back at Camille.

"Impressive illustration of your point."

Ginny rolled her eyes but smiled, and Camille bent to help her pick up the papers. "You need a laptop."

"I know, I know. If I would sign with J&S, I'd have plenty of money for a new computer."

"You don't have to sign. I can give you a technology grant from our community fund." Camille winked. "After all, you are an arts volunteer."

"I'm so confused." Ginny heaved a sigh. "This is supposed to be about business, but you feel like one of us. Where do we stand, Camille?"

"We're friends, Ginny. If you decide not to sign, fine. If you want to sign, I'll include your demands in the contract, including well locations and water testing."

"Bienville Oil's trying to convince us of the same thing."

"So they're back in the running?"

Ginny nodded. "Are you sure J&S will go along with your recommendations?"

"I'll type and print every contract myself — and be there when they're signed." Camille intended to present Uncle Scott with a fait accompli, but she wouldn't drag Ginny into that.

"My artists are a cantankerous bunch. This could take awhile."

Camille tried not to think of the weeks slipping by. "It'll work out. And I want to learn more about your art plans."

Ginny's bright red lipstick highlighted her somber mouth. "I thought from almost the first that God sent you to us."

Camille snorted. "Scott Stephens sent me to you — but he acts like he's God."

"You didn't come to Sweet Olive by accident."

Camille felt uncomfortable. "God's got bigger things to take care of than me: world peace, famine, that sort of thing."

"The Lord goes before us, wherever we're headed." Ginny turned her head. "You brag on the artists in Sweet Olive, how they're as good as famous artists."

"They are!"

"Then why can't you believe what you do is important to God?"

"Ginny, if there were a *plan* for my life, I doubt my mother and I would have been dumped on a street corner while my father ran off to work on an oil well."

The look on Ginny's face shifted to sorrow. "Just because things didn't work out in the past doesn't mean there's no hope for the future."

Camille smiled. "I'm working on it. Can we go back to arguing about your gas rights? That's easier than talking about this stuff."

"What stuff?"

She attempted a careless shrug. "Faith. Friendship. Family."

Ginny seemed baffled. "You dart around like a rabbit running from a hound."

"I'm here because J&S controls my life . . . I'm paying a debt to my uncle." There. She had offered another of her secrets.

"And he depends on you?"

"Not in the way Kylie and Randy — and half of the rest of Sweet Olive — depend on you." Camille ran her fingers through her hair. "At first I wanted to take care of my mother and pay him back for all he's done." She swallowed hard. "And then, I don't know, it became a habit."

"It sounds like it's time for you to do something else."

"That's why I'm in a hurry to get back to Houston." She wasn't sure how much to divulge. "With a corporate job, I'll work in an office with regular hours."

Ginny's face fell. "What about art?"

"The J&S job will pay for my first house." She gave a small smile. "I'll volunteer at a gallery and keep taking classes. By the time I retire, I'll be able to buy a gallery — or at least be part of a co-op."

"Just because you're good at oil and gas doesn't mean you have to do it until retirement. Surely your boss doesn't expect that."

Camille propped her face in her hands. "My father was an oil-field roughneck. Mama says he'd rather sleep in the bed of his pickup than in a five-star hotel."

Ginny didn't rush her.

"In those days, they mainly looked for oil, not gas. He had an eye for it — and a good heart, according to my mother. He listened when she fussed about the need to be a steward of the earth."

Camille pictured her father, reared back in a kitchen chair. "I guess I'm doing this job in part for him."

"Would he have wanted that?"

A whirl of ignored memories flew through Camille's mind — her father bringing her a paint-by-number set, a coloring book, modeling clay. One Christmas, money had been so scarce their rented trailer had no heat, but he came home with an extravagant art kit. And a six-pack.

"You have a gift, Camy," he said as they inspected each item in the metal box. "Don't let it slip away."

Ginny reached out and touched Camille's hand as a tear rolled down her face. *Why did my father waste his talent?*

"Your father would be proud of you, Camille."

"You're supposed to be mad at me, Ginny." She looked right into the big, black glasses. "I shouldn't have approached Lawrence the way I did."

"We make mistakes." Ginny held her hands across the library table. "I wish you could quit putting your life on hold."

"So do I." Camille blinked back another tear. "So do I."

CHAPTER 24

Two small dogs — rat terriers, Camille thought — dashed out. She slammed on the brakes but couldn't see where the animals had gone.

If she rolled forward, she feared she'd run right over them. But she couldn't sit here the rest of the afternoon.

Should she get out of the truck? Camille unlocked the door.

But before she stepped out, Evelyn came from around the house, clapped her hands, and started down the steps with a spryness that gave no hint of her illness. Her smock-like shirt over her clothes billowed like a sail as she ran. A bright green bandanna was tied around her neck.

She yelled, and the dogs ran toward her. Waving, she gestured for Camille to turn in. "Get out of the road, and they'll leave you alone."

Camille sheepishly gave a little wave. "I

was admiring your yard art. The dogs ran out . . .”

Evelyn leaned down and picked up the bigger of the two. “These two chase every car that comes down this road.” She shook her head. “We haven’t had so much traffic down this way since Lawrence was recruited to play college football — before he hurt his knee.”

Sitting in the truck, Camille felt like a giant over the small woman, so she opened the door and stepped out. She scuffed the dirt with her old cowboy boots. The wind, with a hint of fall, ruffled her hair and brought a whiff of that unusual sweet smell she kept encountering.

“I know you were upset with me, but I’m not here for J&S.” Camille reached out for Evelyn’s hand. “I am so sorry for what I did.”

“Lawrence insists I need the money for doctor bills, and he’d like for me to take one of those cruises.” She waved at the pecan trees and ponds across the road. “What a shame it would be to lose all of this for something as temporary as that.”

“Your land wouldn’t necessarily be damaged.” Camille chose her words carefully. J&S had identified the acreage across the road for the well site, land owned by the

Martinezes, but she intended to fight that — as long and hard as it took.

"You should see what they did to my sister's place over in Webster Parish." Evelyn shook her head, her lips flattened nearly into a straight line. "They cut every tree for a mile and tore up the land. Just flat tore it up."

"I admit drilling can be ugly, but land can be restored once the well's in place."

"I'm sure it *can* be restored, but will it be? And how long will it take? Those are the real questions." Evelyn wiped her hands on the smock. "Lawrence, Marsh, and the other young folks will be the ones who have to live with all these changes."

Camille studied Evelyn. No matter what the Martinezes did, changes were coming to Sweet Olive. The idea unexpectedly hurt.

Camille looked at the bright flowers. "Will you please give me a quick tour of your art?" She held up her hands. "Just art. Not gas."

Evelyn followed Camille's gaze to the creations, a hint of a smile coming to her lips. "As long as you don't talk anymore about gas wells or try to slip me a check."

"I am truly not doing a good job in Sweet Olive."

Evelyn stuck her head out so far that she

looked like a little rooster strutting by. "Don't you think we're smart enough to know there's no such thing as free money? Like I told Lawrence, you get something, you give up something. Plain and simple."

"Nothing like a mother's wisdom." Camille smiled.

"What does your mother think about you going all over the country like you do?"

Camille gave a small moan. "About what you'd imagine. She'd like me to put down roots."

Evelyn nodded. "That's what we all want for our children."

"Your son is an outstanding artist."

"Lawrence has grown into a fine man." Evelyn nodded. "He had troubles after his father passed, but he's come through that. He'll make it big one of these days."

"I agree." Camille pointed to the rows of colorful metal stuck in the ground — mostly flowers, birds, and assorted other bright, nonsensical objects. "May I have that tour now?"

Evelyn put her hands in the smock pockets and stared at Camille. "Are you an artist?"

"Unfortunately not. I'm a . . ." She hesitated and then smiled. "Well, you know, I work for the unmentionable."

"You act like an artist," Evelyn said.

"Maybe you should try it. Come on, and I'll show you what I do."

She led Camille to a cluster of intricate roses with stripes painted on them. Wearing red sneakers with mismatched socks, Evelyn looked as though she had sprouted in the display herself.

Looking down, Camille felt the sun on her neck but knew it wasn't the rays warming her heart. "What kind of metal do you use?"

"Recycled tin from barns that were torn down when the first of the wells were drilled south of here. Be careful or you'll cut yourself." The dogs scampered as she spoke.

Camille looked closer, murmuring with delight. "Who cuts the pieces for you?" She knelt for a better look underneath. "How do you join them?"

"I do it all, with a little help from Lawrence." She pointed to a scar on her hand. "Art's not for sissies."

As they drifted through the pieces, Evelyn explained how she'd come to make each one, sometimes in minute detail. While the flowers and assorted other shapes looked random, it became clear that she put great thought — and creativity — into each one.

"You make it look simple," Camille said, getting on her tiptoes to inspect a hodgepodge of orange and black metal poppies. "But they're complex."

Evelyn made a small sound. "I just put a twist on what I see around me."

A car drove by, slowing. The dogs barked. Evelyn waved and the driver went on. "I suppose you'd better go," she said. "Word'll spread fast that I'm entertaining the enemy."

Camille put her hands to her heart. "I didn't mean to cause more trouble."

Evelyn nodded, a serious look on her face. "I was feeling sort of low." She fanned herself and gave a small smile. "What could it hurt if you stayed a little bit longer, right?"

"I don't know," she said as Evelyn put the dogs behind a fence.

"Let's go around back, and I'll show you my art shed."

"I'm not sure Lawrence would like it. Marsh either."

"What they don't know won't hurt them." Evelyn loosened the bandanna and wiped her face with it.

Trailing behind the woman, Camille walked uncertainly up the concrete steps to a small utility shed. From the outside, the little shack looked like a place to store lawn mowers, but it had been transformed into a cozy mishmash of a room.

One wall was covered with faded wallpaper, another with a giant bulletin board covered in photographs and sketches. The plywood floor, painted with pastel squares, slanted slightly, and a box fan in an open window whirred softly.

Evelyn pulled out an upholstered dining chair, its fabric torn. "Take a seat, and I'll get us some water." She reached into a refrigerator similar to the one Camille had in her first dorm room and pulled out an old metal pitcher.

"Our water out here is so much better than that fancy bottled stuff." Evelyn's dark eyes glowed as she turned. "I might even be able to rustle us up a little something sweet."

Camille smiled in return as she settled onto the lumpy chair.

"This is my nest. Always has been."

Evelyn moved with grace, reaching for metal glasses that matched the pitcher. The condensation felt good on Camille's hands, and she took a deep drink of cold water.

"Cookie?" Evelyn asked.

Camille smiled and reached for the plate.

"My mother's recipe. I've been trying for fifty-plus years to make tea cakes as good as she did, but I can't quite get 'em the same."

Camille inhaled, the smell of paint mixed with the cinnamon in the cookie. "Oh my." She closed her eyes briefly. "Your mother's couldn't have tasted better than this."

"Lawrence says the same thing, but I can tell the difference."

"Were you a cook first or an artist?"

"The women in my family have always been artistic, and when I married Manny, Lawrence's father, I started learning. He loved art with a Latin flair — that's what first drew me to him. My family wanted me to paint pictures, but I wanted a different approach." Evelyn chuckled. "My daddy-in-law moved in with us and didn't like my work at all. Complained all the time in Spanish, but my husband was proud of me."

"Are there other artists in the family — besides you and Lawrence?"

"My daughter down in Samford quilts." She pointed to a wall hanging that looked like a sunset made out of hundreds of tiny squares. "That's called 'Evening on the Bayou.' She stitches every stitch by hand."

As Camille absorbed the details of the quilt, Evelyn picked up a basket, about the size of a basketball, and handed it to Camille. "My sister-in-law makes baskets out of pine needles. Marsh bought one as a gift for the governor, if you can believe it."

Camille inspected the delicate handle.

"Isn't Marsh the nicest man?" Evelyn

said. "He's got so much of his daddy in him."

"Is Marsh an artist?"

"He gave it up when he went to law school. But he won a big art competition in high school and got to exhibit with his teacher. Everybody in Sweet Olive went." She frowned. "Of course, his mother was too busy to come."

Camille put the basket down. "I heard he got involved in this case because of his father."

Evelyn nodded. "We've been a headache for him for years, but he keeps helping us."

"You've worked with him before?" Camille set her glass on the table.

"A handful of times. He got us a grant and made the first donation to our art center fund."

"I didn't know you had an art center."

"Oh, we don't," Evelyn said. "But we will one of these days. We're going to renovate an old building and open a gallery. Every one of us will get to display our work."

"What wonderful news! That's the kind of community project J&S loves. We get a chance to give back to the community —"

"But J&S turned us down."

"What?"

"Valerie Richmond said J&S wasn't interested in country art."

"It's a perfect project for J&S."

"She wouldn't even come to our meeting, but she and Lawrence don't get along so well." Evelyn shook her head. "They had a parting of the ways."

"I heard they were engaged." Camille's voice was tentative.

Evelyn sighed. "That woman. She's a climber. Lawrence's ambitions are different." Her face brightened. "All that was before you came to town. Might you consider . . . ?"

"Lawrence is a wonderful man," Camille said quickly, "and extremely nice looking, but I don't know that I'm his type."

Evelyn gave a small cough. "I meant would you reconsider our request for a donation?"

Camille could feel her face flame. "I am so embarrassed."

They both burst out laughing.

"I'd be thrilled if Lawrence caught your eye," Evelyn said.

"Even though everyone's angry with me?"

"You've stirred things up in Sweet Olive. We needed that."

Camille felt a quiet burst of joy. "A local gallery sounds like a wonderful idea."

Evelyn turned her head sideways and

smiled. "You're mighty interested in art for someone who isn't an artist. Lots of folks think art's frivolous. I've never been able to understand that, although I suppose polka-dotted butterflies might strike some as silly."

"I've never favored formal art as much as primitive art." Camille touched a heart-shaped wing.

"That'd be a fine discussion for a Guild meeting. They probably haven't thought about that — except Lawrence. He studied art in college."

"His glasswork is gorgeous. Very dramatic."

"It's a mighty hard way to earn a living." Evelyn mopped her face again. "Since I got sick, I have these hot flashes."

"So you just found out?" Camille asked.

"Only a few weeks ago. I'm a fighter, though."

"I'm sorry . . ."

"It's nice to meet someone who isn't focused on when I'm having chemo or if I'm going to kick the bucket." She made a face and held the aluminum glass to her forehead.

Camille looked around. "Have you considered a window unit?"

Evelyn frowned. "In this creaky old building? The electric bill would cost us an arm and a leg."

"But you could have plenty of money." The words flew out from Camille.

"What are you doing?" a stern voice said behind them, and she jumped, bumping the table with her knee. The water sloshed onto her jeans.

While Camille tried to blot up the spill, Evelyn's eyes lit up, and she stood. "I didn't expect you on a Saturday afternoon, son!" She craned her neck. "And Marsh." Evelyn put her hands on Lawrence's shoulders and looked in his face. "You'd better be staying for supper."

Camille stood stiffly and turned with dread, noticing water had splattered onto her blouse too. Marsh, in a pair of gray slacks and a crisp blue shirt, sucked some of the air out of the already stuffy space. Lawrence, in his usual black T-shirt, looked bothered.

Evelyn stepped back from her son and Marsh and patted Camille's hand, which clenched a soggy paper towel. "Camille and I were chatting about art."

Marsh and Lawrence obviously didn't share her enthusiasm.

"We couldn't believe it when we saw your truck," Marsh said. The formerly inviting room sizzled, and the tea cake seemed to have turned to stone in Camille's stomach. Each of the men stood rigid.

"I drove out here to clear my head," Camille said. "The dogs ran into the road, and I needed to turn around." *Lame.*

"I was lonesome," Evelyn interjected.

"Mama, please." Lawrence turned his attention to Camille. "You can't come out here trying to talk my mother into signing."

"Goodness gracious, Lawrence Manuel Martinez," Evelyn said. "Camille was asking about my folk art. You two can sit down and join us or wait out front."

She threw her son a look only a mother could give. Marsh looked as though he were facing a stern Sunday school teacher.

"Mama, we agreed on how to handle this. You can't invite every landman in town in for tea cakes."

"Does Camille look like a landman to you?" Evelyn raised her eyebrows. "I didn't ask that fellow from Bienville Oil in."

Marsh and Lawrence exchanged a glance, and Evelyn cleared her throat. "Are you listening to me, boys?"

"Yes, ma'am," Lawrence said.

She turned to Marsh.

"Yes, ma'am." He'd probably faced judges easier than Evelyn.

She put her hands on her hips.

"I'm sorry if I was rude, Camille." Lawrence reached over and hugged his mother. "I'm very protective of Mama."

"We have to look out for our mothers, don't we?" Camille said.

CHAPTER 25

Camille's soft words made Marsh think of his own mother. She had certainly never been easy to look out for. But something about the topic brought that sadness to Camille's eyes.

"Lawrence takes such good care of me." Evelyn patted her son's hand. "But he can be . . ." Her laugh was cheerful. "Overprotective, I suppose, is the word I'm looking for."

"That's what I'm supposed to say about you," Lawrence said with a laugh. "Camille, you'll find her a lot tougher to deal with than me. Mama's a feisty woman."

"I give you my word, Lawrence, that I won't ever ask your mother to sign." An impish smile came to her mouth. "Nor you."

The congenial smiles in the room floored Marsh. The other night they'd been furious with Camille.

"You caught me in a weak moment,"

Lawrence said. "You won't get by me again."

"I'll be waiting when you come to your senses," Camille said, but her tone was playful.

A scowl washed across Marsh's face. "Camille, let's be clear —"

"I know," she said, waving her hands, "this isn't art camp." Then she had the nerve to wink at him.

Lawrence stifled a laugh. "Marsh, we all know where we stand. I won't do anything stupid."

Did any of them know where Camille stood? With her hair tousled and water spots on her shirt, she looked right at home in the messy little shed. He was skeptical about a coincidental visit but had a hard time seeing Camille as cunning.

Evelyn's expression was delighted. "Y'all have sure cheered me up, right when I needed it. You boys pull out a chair and have a tea cake."

The wood legs of two ladder-back chairs scraped on the vinyl floor. Evelyn poured Marsh a glass of water and handed Lawrence a Sprite. Camille began to fidget. She crumbled a cookie into tiny pieces and scooted her chair back a few inches.

"I'd better go, Evelyn," she said. "I make your lawyer nervous."

Evelyn cackled. "It's hard to think of Marsh Cameron as a lawyer. These boys used to play ball together."

"She told me you hurt your knee." Camille's voice held a hint of sympathy as she looked at Lawrence.

"I wrecked it." Lawrence rubbed his knee as he spoke. "Then, like an idiot, I dropped out of college. If it weren't for the good Lord — and my mama — I might never have finished."

Evelyn, still standing, patted him on the head. "Not many people can get a degree while working three jobs."

"That's quite an accomplishment," Camille said.

"Marsh is the one who accomplished things." Lawrence gestured at him. "He set up a program in law school to help homeless families, and it's being used around the country."

"He's always looked out for those in need and never takes a dime for it." Evelyn jumped in. "He lives by the Golden Rule."

Marsh pushed his chair back, surprised to feel his face grow warm. He cleared his throat nervously. "It's not that big a deal."

"It sounds like a big deal," Camille said.

"You don't take enough credit for your generosity, young man."

"Thank you, Miss Evelyn. But what were you and Camille talking about?" Marsh kept his voice low and easy.

"Art. Camille's stirred up my thinking."

Marsh looked at Camille doubtfully. She met his gaze before turning to Lawrence. "Why'd you choose art?"

"Art chose me."

"God speaks to us through art." Evelyn placed her hand over her heart. "He touches us with these gifts."

"Art adds meaning, order even, to my world," Lawrence added, smiling at his mother. "What does art mean to you, Camille?"

She clasped her hands. "Appreciating a piece of art always feels like coming home." She squirmed. "I get a weird, giddy, peaceful feeling."

"That's what's cool about Sweet Olive," Lawrence said. "We use gifts we've been given. Money could never buy that."

"Marsh's father should be in on this," Evelyn said. "Bud believes art helps us understand ourselves — and others."

"You've got my clients talking more about their art than settlement checks, Camille." Marsh was bemused.

She blushed. "That's not the way it was supposed to work."

"Sure it was," Evelyn said.

Camille ran her fingers through her hair, leaving a cookie crumb stuck there. Marsh resisted an unwelcome urge to reach over and brush it out.

Her potent smile turned to Evelyn. "I'd better go, but I'd still like to talk about showing your work in Houston."

"I can't imagine anyone would pay money for this stuff," Evelyn said, but she sat up straighter. Marsh could see the hope in Lawrence's eyes as he looked at his mother.

After a flurry of farewells, Evelyn ushered Camille outside, their words drifting through the air as they moved out of earshot.

Marsh looked at Lawrence. "What was that about showing your mother's art?"

"She seems to think Mama's good."

"No disrespect intended, but don't you think Camille's saying that to all the landowners?"

Pursing his lips, Lawrence stared vacantly across the room. "No," he said after a moment. "Camille cares about art. She'd never mislead us about that."

"I hope you're right."

As he and Lawrence walked around the house, Evelyn was taking Camille's business card and promising to mail her a cookie recipe. Camille snapped a photo of a metallic butterfly with her phone before climbing into her old truck.

Evelyn, smiling, met them on the porch. "Isn't she the nicest person? I was wrong about her earlier."

"Camille's a nice woman," Marsh said. "But J&S needs to get a producing well on this land in a hurry."

"You boys fret too much. We haven't had money all these years. I don't know why everyone is so worked up over it." She peered at Camille's card. "If you had any sense, you'd try to get to know her better. She's much more polite than some of those oil-and-gas people who come around, like that old girlfriend of Lawrence's."

Marsh took a swig of the lukewarm water, and Lawrence gave a weak laugh.

Camille caught a glimpse of herself in the rearview mirror and groaned at the crumbs in her hair.

She shook her head and backed out onto the road.

What a revelation. Marsh used his legal skills to help the underdog.

Turning toward Samford, she drove to the house at Trumpet and Vine, its magnetic pull growing stronger each day. She pulled into the driveway and cut off the engine.

Before she could get out, her phone rang. Uncle Scott.

"This is ironic," she said. "You won't believe where I am."

"Wherever it is, it had better involve a contract in ink."

"I'm sitting in Daddy's truck where you picked us up that night."

"I've got millions riding on Sweet Olive, and you're taking a drive down memory lane?"

"I come by here to think."

"I figured that house would have fallen down by now."

She peered out the window. "It's not in very good shape."

"What kind of shape are the contracts in?"

"About the same as this house."

Camille climbed out of the truck and wandered through the yard as they talked. "We're not going to get most of the land-owners." There. She'd said it.

"Unacceptable!" Scott roared the word.

"These are hardworking people with deep roots. They don't want their community to change."

"That's the biggest load of —"

"Sweet Olive deserves to make the decision that is right for it."

"You sound like the attorney for Sweet Olive. Are you working for me or for them?" She heard the click of a lighter as he lit a cigarette. "J&S has a lot riding on this — all over the state of Louisiana. Slattery's been gunning for me for years, and he has clout in the Senate. If we don't do what he wants, he'll find a way to run us out for good."

"And what is it that he wants?"

"You've seen the files."

"We can work around that fancy subdivision of his. There's plenty of land behind it for a well or two."

"Deal killer." The words were harsh. "We can't touch his land."

"That's not the way we do business." Camille spoke through clenched teeth.

"J&S does what it takes. We always have."

"Is that what my father was doing when he died?"

"Johnny was doing his job, and that's what I demand of you. Finish it up and head back to your cushy office job." Scott hesitated. "I'll even fund that other environmental project you're so keen on."

"The new technology?" Camille's pulse raced. "You said J&S wasn't in the research business."

"If it'll help you get off dead center in Louisiana, we'll get into the research business. But if you can't pull this one off, the closest thing you'll come to an office job is a metal shack in Odessa."

Before she could reply, Scott ended the call.

Walking around the house, Camille scuffed the dirt with the toe of her boot. Allison's dream created a fancy gallery. Ginny fought for the people she loved. Marsh helped those in need.

Her own life was going in circles.

How did her mother have faith that things would work out? No matter how much Camille prayed, the answers remained as dim as the dirty glass on the front door.

She kicked a pine cone and headed back to the truck.

CHAPTER 26

Camille was working with one of the children Monday night when the dogs, inside and out, started barking. In her fifth week in Louisiana, she was used to the children's chatter but still didn't see how Ginny got anything done with the overall chaos.

"Aunt Ginny, someone's at the door," Kylie shouted.

Ginny, drying her hands on a bright yellow towel, walked in from the kitchen. "Already?" Her gaze darted to Camille. "It's unlocked!"

A man in his midforties entered first, holding a casserole dish covered with foil. He had scraggly shoulder-length black hair and wore camouflage pants. A short woman of about sixty, with a waist-length gray ponytail, gripped his arm, managing to hold a canvas under one arm and a loaf of French bread in the other.

Scarcely had they stepped over the threshold before two older women — seventy or so — walked in, wearing identical outfits of what looked like homemade scrub pants and tops.

They all looked vaguely familiar.

"Dumplings." One of the women held up a metal pan.

"Sweet potato casserole," the other said, holding up a similar pan.

All four were smiling until they caught sight of Camille, who had risen from her seat at the art table.

"What's she doing here?" one demanded.

"Hello, everyone," Ginny said with an unusual note of gaiety. "Come in, come in." She adjusted her glasses.

"Charlene asked you a question," the man said. "Why is that woman here?"

Ginny looked around as though she didn't know who they were talking about. A rare silence fell over the children.

"Look at the time!" Camille exclaimed. "I'd better be going."

Ginny's brow furrowed. "You said you could stay late today."

"I forgot . . ." Camille nervously straightened the pastels the kids had been drawing with. "I didn't realize you were having company."

"We're not company," one of the twins said.

"Camille's not company either," Ginny said. "She's an excellent art tutor."

"That's well and good, but we don't want her here for the meeting," the man said.

"It's not a meeting," Ginny said. "It's a potluck. I want Camille to join us."

"I can't stay," Camille said quickly.

"I made plenty." Ginny's chin was set at a stubborn angle. "Let me introduce you to the Sweet Olive Artists' Guild."

"Hi." Camille gave a tiny wave.

"This seemed like a good opportunity for you to talk to the group," Ginny said. "I didn't tell you because I was afraid you'd skedaddle."

"Talk?" Camille's voice croaked.

"We heard her at that meeting at the gym," the other of the twins said. "There's nothing left to talk about."

"Camille is an art expert." Ginny looked at the four, who had paused on their way toward the kitchen. "She appreciates our art . . . and has outstanding ideas on marketing it."

"Marketing?" The twins spoke in unison.

"Some members would like to sell their work." Ginny nodded. "Camille understands the Internet and gallery opportunities."

"We wouldn't need gas money if we could sell our art."

"Why would she talk herself out of a job?"

Ginny sighed. "Y'all won't make anything easy. Whether we lease our land or not, some of us want to show our art. We need Camille's insight."

As they talked, someone tapped on the door and Lawrence and Evelyn walked in.

"Ahh." Lawrence flashed his crooked grin. "My favorite landman."

"I didn't know you were going to be here," Evelyn said cheerfully.

Camille was unable to resist smiling at the mother and son. Lawrence wore his usual black T-shirt and his mother was in a pair of bright yellow knit pants, a matching striped shirt, and three strands of hot-pink beads.

"I want everyone to get to know Camille better," Ginny said. "She has an expertise that we are lacking."

The next person to drift in was Marsh's father, Bud, wearing his carpenter clothes. His eyes widened when he saw Camille, and he looked over her shoulder.

"No, Bud, I didn't invite Marsh." Ginny gave him a kiss on the cheek. "This is our regular potluck, not a land discussion."

"I suspect my son won't see it that way."

"Camille's not a secret agent." Ginny took the two jugs of sweet tea he carried.

Camille smiled. "You're a wood carver, right?"

Bud's face creased with a smile that reminded her of Marsh. "I work mostly with a hammer and nails. But I piddle with carving." He pointed to a bust of Mary and the Christ in the back of the room. "That's one of mine."

Camille gasped. "You did that?" She put her hand over her mouth. "That is such an inspirational piece."

"I love to look at it early in the morning," Ginny said. "It centers me, reminds me of God's great love, even on the toughest days." She smiled over at Bud.

"Ginny's my biggest cheerleader," he said.

"Other than your sons," Ginny replied.

Bud grinned. "Marsh and T. J. are biased."

"T. J.?" Camille asked.

"We share an interest in carpentry that his mother doesn't quite understand," Bud said.

The arrival of a handful of artists, including Lillie Lavender, knitting bag in hand, interrupted them. Each person stashed food in the kitchen and sat in the living room. Their conversation whirled around complaints about overdue dues and laments about a Samford antique mall closing. "Charlene and I did pretty well at that store," the twin who introduced herself as Darlene said.

Ginny grabbed Camille's arm and pulled her closer. "These two paint Creole primitives."

Lawrence stepped closer. "You'll never see anything that captures local life as well."

"Did all of you sell pieces at the antique mall?" Camille asked.

"It was hit or miss," Lawrence said. "We'll never earn a living selling art in Cypress Parish."

"Let's talk about that over supper." Ginny shooed Kylie and Randy to the front of a makeshift buffet line.

Evelyn handed Camille a heavy paper plate. "Try the broccoli and rice."

"And peas," Darlene — or was it Charlene? — added.

The artists filled their plates until it looked like a Thanksgiving feast and returned to the living room. They sat on the couch, chairs, and hearth, plates in their laps. The group ranged from a young math teacher to a clerk at a feed store.

Lawrence talked about working in the oil field before college, and Evelyn argued with the twins over who was the oldest member of the club. Even the shyest people talked freely when asked about their art.

Keeping a mental tally, Camille thought Allison could fill a gallery with their work — metal sculpture, watercolors, glass, pottery, wood carvings, and oil paintings. One woman made exquisite figures out of red Louisiana clay. Another did sculptures from cypress boards recovered from Lake Bistineau.

As they talked, Camille's enthusiasm grew. "Whatever happens with your land, you have to share your art with the world."

"You're an artist?" Darlene asked.

"I appreciate art," Camille said.

"She's a wonderful mentor," Ginny said. "The children love her. She wants to own a gallery someday."

"Down the line," Camille stressed quickly.

"What kind of gallery?" Lawrence asked.

The artists leaned in, waiting as Camille shaped an answer. "I plan to work with a gallery back home to learn more about the business and then decide."

"We could use a gallery around here," Lawrence said. "When we try to work with galleries elsewhere, the results are inconsistent."

"In fact —" Evelyn turned to look at Ginny with a question in her eyes.

Ginny nodded.

"Have you thought any more about helping with our art center?" Evelyn said.

"I thought J&S didn't go for projects like that," Bud said.

"Val decided that," Lawrence said. "More likely J&S didn't go for projects like me." A few people chuckled.

Camille looked around the room and back at Evelyn. "J&S will be happy to help — even if you don't wind up signing. We've found that our business does better when our communities do better."

"Marsh put a proposal together," Lawrence said. "In fact, he's been our best fundraiser so far."

"That boy works hard for Sweet Olive," Bud said. "He can deliver the papers to you."

Camille tapped her fingers on the coffee table, her nails free of polish, gauging her words. "I also hope you'll allow me to connect you with a gallery in Houston."

The artists murmured among themselves, their indistinguishable words reminding Camille of a dramatic scene on a television show.

"I don't think we're quite ready for that," Ginny said after a moment. "We need to start smaller."

"But, Ginny, the art here is stunning." Heads around Camille bobbed their approval. "Your whirligigs, for example — they're original and evocative. Collectors will be thrilled."

Ginny shook her head vehemently as the people around her nodded theirs. "That's a hobby, nothing more."

"It could be fun, Ginny," Lillie said, knitting as usual.

"Wouldn't you like to know what the outside world thinks of your work?" Lawrence asked.

"Absolutely not." Ginny looked flustered. "Can we talk about somebody else for a while? That's why I invited Camille."

"There's warm bread pudding in the kitchen," Evelyn said.

The group laughed and moseyed toward the door. Camille moved over to where Ginny stood. "I didn't mean to embarrass you, Ginny."

"It's foolish to talk like that. Lawrence is the professional artist, not me."

"Can't you see how good you are?"

"I play at it." Ginny shrugged. "My role in Sweet Olive is to hold the artists together, not to sell a piece of welded metal."

"Why not do both?"

"You're more pigheaded than I am,"

Ginny said. "Now will you please find someone else to bother?"

Camille grinned and accepted the dessert Evelyn offered her, then took a quick bite. "My mother would love this."

"You could have invited her," Evelyn said.

"Amarillo might be a little far to come for supper. Although, this *is* excellent bread pudding."

They laughed together. "Maybe your father will bring her one of these days," Evelyn said.

Camille pursed her lips. "I lost my dad a long time ago."

"That's hard." Evelyn's eyes were kind as they settled on Camille. "That's how a lot of us got into art. We're our own crazy support group."

Camille stood and made an excuse about getting another napkin. Lawrence followed her into the kitchen. "They're a nosy bunch, but they mean well."

"I like them," she said, leaning against the counter. "They are . . . refreshing."

He grinned. "I'll have to remember that. It sounds nicer than *crazy* or *bossy.*"

She smiled in return. "What are you working on these days?"

"Other than getting up the nerve to ask you out?"

Camille moved back, banging her elbow on the sink.

"Is that a 'no thanks'?"

Camille shook her head. "It's an 'I'm not sure I should go out with one of the landowners.' "

"Think of it as reconnaissance."

"Maybe."

"I'd hoped for a yes, but that's a start." His eyes crinkled at the corners. "Besides that, I'm working on a chandelier."

"Camille, there isn't anything my son can't make out of glass." Evelyn walked into the kitchen with a stack of plates.

"They did a whole display at a museum in Samford," Ginny said, joining them. "Some of his work was even put in an online gallery."

"Did the party move in here?" Bud asked, his hands full of empty glasses. His gaze lingered on Lawrence and Camille.

"We were talking about Lawrence's chandelier," Camille said.

"And I was trying to get Camille to go out with me." Lawrence smiled.

Camille's face grew warm as those in the kitchen — with the exception of Bud — chuckled.

A sweet scent wafted through the October

evening as the artists departed.

"Every now and then I catch a whiff of a fragrance I can't describe," Camille said to Ginny, sniffing. "It seems to be growing stronger."

Ginny inhaled and exhaled with a soft, "Ahh."

She pointed to a plain green bush at the corner of the porch. "Sweet olive. It's especially wonderful when the weather changes." She breathed deeply. "A front must be coming through."

"That?" Camille stood and walked closer to the plant. It had tough, waxy green leaves and small, light-colored flowers. She leaned over and inhaled, but the smell eluded her.

"It doesn't overpower you," Ginny said. "You have to stand back and be aware. And it's a slow grower."

"Are you talking about a plant or a spiritual experience?"

Ginny gave one of the hearty laughs Camille loved. There was nothing subtle about this woman. "You'll have to decide that," Ginny said.

"I smelled this the other day in Evelyn's yard." Camille breathed in and out and in again. "It's a delicate scent."

"That's how the Sweet Olive community got its name. You plant them by your door

or porch, or you're apt to miss the smell."
Ginny sat in the swing, her clogs clapping
the wooden porch as she jiggled her legs.
"I've always thought it was the perfect
symbol for our community — tough, de-
pendable, not flashy."

Camille sat down as well, sliding into a
rocking rhythm on the swing. "And stubborn?"

Ginny gave her loud laugh. "We're ornery,
aren't we?"

"You have your moments." Camille inhaled again. "I wonder if these grow in
Houston."

CHAPTER 27

"Alison Carney," a polished voice said. "May I help you?"

"Allison, hey," Camille said, feeling like they were back in college. "It's Camille Gardner."

"Tell me you're back in town."

"Not quite yet."

"I trust there's not a problem." Allison's words became frostier.

"Not exactly," Camille stammered. "I —"

"You are going to honor your volunteer commitment, are you not?"

"Of course."

"But . . . ?"

"I'm looking forward to working at the gallery," Camille said in a rush, still not pulling out the correct words.

"And we're looking forward to having you . . . if you ever get here."

"I'll give 100 percent when I get back. I've already identified a group of unique folk artists for your consideration."

"That's sweet," Allison replied. "But you know that Carney & Associates doesn't represent many folk artists."

"These aren't ordinary folk artists. They use an array of media with striking results."

"I'm sure they're lovely, but —"

"There are incredible whirligigs, primitive paintings with a fresh eye, and glass that reminds me of Chihuly's work."

"Glass, hmm," Allison said, her tone less terse. "That's quite marketable right now if the quality's good."

Camille was encouraged. "It's excellent. May I e-mail you photos of the work?"

"We're very select in what we present."

"You'll like it," Camille said, clenching her fist. What if Allison didn't like the Sweet Olive work?

Camille paced around the hotel room, sick of cable television. She'd hoped to go to Ginny's to work on art projects with the children, but since it was Wednesday, they had prayer meeting.

Ginny had invited her to go along. "We can always use another pair of hands in the mission class. The children would love to see you."

Camille declined. Helping would only

make her departure that much harder.

"Well, if you won't come with us," Ginny said, "do you have any prayer requests?"

"Prayer requests?"

"People you want us to pray for. That's what we do at prayer meeting," Ginny said with a chuckle.

"I know what a prayer request is." Camille gave an embarrassed laugh. "I don't think I really have any . . ."

"Would it be all right if we prayed for you?"

"Why would you pray for me?"

"We pray to do the right thing about our land," Ginny said. "We can add you to that list."

"Absolutely," Camille said.

Sitting on the end of the hotel bed, she dialed her mother, but the line was busy.

With phone in hand, she looked around the room. For the past seven years, she had lived in rooms like this, and she had photographed every piece of hotel room art she'd seen. Most of it, like the mass-produced European landscapes in this room, were mundane, and she wondered why hotels didn't feature local artists.

Scrolling through the photos, she found the handful of pictures she'd taken Sunday in Sweet Olive. She attached a few to a note to Allison and smiled as she hit Send. Then she dialed her mother again.

"Hey, sweetie," her mom said. "How's my one and only precious girl?"

"I'm okay."

"That's not very convincing. What's going on?"

Camille considered her mother's question. "Work's sort of an extra hassle lately, but I think Ginny and I have patched things up."

"I remember the people in Louisiana being extra friendly."

"Mama, we were only here part of a summer."

"You've only been there this time for a few weeks."

"Good point," Camille said with a little laugh. "You're making me feel happier already."

"Are you still ready to quit traveling?"

"Beyond ready. But this is taking longer than I thought."

"I'm praying about your new job."

"Everyone's praying for me today. I must need it."

Her mother cleared her throat. "Scott called again tonight."

"What'd he want?"

"It was odd. He was asking about you, said he was concerned when y'all talked.

Wanted to know if you'd mentioned any-thing about the Sweet Olive deal."

"He asked about my work?"

"I thought it was strange too. I told him I wasn't sure what was going on but that you are doing a fabulous job."

"He's up to something."

"Your father used to say that Scott came out of the womb negotiating a deal."

"These people are special, Mama. I don't want him to hurt them."

The line was quiet for a moment.

"Then don't let him."

CHAPTER 28

Marsh held up the cup of fancy coffee and gave Valerie a questioning look through the glass wall of her office. A week had passed since the community meeting, and he wondered what she was up to.

She cradled the phone on her shoulder and was writing a lengthy message on a legal pad. Gesturing him in, she slid a file folder over the yellow tablet.

When he handed her the coffee, she mouthed a *thanks* and took a sip. "Ahhh," she said as she wrote on the back of an envelope. Marsh gave a thumbs-up and pointed toward Camille's office. She shrugged and motioned toward the phone.

As Marsh left, he glanced back. Val had already resumed her note taking.

Glancing down the hall, he took a sip of his dark roast. Somewhat to his chagrin, he had found himself looking for ways to run into Camille. He had only talked to her once since the encounter at Evelyn's studio, deliberating over contract details.

Marsh started to leave. Then he turned back. If this were any other businessperson in town, he'd drop in. He stepped toward Camille's office, and Val aimed a small frown his way.

"May I help you?"

The voice startled Marsh, and he turned to see Camille walking in from the lobby.

"I stopped by to see Valerie, but she's busy." For good measure, he nodded in the direction of Val's office, his coffee sloshing. He felt foolish.

"I can have her call you." Camille followed his gaze. "She's been on the phone with her door closed most of the morning."

He gave his head a quick shake. "We'll connect later."

Camille ran her fingers through her hair, which was always mussed enough to show she didn't pay strict attention to it. She looked more like a schoolteacher than an oil-and-gas deal maker. Her only jewelry was a pair of turquoise earrings, and Valerie would have gone naked before she wore those rumpled pants. A pair of heels brought Camille just about to his shoulder, but he liked her better in her beat-up boots.

He cleared his throat. "Have you thought

any more about how the contract might read?"

She nodded slowly. "We're doing the last of the title searches. I should have a document for you to review within a couple of days. I don't expect to get everyone, but maybe we can come up with a compromise."

"My father told me about your art center funding idea. You got their attention with that one. That's a . . . generous offer."

Camille cocked her head. "If it sounds 'generous,' why do you sound suspicious?"

He gave a spurt of laughter. "In my experience, oil-and-gas companies don't usually offer quite so much." He studied her more closely. "Everyone in Sweet Olive is speculating about you."

"Speculation *is* the business I'm in."

On impulse, he reached out and touched her arm. "I have a question."

"Yes?" She tilted her head.

"You had to know some of my clients would ultimately give in," he said. Her face gave nothing away. "So why are you offering them such a good deal?"

Her shrug was so brief he nearly missed it. "Timing's everything. Your clients benefited from our deadlines." She started past him. "And it's the right thing to do."

■ ■ ■ ■

Camille's knock on Ginny's door Thursday evening was deliberately tentative. She liked to watch the students draw before they noticed her.

However, no one was seated at the art table today. A child wailed from the direction of the kitchen, and two or three children played an unusually frenetic game of chase.

She knocked louder. The dog walked up to her, licked her hand, and ambled off, and Randy, a smear of blue paint on his face, wandered to the door. He stared at her for a second. She picked up the cowbell and rang it, laughing, but he ran off, chasing a ball that rolled across the room.

The crying intensified, and Camille opened the door. "Hello. Ginny?"

At the sound of her voice, the yard dog ran at her in an unexpected barking frenzy. The inside dog skidded around the corner and reared up on the door, his shrill yaps adding to the noise.

"What in the world are you barking at?" Ginny's voice was agitated. She held a child of about eight or nine — too large to be carried — in her arms.

Camille gave a wave. "It's me." When she pushed the door open further, the dog on the porch dashed inside and started wrestling with the smaller animal. A cat darted through Ginny's legs, hissing.

"Can you stay with the students until my sister-in-law gets here?" Ginny said, perspiration shining on her forehead. "Sammy's cut his arm."

As Camille looked closer, blood oozed down the child's arm and onto the smock-like shirt Ginny wore. "Certainly," she said, noticing the children's scared expressions as they looked at Sammy. "We'll have fun."

Kylie gave a tentative smile, but the others shook their heads and looked reluctant. Randy nodded. "She likes my pictures."

"Let's see what everyone's working on." Camille sat at the table as Ginny mouthed *thank you*.

Camille started the children — four elementary students and two preschoolers — on a colored-pencil project and was charmed by their color choices and design eye. Maybe there *was* something in the water . . .

She was so engrossed in the children's paintings that she jumped when the storm door slammed. "Mommy!" Randy said, and ran toward the front of the house, throwing his arms around the woman's knees. Camille remembered seeing the children hug the woman at the art festival.

"Hey, buddy. How's my little man?" The woman took a step toward the art table, Randy clinging to her knees. "Kylie, aren't you going to give Mommy a hug?"

Kylie ignored her, picking up a black pencil and scribbling bold blobs on the paper.

"What's wrong, sweetheart?" Camille asked.

The woman seemed to notice Camille for the first time. "Who are you?"

"This is Miss Camille." Randy tugged on his mother's oversized purse.

"I'm Camille Gar—"

The woman's eyes narrowed. "You're that woman giving out checks."

"I work for J&S Production. I'm here as a volunteer today."

"Where's Ginny?"

"There was a minor emergency, and she had to leave. Could I help you with something?"

The woman smirked. "More likely, I could help *you*. I'm Janice Procell, one of the landowners. I watched that fight at the gym, and Drew told me you're a spitfire."

"Drew?"

"Drew Cross, my boyfriend," Janice said as though she'd admitted to dating a movie star. "He says you're playing us, but that woman who works with you is much more reasonable."

Camille looked at the children, all of whom had gone back to their projects except for Kylie, intent on drawing what looked like a series of tornados, and Randy, still tugging on Janice's purse.

"Perhaps we can discuss this when Ginny gets back?"

Janice's mouth was set in a sour expression. "The land's mine. She's using that Saint Ginny act to steal from me and my kids."

Camille kept her face passive. "I'd be happy to look over your deed another time," she said, keeping her words quiet.

"Kylie, Randy," Janice barked, "get your things." She was a short, thin woman, who looked like life had been hard on her. Her hair was pushed back with an elastic headband, and her cropped pants revealed a tattoo of a dragon on her ankle.

"But class isn't over," Kylie said, her face stricken. Randy moved back toward the table.

"Ginny didn't mention you'd be taking them." Camille stepped between the children and Janice.

"I hardly need an appointment to pick up my own children." Janice snapped her fingers. "Don't make me count, Kylie. We're leaving now."

Tears came to Kylie's eyes as she stood.

Camille looked around, more tense than she'd been in the most hostile of J&S negotiations. She could think of only one thing that might keep the woman here. "Now that I think about it, we do need to discuss your claim. Why don't we go into the kitchen and discuss the options?"

"That's more like it."

As soon as they were seated, Janice began to wring her hands. "Everybody's going to get money, and I want mine. This is Procell family land, and my children deserve their share."

"I understood that Ginny was handling that for the family."

"Todd wouldn't want it that way."

"According to our records, the arrangement was stipulated in his will."

"We were getting back together." Janice seemed genuinely dismayed. "Then he got himself killed."

"I'm sorry for your loss. Your children are precious."

Janice nodded. "Ginny's been a big help,

but I need that money to provide for my babies. It's hard without Todd."

Camille merely nodded.

Janice strolled out of the room and gave the children a hurried good-bye. "I'm not going to be able to stay after all. I'll see you sweet peas later."

"Will you come back tonight?" Randy followed her to the door.

"We'll see," Janice said.

Kylie looked at Camille, her little lips pursed. "That means no."

"Be good for Miss Camille," Janice said. As the front door closed, a pall fell over the room.

"I'm glad she's gone," Kylie said in a trembling voice. "I hate her."

"Oh, Kylie," Camille said, putting her arms around the child, "of course you don't."

"I want to stay with Aunt Ginny."

Camille stroked her soft, curly red hair. "It'll be all right."

"I know." Kylie sniffed as she spoke. "Jesus is watching out for us, even when Mommy can't."

Drawing in her breath, Camille pulled Kylie closer. "What a smart girl you are."

The look on Kylie's face was like stumbling across a familiar, faded photograph.

Camille had worn that look almost con-
stantly until she'd turned fifteen.

CHAPTER 29

Camille walked up Lawrence's driveway early Saturday, bypassing the teal-and-brown house.

His studio was nestled between two huge pine trees behind his house, a plain brown metal building. The blue door stood open.

Climbing the concrete steps, she called out, more nervous than expected.

"Camille!" he said, rising from a work table just inside the door.

She looked past him to a row of tiny glass flowers. "Those are gorgeous."

"I said I'd never design jewelry, but I need to earn more money." He guided her to a nearby mirror and held one of the flowers up to her ear. "Do you think women might be interested in something like this?"

"Absolutely."

"I'm thinking of signing up for a booth at several of the regional art shows." He tilted his head, his black hair blowing slightly in the breeze from the doorway. As usual, he wore a black T-shirt — and wore it well. "I just have to figure out my schedule."

"That's why I asked to come by."

"Time on your hands?" He smiled.

"I wanted to follow up on an earlier conversation."

His expression froze.

"What's wrong?" Her face heated up, and then she nodded. "Don't worry. I'm here to talk about art, not gas."

"I was an idiot to take the check. You're in the gas business."

Camille fingered the delicate glass flower. "That's behind us. I want to talk about the future."

He nodded toward the open door. "Let's sit outside and enjoy this day. The sky. The light. Even the temperature is nice. It's the gift of early October in Louisiana. We've actually survived another summer."

They chatted as they strolled up the drive, sunlight gleaming on his glasswork. The sun had shifted during her weeks here, and it gave a magical glow to a new sculpture of a bird.

She turned to face him. "I heard from the gallery owner in Houston," she said. "She wants to talk further about your work."

He sauntered over to the closest of his

stunning bottle trees, touching it with what almost looked like affection. The contrast between his big, masculine hand and the vibrant glass captivated her.

"I don't know about a big-city gallery. I tried selling a piece or two in New Orleans, and it didn't work out so great."

"It all depends on the gallery," Camille said, her energy surging as she spoke. "The right place can connect you with people who appreciate your particular style."

He smiled. "You sound like a matchmaker."

"That's sort of what it is."

He guided her to the swing where she and Ginny had sat on the first day she came to Sweet Olive. "Tell me how it would work."

"I'll send more pictures to the gallery, and the owner will decide what she wants. She'll pay you — and then sell them at her price."

He frowned slightly at that and was silent.

Camille turned to look at him. "I don't want to talk you into something else you're not comfortable with."

"I'm not a wishy-washy guy by nature, and I sure don't think of myself as weak." He sat up and rubbed a scar on his hand. "I work with molten glass, one of the most dangerous kinds of art."

She waited.

"When Mama got sick, though, I panicked. I took the head waiter job at the Samford Club, asked Slattery to increase my hours, worked more for Bud Cameron. You name it."

"And took the check."

He leaned forward, his elbows on his knees. "She'd had her first round of chemo the day before." He exhaled. "I thought that money would make everything all right."

"But you changed your mind."

"I'm not much of a word guy, and this is hard to explain." He paused, and she forced herself not to rush him. "When you came to town, we were all about to give up. Your interest in the art made us take a fresh look at what we've got."

"But I wanted you to take a fresh look at your mineral leases," she said.

He shook his head. "Up here, we believe things happen for a reason. We needed you to make us consider new possibilities."

The swing eased back and forth. He smiled over at her. "You understand Sweet Olive."

Fingering the swing's chain, she looked out at lawns filled with art as far as she could see. "The strangest thing? I feel like Sweet Olive understands me."

He wrinkled his brow. "We don't want you

to leave."

"But I have to."

"Do you?" he asked.

Scott's call came Saturday evening.

"Camy! I hope you're doing something fun."

"I'm in my room studying the geology maps for the Cypress gas field." There was a loud cheer in the background. "Where are you?"

"In a bar in El Paso," he said. "There's a football game on, and I'm having trouble hearing."

"Step outside. I have questions that need answers."

"You'd better have signatures for me," Scott said. "Tell me you've harvested more names."

"Like I told you the other night, we have to find a way to move the well sites," she said. "There must be other land available."

"The records I gave you clearly show the available land."

"We've changed sites plenty of times for powerful landowners all over the country. Why can't we do that here? I recommend we adjust the plans. Otherwise we'll be putting them outside someone's bedroom window."

"I've got an idea."

"I knew you'd think of something."

"I'm thinking," he said, his voice sarcastic, "that these goofy artists can look out their windows and enjoy the view of all that money they'll be making. We can't go farther south with them."

"Really? That's your answer? Have the engineers looked at the water supply?" she asked. "We're unlikely to get water rights with this batch of leases."

"Camille, I sent you there to do one important thing, and all I'm hearing is excuses."

"These are legitimate concerns."

"You, of all people, should know how hard it is to make money in oil and gas these days. Lawyers. Environmentalists. Government regulations. Oil deals being fought in some idiot's kitchen. Give me a freaking break."

"But we've always made money by treating people right."

"Your head's out of the game," Scott said. "I thought you would make up to me for that mess you made on television."

"I always give you my best."

"Then let's see some names on contracts." The crowd roared behind him. "The Cowboys just scored. I've got to go."

CHAPTER 30

Allison's plane was late, giving Camille time to worry that the hasty invitation had been a mistake. And maybe she should have rented a car.

Perhaps she should have mentioned the gallery owner's visit to Ginny.

When Allison stepped out from the baggage claim area Monday afternoon at the small Samford airport, she pulled a large suitcase, a leather purse slung over her shoulder. She wore a black wraparound dress and a frown.

"Allison! Over here!" Camille yelled, and the frown grew as Allison eyed the truck. Hopping out, Camille smiled and tossed the suitcase into the back.

"Will it be . . . *safe* back there?" Allison wrinkled her nose as she spoke. "I'd prefer to put it up front, if you don't mind."

Camille reached for the bag. "It'll be tight, but we'll make it work." The suitcase wedged between them, Camille let out the clutch and pulled out. "Thank you for squeezing this stop into your trip," she said. "You're going to love these artists."

Allison gave a weak laugh. "It's not the artists I care about. I just hope their *art* is as good as you say."

"You won't find work like this anywhere else."

"I see a great deal of fine art," Allison said. "Very fine art." She crossed her tan legs at the ankles and looked over at Camille. "But I admire your enthusiasm." She looked around with a hint of interest. "Besides, I've never been to North Louisiana."

"The people are friendly. The countryside is beautiful, full of trees and lakes. The food's outstanding and —"

"I didn't realize you had such deep ties to this place." Allison arched her perfectly shaped eyebrows. "You sound like a travel brochure."

"I don't have ties here, but it's been a nice stop."

"So tell me about Lawrence Martinez. I'm oddly pulled in by the photos of his work — and he's had web exposure."

"He's phenomenal," Camille said. "He lives next door to his mother in Sweet Olive and —"

"Next door to his mother? I can't imagine a mama's boy being much of an artist."

Camille couldn't hold back her laughter. "I wouldn't call Lawrence a mama's boy. Every woman in Cypress Parish has a crush on him." She paused. "He's exceptional, but I also want to introduce you to Ginny Guidry. She makes whirligigs that would be an asset to any folk-art collection. She doesn't realize how good her work is."

"She's undiscovered?"

"She's shown a piece or two at small local shows, but her work's not been sold in a gallery."

"I prefer to deal with people who have already been vetted."

Camille ran her fingers through her hair. "I thought you wanted fresh talent."

"I seek artists who have already made it through the lowest levels and are moving up. My goal is to snatch them right before they hit it big."

"But your gallery has a reputation for finding unknown artists."

Allison's shoulder-length black hair scarcely moved as she nodded. "They are unknown until I represent them. Beginners can be so unsophisticated and needy."

"Ginny's not needy, that's for sure."

"The thing about new artists," Allison

323

said, letting loose a dramatic sigh, "is that they hound you. They want to show their work. They want to know if you've had any nibbles. They want to know if you've sold something. It's exhausting."

Camille thought of Ginny, rushing off to her day job, coming home to teach classes and moderate community meetings, sandwiching her own art in between. "I suppose it's just as well you're not interested." Camille added a fake sound of regret to her words. "Ginny's stonewalled other attempts to show her art. She probably wouldn't be a good fit anyway."

"Other people have been interested, you say?" Allison perked up.

"At least one collector that I know of." Camille figured it was acceptable not to mention she was talking about herself. "Ginny's particular about how her work is shown."

"So it's exhibited privately?"

"You might say that." Camille hid a smile.

"Perhaps I was too hasty." Allison threw her hands up. "I'm yours for the next few hours. Show me whatever you like."

Saving Ginny's artwork for last, Camille drove through Samford, past the intersection of Trumpet and Vine.

Allison pressed her lips together in a stark straight line, her carefully shaped brows following suit. "I bet you'll be happy to get out of here. This place is a — well, let's say it's seen better days."

Camille looked at the vacant house and deserted church, both forlorn in abandonment. The shabby convenience store and park weren't much better. "The area has charm," she said, surprised at her rush of defensiveness. "And the people are extremely creative."

As they drove around the curve into Sweet Olive, the row of bright houses ahead, Camille held her breath.

"How quaint," Allison said. Then she caught sight of Lawrence's work. "This is more like it." She grabbed the door handle, and for a split second, Camille thought she was going to jump out of the truck.

"Lawrence blends a folk-art approach with a modern twist." Camille pulled to the side, distracted by the sight of Valerie's BMW.

"It's very effective," Allison said.

"I've never thought of art as being 'effective.'"

"Don't worry. You'll learn."

"But —"

Before she could continue, Lawrence

rounded the corner from his studio, in a pair of slacks and a shirt and tie. "Oh my." Allison opened the door in a rush. "He is a hunk."

Camille couldn't suppress the thread of disappointment that ran through her at the sight of Lawrence dressed up. She preferred his black Ts and cargo pants.

As Lawrence clasped Allison's outstretched hand, Valerie appeared. She wore a black silk blouse, tight black jeans, and bright red heels, her hair piled on her head in artful confusion. Her smiling gaze passed over Camille, focusing on Allison.

"Valerie stopped by to get your questions answered, Camille," Lawrence said.

"My questions?"

Valerie waved her hand, as though drying nail polish. "Don't worry. I found out what we needed, Camille."

"Are you an artist too?" Allison asked.

"Only if you consider finding oil and gas an art." Valerie gave a tinkling laugh. "Camille and I work together at J&S Production." Valerie released a sympathetic sigh. "We had no idea this deal would take so long." Her voice dripped southern charm and she drew out the word *long.*

"Valerie," Camille snapped. "This isn't your concern. I'll see you at the office." She looked forward to sacking Valerie before she departed Sweet Olive, no matter what Scott said.

Allison seemed to be torn between looking at the glass on display in the yard and at Lawrence, who tugged at his tie.

"The boss has spoken," Valerie said. "It was a pleasure meeting you, Allison. Will you be in Louisiana long?"

"Only a few hours. I hope I can get out on the last flight to Dallas. The Samford airport's rather . . . small." Her lips narrowed.

"Isn't it impossible to get here?" Valerie said. "I'm driving over to Dallas myself later today."

She was?

"Is it possible . . . ?" Allison looked at her diamond-encrusted watch and leaned toward Valerie.

"I'd be delighted for you to ride with me, if you don't mind small cars." Valerie pointed at her shiny sportster.

Allison looked from the car to Camille's pickup. "I expect to be finished here by early evening. That will help me immensely."

Why have I never realized Allison is a Texas version of Valerie?

"If you're in a hurry, we'd better head to my studio." Lawrence pulled off his tie, his face impassive. "Camille, you might want to notify Ginny."

Ginny's bright red lips were stern when she sauntered out into the yard to meet Camille and Allison. She wore her rattiest pair of denim overalls, a gigantic bleached spot over the left knee. Her hair was in two fat braids.

"This is the gallery owner I mentioned on the phone," Camille said.

"You're the artist?" Camille realized with a start that it was the first true note of delight she'd ever heard in Allison's voice.

"For better or worse," Ginny said.

"Where does your inspiration come from?" Allison said.

Camille tensed, waiting for Ginny to respond with her down-home disdain. Instead she gave her hearty laugh. "Most of my ideas come from trying to put the pieces of everyday life together." She gestured toward the house. "Would you like to see my collection of local art?"

Allison swept past Camille. "That would be lovely."

"Are Kylie and Randy here?" Camille trailed the two, feeling oddly out of place.

"Evelyn took them to the library," Ginny answered over her shoulder before launching into a discussion of gallery operations with Allison.

"Camille, you were not exaggerating about these people," Allison said as she studied one of Bud's sketches. "We could mount an entire Sweet Olive exhibit."

"I'm not sure." Camille was afraid to look at Ginny.

But Ginny seemed intrigued. "What would that involve?"

Allison reached into her handbag and pulled out a small leather calendar. "Camille can catalogue our acquisitions." She tapped the date with a pink-polished nail. "And oversee the shipping process. With her return to Houston coming up, it'll be tight, but we'll make it work."

Ginny fingered one of her braids, looking at Camille.

Allison glided back through the living room, murmuring to herself and jotting in her notebook. "Camille promised me a treasure trove, and she's true to her word."

"That's a matter of perspective," Ginny murmured.

"I told you I needed to get back to Houston," Camille said. Misery sank in her stomach like a brick.

"I thought you were staying until Sweet Olive worked out its leases." With her fierce glare and overalls, Ginny only needed a pitchfork to look like a country warrior.

"We've stalled. I e-mailed my boss today, suggesting we put Sweet Olive on hold." She was prepared to fight his response.

Allison's pale lipstick turned into a smile. "I'm looking forward to teaching Camille about the art business. She's going to owe me big-time." The playful laugh Allison added didn't keep Camille from thinking of Valerie.

"This is some coup," Allison said. "The other Southwest galleries aren't going to know what hit them."

Camille could hardly listen to Allison. She put her hand on Ginny's arm. "I'm sorry —"

Ginny pulled away. "Enough with the apologies."

Allison gestured at the room — painting, pottery, glass, fiber, baskets, and Bud's carvings. "Some of these pieces are crude, but I'm willing to take the entire lot."

Camille's heart pounded. "These aren't crude. They're real. They're valuable."

Ginny picked up a pottery vase, caressing it. "Most of these are gifts from friends. I'll never sell them." For one of the first times since Camille had met her, Ginny seemed shaken.

"We can hash out details over the phone. I'll get a commission, but you'll still come out very well."

"I'll need to talk to the other artists . . . and pray about it."

"Pray?" Allison rested her chin on her hand and looked Ginny over from feet to braids. "That could give us a hook." She held up her hands as though framing a sign. " 'The Spiritual Bayou Woman Finds Meaning in Her Metal Designs.' If we spin this right, we'll get national press."

"No." Camille wished she could shove Allison out of the house. "Ginny isn't some doll to be paraded around."

Allison nodded. "We'll have to work with what we've got, but there's definitely raw potential here."

"I made a mistake." Camille's voice was almost a wail. "Let's forget this ever happened."

Ginny gave a grim chuckle. "I've been praying for God to open a door for you, and it looks like He's opened one for me instead."

"No," Camille whispered, nauseated at the idea of Ginny's image in Allison's hands.

"I don't understand what's going on here." Allison flipped her hair back. "Are you driving up the price? Because that is highly unprofessional."

"You're the one who said I should believe in my work, Camille." Ginny adjusted her black glasses. "It's time for me to move on with my life."

CHAPTER 31

Camille splurged on a collection of water-color pencils for the children. They could paint the lines with water, giving their work an impressionist look — and she knew Kylie and Randy would love them.

She also picked up several sets of markers and crisp white paper and paid cash out of her own pocket. She was excited to get to Ginny's to talk about possibilities other than Allison's gallery. Maybe Camille could convince area hotels and restaurants to display pieces, with information on the artists.

Thinking about the night before, she popped the clutch and killed the truck, something she hadn't done in weeks.

Valerie had wheeled into Ginny's driveway like a white knight rescuing Allison from an attack of peasants. "Send me the list of each of the items and the asking price," Allison said as she climbed in the car. "We'll make the best of this."

Camille had sank into the swing, drawing in a breath. She was unable to smell the sweet olive. Even the whirligigs were silent.

"I'm going to miss you so much." Ginny eased into the swing like she was getting onto a ski lift. "When exactly are you leaving?"

Camille swallowed. "I don't know what I'm doing." Scott had called in fury at her suggestion they pull out.

"I shouldn't have been so rude about Allison. She caught me off guard. I guess I've had one too many surprises lately."

Camille cleared her throat. "I should have told you I invited her."

"You really think my windmills are good, don't you?"

"The best. I'd be proud to sell them — although I'm beginning to think the Houston gallery isn't going to work out." Camille cut her eyes at Ginny. "For a variety of reasons."

Ginny laughed. "Seeing her in my living room was kind of like seeing a vegetarian at a beef convention."

Camille gave the swing a push with her foot. A breeze blew across the porch, carrying the sweet scent. The yard art rustled in the night.

Camille had left with a promise to return the next night to clear everything up, and she was eager for the visit. Rolling her window down a few inches, she savored the hint of fall, a less-than-stifling breeze, as she headed north on Vine.

The oversized houses on small lots signaled that she was close to her cutoff to Sweet Olive. She drank in the sight of the sun setting in the distance.

Then she narrowed her eyes, her head flying around as she tried to get her bearings. She was looking east; that couldn't be the sun setting. She stared as the fireball exploded in the sky, leaving a large flame burning in the distance.

Gunning the truck, she hunched over the steering wheel and craned her neck for a better look. A pillar of thick smoke rose into the sky. She frantically tried to pinpoint the location, but the distance made it hard to tell.

She roared on, trying to call Ginny but got a fast busy signal.

Everything looked normal at her first turn, but the fire blazed on the horizon. Even from here, she could see it spitting sparks.

She pulled onto the shoulder when two sheriff's cars, lights flashing, zoomed past her. Before she could get back on the road, a fire truck appeared, its siren sounding like a foghorn.

"Please, please, God. Keep the workers safe. Watch over their families and these first responders. Oh, Lord, please. Not Ginny's place or Evelyn's. Not Lawrence's studio, filled with such beauty, or Lillie Lavender's. Not the tiny church."

Her mother's voice rang in her ears. *Trust the Lord, and do good."*

No matter how bad times had gotten, even with her husband's abandonment and death, Beth Gardner did not waver. Her faith had fueled Camille through every challenge, and she hoped it would help her handle what she saw unfolding in the distance.

Speeding up, Camille fell in behind the fire truck. A deputy of some sort, wearing a yellow reflective jacket, had already set up a barricade of two sawhorses, conferring quickly with a fireman who stuck his head out of the window.

Camille tried to follow when the truck lumbered through the roadblock, but the man stepped into the middle of the road, holding up his hand. "No civilians allowed."

"I have friends in there."

"You need to clear the road."

A Louisiana state police car was in the process of pulling around Camille's vehicle, its bright blue lights nearly blinding her. She opened her door and leaned out.

"Lady, this entire area's being evacuated," the officer said. "We have another hazardous situation on our hands, so you need to get out of here."

As he spoke, three pickups turned onto the road, giving quick beeps of their horns and passing on the shoulder.

The officer gave each a quick salute.

"Is it bad?" the last of the drivers asked, rolling as he spoke.

"They're saying it's toxic. These well accidents are getting worse."

The driver gave a wave and peeled out, his taillights almost the same color as the ball of fire over the trees.

"They got in there," Camille said, her voice ragged. "Why can't I?"

"Those men are volunteer firefighters."

A minivan with a young couple pulled up. "What's burning?" the woman called.

"That new gas well, the one just outside Sweet Olive."

Camille gasped. The fire was close to the artists' houses. A small group of cars and trucks gathered on the shoulder, and people got out of their vehicles, their voices pitched high.

The officer unhooked a flashlight from his belt and pointed it at Camille like a baton, but she spoke before he ordered her to move. "That's my well." She fumbled for the ID badge the guard at work had insisted she have made. "I work for J&S. I report directly to the owner." The words flooded out.

"Only authorized personnel allowed." He shook his head.

"I am authorized."

She felt almost sorry for him as he studied her. A beat-up pickup had pulled almost to her bumper and was honking. The driver spit a stream of tobacco onto the road.

The officer made a sound in his throat and stepped closer to Camille. "Show me that ID again." He pulled a small notebook and pen out of his jacket pocket. "Camille Gardner." He wrote her name as he spoke. "The command center is in the school parking lot. Don't get in the way of people trying to save fools like you."

He walked back to the sawhorses, moving one enough for her to drive through. When she looked in her mirror, he was arguing with another driver.

Seeing no lights at Ginny's or Lawrence's, she skidded down to Evelyn's place, the truck fishtailing in her haste. Evelyn answered the door with a washcloth over her mouth and nose, her eyes red, her head bare, the dogs at her feet.

"Lord have mercy, Camille. What are you doing out here?" Evelyn pulled her in by the arm and slammed the door, as though warding off a monster.

"Are you hurt?"

"I'm fine, but Lawrence must be sick with worry. He's at work, and the phones aren't working."

"The authorities are evacuating all of Sweet Olive," Camille said. "I'll give you a ride. Does anyone else need a lift?"

"I'm not sure where Ginny is."

"Let me go to the school and see what I can find out." Camille took Evelyn's hand. "I'll get you some water, and I want you to rest until I get back."

"I do feel shaky."

Camille helped her to the living room and sprinted into the kitchen for a glass of water. As she opened the cabinet door, she saw a note card stuck to the refrigerator door. Marsh's name was printed at the top in dark blue, and he'd written a note to Evelyn thanking her for a batch of cookies and for the pleasure of working with her.

"I'm honored to handle your drilling issues," it said. "Try not to worry. It's all going to work out." He'd signed only his first name with a scrawled flourish.

Repeated calls to Ginny's cell phone didn't go through. Neither did calls to Valerie, Lawrence, or the J&S corporate headquarters in Houston. "All circuits are busy. Please try again," a recording said repeatedly.

The school parking lot looked like a psychedelic circus: red and blue emergency lights colored the area. The smoke was acrid, and a handful of people wore surgical masks. Camille walked through the crowd but recognized no one.

"We'll take statements shortly," she heard a female deputy say. "First we need to get them to the hospital."

"Burns?" she heard another officer ask.

"Mostly smoke," the other said.

Seeing someone go into the gym where the meeting had been held, Camille followed, unsuccessfully trying Ginny's number again. The folding table sat where it had the other night, but this time a deputy occupied it. A police radio lay nearby, squawking updates Camille couldn't understand.

Every few seconds, the deputy wrote something down.

Unwilling to interrupt her, Camille turned to a man standing nearby, wearing a blue Bienville Oil jumpsuit covered in soot. "Do you know what's going on?" she asked in a hushed voice.

"A J&S well blew out."

"Was anyone hurt? The workers —"

"Three guys went to the hospital," he said. "The others insisted on staying. They can't get it capped, and a lot of people won't leave."

Camille gasped. "We'll get hotel rooms."

"They're planning a shelter at a church in Samford. These folks can't afford a hotel."

"J&S will pay."

"You're right about that," he said.

"Oh, Camille." Ginny swooped in from the side of the room, carrying an armload of bottled water. "You shouldn't have come out here. They're making people leave."

"Are you all right?" Camille rushed up to hug her around the water.

"For the moment. Janice rushed over for the kids. They were more upset about missing your art lesson than about the fire."

"I was on my way when I saw a giant flash. I was afraid it might be one of your homes."

"Have you heard anything about how it's

spreading? We can't lose the art —"

A voice interrupted. The sheriff shouted through cupped hands, "It's imperative that everyone vacate the premises immediately. The command center is being moved to the Emergency Response Shelter in Bossier Parish."

Dropping his hands, he strode over to Ginny and shook his head as he accepted a bottle of water. "Ginny, you need to convince folks to leave. We don't know what we're dealing with."

"Most of these folks have never stayed anywhere other than their own house," Ginny said. "It would take a bigger blast than this to get them out."

"Air quality's poor. The youngest and oldest are at risk for breathing disorders." He lowered his voice. "That well could burn for days."

"I've got to get Evelyn," Camille said.

He seemed to notice her for the first time and frowned. "J&S has a mess on its hands, Miss Gardner. We've notified your disaster team."

"The team can handle well logistics, but I need to make sure the residents have what they need." Her breathing was shallow. "We'll reserve a block of hotel rooms and set up a conference center where people can contact their relatives."

Within twenty minutes, Camille pulled back up to Evelyn's house. Alarmed when Evelyn didn't answer the door, Camille knocked louder and tried to push it open, but it was locked. She peered through the window, but a sheer curtain blocked her view. She ran around the house and tried the back door, but it was locked too. So she climbed up on the porch rail and looked in the transom, afraid of what she might see.

Before she had her footing, the house seemed to bounce, as though it had sprung off a trampoline. A shelf of empty jars rattled nearby. Camille was falling when the door crashed open.

"Oh my word, child." Evelyn rushed over to where a stunned Camille lay. "Are you hurt?"

"No," Camille croaked. Holding her left arm, which felt like someone was sticking hot needles in it, she got to her feet, her legs wobbling like a newborn colt. "I'm so happy you're all right."

"Did you feel the house shake?" Evelyn looked around, her eyes wide. "Did the well explode?"

"I don't know." Camille tried to stand. "We've got to get you out of here. The well fire's a health hazard."

Evelyn looked as though she might argue but nodded. "We'll leave as soon as we wrap your arm."

Camille's arm hurt so badly it brought tears to her eyes, and she shook as she followed Evelyn into the house. "We're getting you a hotel room. Sweet Olive neighbors will be on one floor, so you can stay informed."

"We don't need to spend money on a hotel room. I don't plan to be gone from home long, and I can't leave my dogs."

Camille's energy drained with every throb of her arm, so she merely smiled and agreed, while Evelyn chatted and put ice on her arm. Loading Evelyn's suitcase, she fished in her purse for ibuprofen, swallowed four, and herded the terriers into the truck.

By the time they got to the barricade, which had now turned into a full-fledged checkpoint, the pain was so bad she felt faint. The noxious fumes from the fires, which were bigger now than when she'd first seen them, made her queasy.

She pulled over to speak to the deputy, who made a *tsking* sound when he saw the bandage. "I told you not to go in there, ma'am. Were you injured during the earthquake?"

"Earthquake?"

"Three-point-three on the Richter scale," he said.

"Is everyone accounted for?"

"Is that Ms. Martinez you have with you?" he asked.

"Hey, Jonas, it's me," Evelyn chirped, brushing against Camille's arm as she leaned over to speak. Camille tried to smile.

"She's the last one coming out tonight," he said. "Half are already out, and half say they're not leaving." He waved a hand, as though trying to clear the thick air. "Like I told Mr. Cameron, I wish they all had the sense to get out."

"Most of us old folks like to sleep in our own beds." Evelyn smiled.

By her headlights, Camille could see the crowd had grown. Regional television stations had set up satellites and were doing live feeds. Bright lights illuminated reporters speaking urgently into microphones or scrolling through notepads. Drew Cross was talking loudly to Marsh.

Camille leaned back on the headrest and closed her eyes.

"Look at that Cross boy," Evelyn said. "He's probably stirring up trouble."

Pulling the truck around the deputy, Camille edged onto the grass. "I'd better get an update. I'll be right back."

She concentrated on putting one foot in front of the other as she approached the lawman.

"Camille!" Marsh's voice was close — and startled.

She stumbled, hitting the ground hard.

Chapter 32

The hospitality suite was chilly and impersonal.

Valerie had lined up a row of dining room chairs from a banquet room along one wall. To Camille, they conveyed the look of a firing squad.

Which might be appropriate.

An urn of coffee brewed on a small table, and soft drinks were iced in an oversized plastic bowl. "I still don't see why we needed a fruit tray *and* cheese," Valerie grumbled, plopping down on a small couch that looked like a dorm-room futon.

Camille winced, both at Valerie's tone and the pain. Not only had J&S disrupted an entire community, but Camille had managed to break her wrist and dislocate her shoulder. "Are you certain everyone got word about the free rooms and the vet for their pets? I can't bear for anyone to be stranded without a place to stay."

"Why are you so obsessed about that?" Valerie said. "Mr. Stephens said we should only put up the people who were forced to evacuate, not those who want a fancy vacation."

"You spoke to Scott? I texted him from the emergency room, but the service was so poor."

"He's asked me to keep him informed," Valerie said, hesitating. "He checked on your condition a dozen times overnight. He acted . . . almost worried about you."

Camille exhaled the breath she hadn't known she was holding. "When will the pizzas be delivered?" She arranged the napkins Val had left in the packages.

"Within the hour." Valerie grabbed her phone out of her purse.

"Maybe we should have gotten fried chicken instead," Camille said. "We still could."

Making a production out of fluffing a throw pillow, Valerie huffed. "I don't think these people are going to be all that interested in food."

Camille adjusted her sling.

Valerie looked at her phone. "Here's a new report. Wind has shifted. Woods still burning. No houses on fire. My father's about to have a fit about smoke at his Cotton Grove subdivision."

"And the workers at the well?" Camille's voice bordered on hysterical.

"Everyone's accounted for, and Evelyn's been released from the hospital. A couple of workers were held overnight, but they're out now."

"Thank You, Lord," Camille murmured.

"Are you *praying?*" Valerie said.

"If this won't make you pray, nothing will," a thin voice said from the door, and Camille whirled so quickly that her arm felt like she had held it in the fire. Her head spun.

"Evelyn!" She rushed to the door. "Let me help you sit down."

"I'm better off than you are." Evelyn nodded at Camille's sling.

Lawrence was behind his mother, his eyes concerned. "A cast and a black eye?"

Camille touched her cheek with her uninjured arm. "I think we've proven I'm not good in a crisis."

Neither he nor Evelyn appeared amused. "You scared me to death," Evelyn said.

"The media's having a field day with that one." Valerie looked at Lawrence. "Worst injury of the day goes to the J&S executive."

"She rescued me," Evelyn said. "She could

have headed back into town and left me out there."

"That's not Camille's style," Valerie said, and the words did not sound like a compliment.

"You two put all this together?" Lawrence walked over and took a cube of cheese. "Is it true that Camille called a caterer from an operating table?"

Camille rolled her eyes. "I was waiting for a doctor so I set a few things in motion." She pulled a grape from the tray and nibbled on it to keep from chewing her fingernails. "Valerie told me that half of Sweet Olive camped near the road last night."

"We're a stubborn bunch," Lawrence said. "But Marsh convinced people to come here today. He said we might as well get a shower and a good meal — and let you pay for it."

"Are they furious?"

"I've seen them madder — the time they closed schools for a week for a hurricane that never hit." Evelyn paused and captured Camille's gaze with her own. "They're upset, but they don't blame you for this."

"It's my fault," Camille said. "I represent J&S, and we brought this pain into your lives, into your homes."

"Don't be ridiculous," Lawrence said.

"Where's Ginny?" Camille asked.

"She and Marsh are meeting."

"We've got meals and other vouchers," Camille said. "Can you think of anything else?"

"A few big, fat liability checks," Valerie muttered.

As the residents trickled in that afternoon, the room took on the air of a funeral parlor visitation. At moments, people were distraught, demanding answers and tearfully recounting the events of the night before and the long day. At other times, they joked and snacked, greeting neighbors as though they had been apart for weeks.

They bombarded Ginny with questions when she stepped into the room early in the evening, but she seemed intent on reaching Camille.

"You should sit down," she said, hurling herself across the room, her hair bouncing on top of her head. She wore a long skirt and an oversized purple T-shirt, and her eyes were tired.

"Has someone else been injured?" Camille gasped the question.

Ginny shook her head and moved in for a careful embrace. Camille tried not to wince, the sling and cast in the way. "Are you all right?" Ginny asked.

"I'm heartbroken. I'm so sorr—"

"Stop with the apologies, Camille." Ginny spoke over her words. "They say it was a faulty piece of pipe. It overheated and blew up." She put her hand at the small of Camille's back and nudged her toward the couch, putting a pillow under her arm.

"I'm supposed to take care of you, not the other way around," Camille said.

"I don't need taking care of."

"You're exhausted," she said, as Ginny sat down next to her. "Where are Kylie and Randy?"

"That's one of the blessings out of this." Ginny leaned her head back on the couch. "Janice was terrified when she heard about the fire and got to my house before anyone else. She's taken them to her sister's house in Alexandria for a couple of days. She acted . . . better."

"I bought them some new art supplies," Camille said, her voice thin.

"It could have been so much worse. The fire's nearly out. We should be able to go home tomorrow. Now we need to put you to bed."

Camille started her usual denial but stopped midsentence as Marsh walked in. He wore faded jeans and an oxford-cloth shirt, untucked, sleeves rolled up. He had no socks on with his loafers.

The careless clothing was offset by the serious look as he strode over. "How are you, Camille?" He looked her up and down.

"Thanks for driving me to the hospital."

"It was the least I could do." He grinned. "It's been a long time since a pretty woman fell at my feet."

"I doubt that."

"What'd they say at the hospital?" Marsh said.

"That I should be more careful when I peek in someone's window."

"I hated to leave you in the ER, but I had to get back to Sweet Olive to make sure my father was all right." Marsh pulled up a chair, sitting knee to knee with her. "In case you're wondering, you've called the sheriff so many times that he's about to block your number."

Camille's chuckle was weak. "At least they restored phone service."

"You could have been seriously injured."

"Then I would be out of your hair."

"Don't joke about things like that," Ginny said.

Camille looked from one to the other. Business would intrude soon enough, but she liked the way they huddled close to her. She turned slightly, bumping Marsh's knee.

"I slipped and fell. It was my own fault." Camille attempted to sit up straighter. "We need to discuss how long it will be before people can get back into their homes — and what we'll need to do to compensate them."

"The fire inspectors have to sign off on letting people back in," Valerie said, walking up, her eyes glued to her phone. "They haven't gotten the fire completely out."

Everyone in the room flocked to where she stood. "I knew it was a bad idea to come here," Charlene, the bossy one of the twins, said. "I'm not sitting around while my home burns."

"You are not going in there," Darlene said.

Camille got to her feet slowly, steadying herself with the hand that wasn't bandaged. "Please, stay here where it's safe."

"We're not getting enough information," Drew Cross said. "We don't know any more than we did last night."

"We'll relay it as quickly as it arrives," Valerie said.

Camille held up her hand, swaying slightly. "I'll go to the site and give everyone regular reports."

"Absolutely not," Marsh said, and Camille noticed Valerie's head jerk back slightly.

"I'll go." Valerie lifted one shoulder, her gauzy shirt flowing with the movement.

"Mr. Stephens requires constant feedback anyway."

"I'll go with you," Lawrence said.

Within a few hours, the residents had scattered to their rooms with the promise they would be notified in person if there were any changes.

Marsh had gone home to let his father into his house.

The fire smoldered on, pictures from Valerie dinging on Camille's phone.

Two firefighters were taken to the hospital for burns and smoke inhalation, and Valerie had set up a communication center on the road where a deputy was stationed.

"I appreciate your help with this," Camille said in a broken-up cell call.

"The Houston office sent an e-mail with emergency protocol, and my father insisted businesspeople deserve to know what is going on."

For the first time, Camille was relieved when the call dropped. Leaving Sweet Olive would be heart wrenching. Leaving Valerie would not.

In the hotel suite, Camille paced until Ginny complained that she was making her nervous. Then she stared out the window at the parking lot and paced more. She was so tired she hardly felt her wrist and shoulder.

Ginny, the only other person in the room, was sandwiched between the arms of the small sofa, eyes closed and breathing steady. Camille couldn't imagine how she slept in that awkward position, her arms up under her head and her legs bent. Her long hair hung over the couch arm.

Camille had never seen Ginny slow down. In the wee hours of the night, she looked vulnerable, like one of the children she cared for.

Getting a blanket and pillow from house-keeping, Camille covered Ginny. "Sleep well," she murmured.

"Shouldn't you be doing likewise?" a voice whispered in her ear.

A sharp pain ripped through Camille's shoulder as she jumped back into Marsh.

"Careful." He put his arm around her waist.

"What are you doing back?"

"You don't like to accept help, do you?"

Camille let him guide her to the other side of the room. His touch was light, his voice kind. "How's the arm?"

Resisting the urge to shrug, she twisted her mouth as she sank into a chair. "Not too bad."

"You're a tough thing." He sat in the seat

next to her. "No wonder you wound up in the oil-and-gas business."

She snorted. "If I were tough, I wouldn't *be* in this business."

"You risked your life for Sweet Olive."

She closed her eyes and put her hand on her neck. "I owe my life to Sweet Olive."

At this moment her future seemed as unclear as the smoke-filled sky, but whatever happened would be tinged with lessons from the wise artists.

Camille's mother called for the third time early the next morning. "I saw you on television again. Your interviews are gripping."

Camille moaned softly.

"Are you sure you're all right?"

"Mama, like I told you six times yesterday, I'm good." She glanced down at the sling and cast. "I'm worried about what Uncle Scott's going to do when he sees all those news reports."

"Quit worrying about Scott. You need to come home."

"Home? I have a job to do. And another one in Houston."

"I want to take care of my girl for a while."

Camille smiled. "You always take care of me."

The next call was from Allison, who alternated between excitement at seeing Camille on national news and concern that the art had been damaged. "If there's a silver lining to this, it's that you'll have time to crate the Sweet Olive art." Allison gave an exasperated sigh. "But let's figure out exactly when that will be."

"I don't know, Allison." Camille adjusted her arm. "I don't know."

"We might work this into a dramatic marketing piece. Did any of the art burn?" Allison stopped, as though she had just realized the jeopardy. "Ginny's house was not damaged, was it?"

Camille drew in a deep breath, feeling as though she could smell the thick smoke. "I don't think I'm going to be able to fill in at the gallery anytime soon."

"Are you serious?" Allison shrieked. "Are you taking the artists to another gallery?"

"I'm not taking the artists anywhere at the moment," Camille said tiredly.

"You'd better not steal them away from me," Allison said. "We had a deal." She hung up.

CHAPTER 33

The house at Trumpet and Vine looked different at various times of the day.

At dawn, when sleeplessness forced Camille out of bed, it had a calm dignity. The street corner wasn't noisy yet, and the sun wasn't bright enough to show its flaws.

By lunchtime, it looked like a middle-aged aunt, sagging but approachable.

For some reason, Camille liked it best in the evening.

Tonight the traffic was steady enough to be lively but not so heavy as to be intrusive. With the days getting shorter, the house had already fallen into shadows.

She pulled the truck into the drive and leaned her head back, favoring her injured arm. The quiet darkness calmed her after another day of dealing with fire fallout, including a nasty scene with Slattery and a terse voice mail from Uncle Scott.

At least everyone was safe and back in

their homes, ready to resume their lives during the weekend ahead.

Taking a deep breath, she got out. The traffic light had switched over to flashing yellow and she stood there as it went bright, dark, bright, dark.

As a car slowed nearby, she looked around self-consciously and crossed the street to the convenience store. She thought the same old man watched TV behind the counter tonight as he had done when she was fifteen.

He didn't speak when she bought a fried pie and a cup of decaf coffee, half looking over his shoulder at a news program as he took her money.

Camille stepped toward the door before stopping. "Excuse me."

The man didn't respond but a tiny, wrinkled woman leaning on a walker gave a nod. "Bill, the young lady needs something else."

"I wonder if you know anything about that house across the street?"

"Like what?" the man snapped.

"Is it still for sale?"

"Sign still there?" he asked.

"Um . . . yes, I believe so." Camille knew it was. She looked for it every day.

"Then it's still for sale. Will there be anything else?"

"Bill!" the woman said, gliding closer to Camille. "Someone finally made an offer on it."

"You don't know that," the man said.

"I talked to the real estate agent myself," the woman said. "He was in here for a biscuit yesterday . . . or was it Tuesday? Are you interested in buying it?"

"Oh no," Camille said.

"Then why are you taking up our time?" The man turned back to the television.

Camille put her hand on the door.

"He gets wrapped up in the TV," the woman said apologetically. Her smile was strong, although her body looked frail.

"No problem," Camille said, but she didn't open the door. She felt frozen, looking out at the duplex.

"I'm Martha. That mean old coot's my husband, Bill. His sister used to live in that house." She scrutinized Camille, her eyes lingering on the cast.

"I'm Camille." She chewed on her lip. "Was your sister-in-law Mrs. Maxwell, by any chance?"

Martha's eyes got large behind her thick glasses. "You knew Edie?"

"My mother and I knew her. It was a long time ago."

"She passed away three years ago," Martha said. "Heart attack. Not a day goes by that I don't think of her."

"She was a nice person," Camille said. When Uncle Scott had offered Mrs. Maxwell a wad of cash, she had shaken her head. But Camille had seen him slip it into the apron pocket while scolding her mother for taking too long to get in the big truck, a red Silverado.

"She was good as gold." The woman walked from behind the counter, moving the walker steadily with each step. "What was your mother's name?"

"Beth Gardner. She lives in Amarillo now."

The woman tilted her head and seemed to be waiting. "And you're Camille Gardner?" she asked, as though trying to place her. "What brings you to Trumpet and Vine at this time of night? Mostly we do daytime business."

Camille shrugged. "I'm new to town. I was driving by."

"This used to be a lovely neighborhood," Martha said.

"Well, it sure ain't anymore," Bill said.

Camille nodded. "Life changes, I suppose."

"Did you ever go in Edie's little gift shop?" Martha asked. "She lived upstairs

362

and had the shop on the bottom floor."

Camille nodded slowly. "Once." She still had the tiny souvenir pitcher Mrs. Maxwell had given her, its handle now glued together and its spout chipped.

"I hope the new owners are good neighbors," Martha said. "Wouldn't it be something if this corner sprang back to life?"

Camille held back a moan. The store owner must be quite an optimist if she held out hope for Trumpet and Vine and the duplex in particular. The yard was mostly dirt, and a big limb lay on the roof. Torn screens were flopping on two windows by the porch, and a cat sat on the wooden ledge.

As Camille exited, Bill locked the front door of the store behind her.

Propelled by dismay that the house had sold, Camille lurched to the duplex. She felt like she had gone back in time and been disappointed anew.

Had she ever gone in the shop? the lady had asked. Once. The place was branded into her memory, despite all of her efforts to forget it. She crept around back for a closer look.

Her mother, a part-time cafeteria worker, had insisted — in a calm, firm voice — that they accompany her dad on a summer wildcatting trip to Cypress Parish.

Even at fifteen, Camille had not complained when they cleared out of their apartment in Abilene and headed east. They had moved so much that she didn't have friends to part with, and her entertainment was portable — a sketchbook and watercolor paints.

They set up camp at the Takin'-It-Easy RV Park on the south side of Samford, occupied mostly by oil-field workers who didn't look like they had ever taken it easy. But despite litter and domestic arguments in nearby trailers, the site had appealed to Camille. Magnolia trees flanked the entrance, their big, white blossoms giving off a wonderful scent.

While her dad crawled around on drilling sites, she and her mama sunbathed at the tiny pool at the RV park, a rare treat, and Camille picked up a few dollars watching a smattering of young children while their parents worked.

After only a few days, her short babysitting stints had turned into art lessons. With excitement, she planned an exhibit for the end of summer and saved money to buy treats for their "graduation."

For the first time in years, her mother didn't have a job and her father was home each evening, happy and seldom drinking.

Until that day in mid-August, when the scorching sun sent her back to the little trailer for Kool-Aid. Her father, his eyes bleary and his breath foul with beer, was throwing their belongings into two cardboard boxes and a suitcase they had bought at a garage sale when Camille was in fourth grade.

He had shielded his face from the bright light when she opened the door and then fussed at her for surprising him. "Where's Beth?"

"At the pool." She ignored the flood of dread in her stomach. "Wanna join us?"

"Go get her. We're leaving."

The words themselves weren't all that different from versions he had uttered a dozen or more times. But his voice sounded different — upset, weary, even defeated.

The next hour was a nightmarish blur, a whirl of shouts, tears, and misery. No matter how hard her mother pleaded, her father wouldn't budge. A well fire near Tyler needed his immediate attention.

"I've got to go now," he said, "and try to save the company."

"Isn't that Scott's job? It's his company now."

Her father popped the top to another beer

and took a long gulp before answering. "It's going to take both of us."

"Then let's get going. Camille, run tell the children good-bye. I'll finish securing our things."

When her daddy set the beer can on the counter, Camille knew he was leaving them again. He exhaled. "This one's dangerous. I can't take you with me."

For a moment, worry for her father and relief dueled within Camille. She liked this place. She wanted to stay.

"Scott says we'll need the camper," her father said. "The well's isolated and it'll be the only place for the guys to crash." He held up his hand when her mother started to speak. "J&S owns it."

"Owns us," her mother murmured.

"Not for long. I'm this close to getting out." He held his thumb and index finger about an inch apart. "I have something in the works, and we'll never have to move again — but first I've got to take care of this fire."

"You've been drinking, Johnny. You shouldn't drive. You shouldn't —"

"I only had a couple of beers, Beth." He rubbed his neck. "The fire's a bad one. They need me."

"Where will Camille and I stay until you

come back?"

He pulled her mother close and nuzzled her neck. "Scott's been in Bogalusa oversee-ing a pipeline leak. He'll pick you up on his way through Samford and drop you in Longview."

"Longview?" Camille tried to remember if they had lived there before, the Texas towns running together.

"That's our next stop, baby girl." He drew her into the embrace with her mother. "I'll meet you there."

Her dad drove the old truck off, camper in tow. He waved and blew a kiss as he left. "Draw me another picture, Camille," he said as he rolled through the gates of the park.

A neighbor whose husband worked in the oil field too offered to take them to the corner where they were to meet Uncle Scott. "We sure are going to miss y'all. Abby says she's going to be an art teacher like Camille when she grows up."

Camille wiped back a tear as the woman, her old car needing a muffler, drove off. Her mother sank onto a concrete bus bench outside the convenience store and tugged on Camille's arm. "We'll quit moving around now that you're in high school. Dad-dy's going to find us a house with a yard."

"Right. And I'm going to own an art studio and you're never going to have to work again."

"Oh, sweetie." For the first time she could ever remember, her mother began to weep. "Everything's going to work out."

Camille kicked one of the boxes holding their meager belongings. "If you say so . . ."

"Your father's a good man, but he has a job to do."

"Other people's fathers don't leave them on street corners."

Her mother put her head in her hands and sobbed. Shame washed over Camille, and she wrapped her arms around her mother, wedged against her on the hard bench. "I'm sorry, Mama. Don't cry. Everything will be all right."

She kept saying that when they went into the store for a snack. When the afternoon sun blistered their noses. When Uncle Scott still didn't come.

"I don't even know how to reach him," her mother said, a fresh round of sobs coming.

In that moment, Camille vowed never to make her mother cry again.

"Everything's going to be fine." She dug out her babysitting money. "How about some ice cream?"

At dark, a woman — "Edith Maxwell, but my friends call me Edie" — came out of the duplex/gift shop and offered them a meal and a place to sleep.

Worried that Uncle Scott wouldn't be able to find them, Camille taped a sign on the bus bench that said *Over There* with an arrow. From the pay phone, they had placed calls to every J&S employee they could think of until their change had run out, gaining no information except that the fire in Tyler raged out of control.

Her mother had slowly regained her composure, shelling peas with Mrs. Maxwell, and Camille sat on the steps.

"God knew we needed you, Edie," her mother said, her smile almost back to normal.

At midnight, when Scott still had not appeared, Mrs. Maxwell pulled out the rollaway bed, and Camille snuggled there until her mother drifted off to sleep. Then she went back to the stifling porch to keep watch.

Uncle Scott's arrival, at that dark moment before dawn, awoke Camille from the chair, and she ran into the yard to flag him down. Although she had never felt close to him, this morning she rushed to his fancy new pickup and threw her arms around him.

He smelled like cigarettes and sweat and wore an expression she hadn't seen before.

"Your father's had an accident, Camy. Where's your mother?"

From that moment, she was in Scott's debt, her dreams of an art career blown away by an oil-field fire.

Marsh rounded the corner of Vine with a cramp in his left leg. That's what he got for waiting so late to run. The well fire had occupied most of the day with a conference call with the Baton Rouge office, the founding partner shouting about the bad press.

Marsh groaned. He must be getting old when a Thursday night jog sounded like the perfect evening.

He glanced over at the convenience store, closed for the evening. Wiping the sweat from his face, he stepped back into the shadows as he saw someone walking around the rear of the house across the street.

Looking closer, he frowned. A pickup that looked like his father's was in the driveway. Maybe his dad had stopped to check something for Ross — for surely Camille wasn't there.

He cut across the street and padded around the side of the house, his dad nowhere in sight, the truck shrouded in shadows.

As he looked closer, though, he could barely make out someone on the back steps, jiggling the door handle. The person was obscured by a bush, but it was not his father.

"Finally," a woman's voice said softly.

"Camille?"

But she had already stepped across the threshold.

Marsh was curious by nature and good at figuring things out — but this one had him flummoxed. Following her into the house, he watched as she stepped into what must have been a dining room. With her back to him, she stood in the doorway for a long moment. Then she rubbed her hand along the wood trim.

This woman was crazy. Anyone could walk up on her standing there like that.

He took a step. "Hello."

"Ugh," Camille grunted, whirling around, coffee flying out of the paper cup in her hand. "Marsh!" She grabbed her hurt wrist. "What are you doing here?"

"That's the question I was about to ask you."

She gave a nervous laugh, the flash of a streetlight outside illuminating her face. She wore those same ragged jeans and cowboy boots tonight with an art festival T-shirt of some sort. Her hair was sticking up, and she looked fantastic.

"Did *you* buy this place?" he asked.

"No." She stepped back. "I've been intrigued by it and couldn't resist a look around."

"At this time of night?"

"I've been busy," she said. "Our deal can't be too far off, and I wanted to see it before I left." She raised her eyebrows. "You?"

"Ross is the agent for this property, and I thought he had a prowler. I can't believe it was unlocked." He reached for his phone. "I'd better let him know."

"Marsh . . ." Her voice had a begging tone he had not heard her use before. "Please don't. Okay?"

"He needs to know it was open. There's not much to steal in here but nonetheless —"

"It wasn't open." She spit the words out. "I broke in."

He tilted his head.

"I don't think I damaged the lock. If I did, I'll pay for it."

A couple of seconds ticked by. "Say something," she said. "You're making me nervous."

"You weren't nervous wandering alone through a dark, vacant house?" Nerves made him sweat.

Marsh considered himself a discerning sort of guy. Trying to understand Camille Gardner was like doing a puzzle with his eyes closed. Just when he thought he had her figured out, she did something like . . . well, break into an old house at night.

He, a man who made his living cross-examining people, floundered.

She moved toward the front of the duplex, looking up at the ceiling.

"What am I missing?" he said, half talking to himself. "What are you doing here?"

She fanned her face. "Let's sit on the steps." She pulled on the ornate front doorknob, a remnant of a finer day.

"You've been in here before." Marsh closed the distance between them and put his hand on top of hers.

Her shoulder was right under his chin, her hair damp at the back of her neck. He moved in another notch and drew in a deep breath. She did not move away. Her breathing sounded soft and steady, while his felt uneven.

Camille followed him onto the porch and sank onto the steps. She nudged at an ant bed with the toe of her boot. "We lived in Samford for a few weeks one summer." She stared off into space.

"I had no idea."

"Your investigation into my background didn't tell you that?"

"There's not much about you online." He gave a grin. "For example, there's not a hint of any burglaries."

"I should have asked Ross to show me the house."

"That's what I usually recommend." He was surprised by how much she made him want to smile.

She looked at him intently, sitting so close that he could watch the way her eyelashes swept down as she talked. "It's sort of a long story," she said after a moment.

He glanced down at his watch.

"That's an incredibly irritating habit."

Marsh unfastened the watch, gave her a steady look, and tossed it out into the yard. "I'd like to hear the rest of your story."

"You're crazy," Camille said but moved closer, looking up at the beaded-board porch ceiling. "My father was a wildcatter and always had a well he wanted to check on. Until recently, I thought he cared about the oil-and-gas business more than he did me and Mama."

She fidgeted with the hem of her jeans. "He was called away to a well fire. He burned to death." She swiped at her face.

374

"His clothes melted on him."

Marsh slid an arm across her shoulders and cradled her head. "I'm so sorry for your pain, Camille."

She put her good arm around herself, drawing into a ball against his chest. "It was worse for my mother. I'd learned to live without him a long time before that."

"What'd you do?"

"The same thing I always did — called my uncle."

"Did he help you?"

"Always." Camille grew still against him and then lifted her face. "I got your shirt wet. I don't usually cry."

"That's what all women say."

"This place has made me emotional. My mother asked about it." She shrugged. "I wanted to see it too."

"Does your mother live in Houston?"

Camille shook her head. "She eventually went back to Amarillo, where she grew up. She has a nice little house and lots of good friends from church. It was sort of a fresh start for her, even though she never remarried."

Marsh shifted so he could see her face more clearly. "Did you make a fresh start too?"

She gave her head a quick shake. "I'm still

working on that."

"With your interest in oil and gas, you must take after your father."

"I suppose," she said.

"Is that a bad thing?" He turned so his face was almost touching hers.

"Before coming to Louisiana, I thought so. I suppose you could say my father was like a good gas well that never produced to its potential." She gave a choked laugh. "Daddy made some colossal mistakes — including the one that cost him his life . . . but he loved me and my mother."

Camille pulled away slightly. "How about you? Is it true that you're a lot like your father?"

"If I were half the man my dad is, I'd be happy," Marsh replied.

"What about your mother?"

"My parents are as different from each other as that store over there is from Nieman Marcus. The only thing they have in common is me. Thankfully they figured that out before they killed one another."

"How old were you when they split up?"

"Five," he said. "I pretty much spent my childhood shuttling back and forth between Samford society and Sweet Olive artists."

She touched his face. "No wonder you're so comfortable in both worlds. But that must have been tough."

"For years I felt like two people. I watched what I said and how I said it. I even worried about what I wore." He gave an embarrassed laugh. "I didn't want to look too sloppy at my mother's or too dressy at my father's."

She frowned. "Where does your brother fit into all of this?"

"My mom married Doc — Roger Aillet — a year after the divorce. T.J. — Thomas Jacques Aillet — was born when I was seven." He stared up at the flashing traffic light. "When he got old enough, he begged to go with me to my dad's. He always seemed more at home at my dad's than in the Samford house."

He glanced down at his empty wrist. "This is weird."

She started to stand. "Let me get your watch."

Marsh shook his head. "I've never told one person — not even Dad — what I just told you, the one person in the world I'm supposed to keep at arm's length."

"Now we're even." Camille put her finger to her lips and offered a small smile. "Except you know the secret of my criminal tendencies. I swear I'll never break into another building."

He stood, tempted to pull her back up against him.

"Do you need a lift?"

He looked at her and the truck and threw wisdom out the window. "Could I interest you in a burger?"

Camille and Marsh left the diner after midnight with loud farewells from the robust owner. "Bring your girlfriend back anytime!" Camille felt like she was back in high school and had somehow become the popular girl.

"He likes you," she said, sliding behind the wheel.

"He and my dad have been friends for years. I did a small favor for him in court once."

"It must not have seemed small to him," she said.

"I only did it because my father asked me to, and it only took a few hours. I groused about it so much around the office that you'd have thought I'd spent weeks on it." He gestured to show her the route to his house.

"I'm ashamed of how I felt about the case," he said.

"What do you mean?"

"I was annoyed every minute I wasn't getting paid. I made a big deal about it to my dad, making sure he knew I was only doing it for him."

"I bet that went over well."

Marsh grinned. "He told me he'd rather hire another lawyer than listen to me whine. I got the message and won Sam a little settlement. That's not a secret, by the way. He tells everyone about it. And I do mean *everyone*."

"And that embarrasses you?" Camille slowed as he directed her onto the lovely tree-lined street.

"I don't want to be the big, selfish lawyer, but I do want to take cases where my work has impact."

"Are you talking about Sweet Olive?"

"That case has big implications. Little community fights big oil. You know that."

She made a small noise. "But you haven't handled this case like that."

"So my charm is working?"

"Occasionally." She couldn't hold back a smile. She turned by the Richmond home and wound back to Marsh's street.

"Do you think it's safe to turn into my driveway?" he asked with a grin.

She patted the steering wheel. "We've bonded since I came to Samford."

A tingle ran up Camille's spine as she

pulled in. She had not realized before that the house resembled one of her most recent art purchases — a watercolor of a bungalow by a Florida artist. When she bought it, she had imagined stepping into the space.

"You have a lovely home," she said.

"Thanks. I bought it the second I could. I needed a place to call home."

"Whose work is that over the fireplace?"

"Evelyn traded me that for a small job I did for her," he said. "I came out better than she did."

"I didn't know she painted."

"Folks in Sweet Olive do a little of everything," he said, opening the passenger door.

On impulse, she grabbed his sleeve. "Thank you for an . . . interesting evening. I never knew breaking and entering could be so much fun."

He stepped from the truck. "The pleasure was mine."

Going into the house ranked as one of the stupidest things she'd ever done. Being caught by Marsh made it worse. Spilling details about her past compounded it.

Not only had she chosen to open up to the landowners' lawyer, she was pretty sure she was falling in love for the first time in her thirty years.

That was about as smart as the time her father wanted to turn an old well site into an amusement park.

Maybe the fire and her injury had frayed her. Or perhaps Uncle Scott was right. Maybe she was getting soft. And maybe she should have told Marsh her other secret.

CHAPTER 34

Marsh arrived at the Samford Club nearly thirty minutes early Tuesday, surprised that his palms were sweating.

This wasn't a lunch he looked forward to.

Lawrence greeted him at the elevator. "Let me show you to your table, Mr. Cameron," he said, a big smile on his face.

Marsh drew back. "What's up with you?"

"Today," he said, reaching out to high-five Marsh, "is my last day as a waiter. I am officially retiring from food service."

"Did you decide to take the J&S deal after all?"

Walking toward a small private dining room, Lawrence shook his head. "I'm certainly not spending that money yet. Like Mama always says, 'we lived without the money before.' We'll get by."

He looked like a quarterback who had scored the winning touchdown. "Camille restored my confidence about my glass.

Even though the gas deal's not certain, I have to give my art a chance."

Marsh raised his eyebrows and tried to look unconcerned. "Are you and Camille . . . involved?"

"You sound like my mother," Lawrence said with a laugh. "There's way too much going on right now, with the leases, the gallery possibilities . . ." He shrugged. "Besides, Camille doesn't seem that into me."

"You're telling me Camille's immune to that rugged artist image you work so hard at?" Despite his attempt to be unaffected, Marsh's voice sounded gruff. His relief ballooned.

"She seems to go more for the suit-and-tie type. I don't get it." Lawrence paused. "For the next few years, I'm putting my time and energy into my glasswork. I don't know anything about business, but I'm going to give this a shot."

"I know where you can find a cheap lawyer."

Lawrence nodded. "You need to go ahead and open your own firm too. We're not getting any younger, buddy."

Pulling out a chair, Lawrence sat down. It was the first time Marsh had ever seen him do that on the job. "I want to finish up Sweet Olive first," Marsh said. "Something's not quite right."

"Give it up," Lawrence said. "I've realized we can't control what everyone else does. People have to do what's best for them."

"I've got to make sure all the property titles are clear, no matter what happens," Marsh answered. "Your children — or your children's children — shouldn't have to fool with all this."

"Camille cleared the title on the Martinez land before she gave me that check," Lawrence said. "Does this have something to do with the questions you've been asking about Ginny's property?"

"Let me do a little more digging before I say more. It's probably nothing."

Val stepped into the room. "What are you two talking about?" Her voice had an accusing tone, and Marsh wondered how much she had heard.

Wearing a fancy suit with the pearls her parents had given her for her twenty-first birthday, she looked beautiful — but different. Marsh had always thought of her as the most beautiful woman in Samford, but she seemed artificial compared to Camille.

"I'd better get back to work," Lawrence said, not meeting Valerie's eyes. "Keep me posted, will you, Marsh?"

"You're walking out?" Valerie grabbed his

arm as he started by.

Lawrence looked down at her hand. "Do you need something?"

"I need to know what you two were whispering about." She stamped the toe of her high-heeled shoe. "You're talking about Camille, aren't you?"

"Val—" Marsh said.

"Grow up, Val," Lawrence said.

Valerie put her hand over her mouth.

"I've got to get to work." Lawrence pulled the door shut behind him.

"Well, that was . . . unexpected." Val plopped into a chair without her usual elegance. As she placed the napkin in her lap, he noticed that her hands were trembling. "Are we here to talk about the J&S deal or for you to dump me too?"

He frowned. "Let's don't say something we'll regret."

She let out a huff of breath. "You think I'm a loose cannon."

He eased into the chair next to her, not pulling it up to the table.

"I won't bite."

He scooted closer and put his hand on the back of her chair. "Why are you acting so sneaky?"

She didn't meet his gaze. "So it's business we're talking today."

"We've been friends a long time. You're up to something."

"That J&S job should have been mine. I know the way Scott Stephens works, and I intend to deliver." She flipped her hair over her shoulder with her hand. "With or without your help."

"Val, Camille's worked hard for the right deal. If you mess that up, it hurts J&S and the people who live around here. Doesn't any of that matter to you?"

She was quiet for a second and then shook her head. "Camille is too tight with the artists in Sweet Olive, and you know it. I'm looking out for J&S."

"And for yourself."

"Aren't you?"

He looked at the hunting scene hanging on the far wall, English hounds and fancy gentlemen on horseback. "I'm trying to do what's right."

"You're throwing away the state commission appointment." Her voice revealed her disgust. "You're more interested in keeping your daddy and Camille happy than your firm."

He narrowed his eyes. "I'm serving my clients."

She chuckled, not the light, tinkling laugh he usually associated with her, but a stiff sound. "Corporate firms want their partners to be loyal to them no matter how perky the opponent is."

"This isn't about Camille."

"Are you sure?"

He glanced at his watch. "Do you want to order?"

"I want you to tell me why you called this meeting." She waved her arm around the room. "You're obviously going for something quiet and private, with a hint of professional."

"I'm concerned about you."

"Oh?"

"You need to move on with your life." That seemed to be the theme of the day.

"So you can have a clear shot at Camille?"

"Quit obsessing on Camille," he snapped. "This is about you, Val. You're systematically destroying your life."

Her nose wrinkled. "My, my. Where'd that come from?"

"First there's Lawrence." Marsh plowed on. "You were engaged, and that means something. You treat him like dirt."

"We were kids. You've dated plenty of people." Her mouth twisted. "Although you've never gotten serious." She lowered her lashes. "I'm waiting for you."

"Quit fooling around, Valerie. We dated

and we had some fun. But we're not going to be a couple."

She pushed her chair back. "Is there anything else, or is this lecture over?"

"What do you know about the Sweet Olive leases?" His tone was abrupt.

Valerie smirked. "The artists aren't likely to sign anything. You're trying to get the well sites changed, you've convinced J&S to consider water from the Red River, and Camille is not going to win."

"Aren't you and Camille on the same team — that J&S team you keep talking about?"

"I'm dealing directly with Scott Stephens." She made a point of glancing at her diamond-encrusted watch.

"Val, do the right thing here — not only for J&S but for your life."

She unleashed one of her legendary smiles on him, her teeth sparkling. "We'll see," she said and glided out.

So much for lunch.

Truth was, Marsh did talk about his cases with one person.

His father.

While he didn't divulge legal secrets, he often sought his father's counsel.

A contractor by trade, Bud Cameron

wasn't very interested in business, and you couldn't pry a confidence out of him with a pair of pliers. But more important, he understood human nature in a way most of Marsh's colleagues did not.

He found his father in his shop, adjacent to his house in Sweet Olive.

Marsh's mother, who never missed an opportunity to criticize his father, liked to say that Bud wasn't happy unless he was playing with tools. She believed smart men "worked with their brains and not their hands" and thought her ex-husband had wasted his life.

She'd traded him in for a doctor, moving from the small old cottage to the gargantuan house near the Richmonds. With his law practice, Marsh moved regularly in the same circles as his mother and the eye doc. T. J., though, had chosen carpentry as his profession — a blow to his mother.

She was socially connected and went to all the *right* parties. But his father was actually the one plugged in deeply. Most days, he knew more about what was going on in Samford than the mayor.

"Don't usually see you this time of day on a Tuesday," his father said, as Marsh walked into the wood shop. The smell of sawdust and varnish tickled his nose as his father gave him an exuberant hug. "You knocking off early?"

Marsh stepped back and shook his head. "I needed a break."

His father's eyebrows rose. "You're just in time to help me with this board."

Marsh loosened his tie and moved into place. "You carving?"

"Carpentering. Got to make some money to pay for my carving habit."

"Gas lease money would help." Marsh moved carefully across the cluttered room with his end of the heavy board.

"Not going to happen." His father eased the wood onto a sawhorse as he spoke. "So if that's what brought you out here, you probably need to try someone else."

"I never expected you to lease your land." Marsh grinned, picking up a small saw with his grandfather's initials carved in the handle. "Just doesn't suit your personality."

Bud nodded at the tool. "You want to hire on with me and T. J.?"

"That's a tempting offer on a day like today. But I'm not very good with a hammer."

His father shook his head and went back to his work. "You're handier than you let on."

"Dad, do you trust Slattery?" he blurted out.

"Why would you come out here to ask a question like that?"

"Probably for the same reason you're not answering."

"Slattery's the smartest man in North Louisiana, and he looks out for Slattery."

Marsh lowered himself to his favorite spot, a beat-up wooden stool that had been in the shop as long as he could remember. The very act of sitting there, surrounded by the essence of his father, calmed his nerves.

Tools and gadgets filled a Peg-Board, and Marsh could identify most of them. The homemade toolbox, its handle worn smooth through years of use, had belonged to his grandfather.

Sawdust covered the plywood floor, and an unused push broom sat in the corner. The carving table was covered with an assortment of partially completed figures, including several dogs — his dad's favorite subject.

His father took a seat in a tattered platform rocker that had migrated from his house to the shop years ago. This afternoon the light from one of two big windows backlit the chair and his father, giving him the look of down-on-his-luck royalty.

Somewhere along the line, the chair had been reupholstered in gold-striped vinyl, and many of Marsh's favorite memories of his father were here — drinking coffee, whittling, reading his Bible early in the morning.

While many men clipped cell phones to their pockets, Bud Cameron always wore a tape measure. It was there today, on his father's old painter's pants, a reassurance.

Unhurried, his father would give him as long as he needed to say what he had on his mind. He and T. J. joked that Job could only wish for as much patience as Bud Cameron had.

"I need your advice," Marsh said finally.

"I didn't think you drove up here to borrow a hammer. What's going on?"

"Where do I start? Sweet Olive's contract, my law practice, Camille." He gave his father a sheepish smile. "Somehow this keeps coming back to Camille."

His father gave a brief nod. "I can see why. She's got spunk. Ginny wants us to find a way to keep her, and Lawrence has a crush on her."

"She and I are on opposite sides of a deal," Marsh continued hurriedly. "Or, we're supposed to be."

"She could turn out to be what Sweet

Olive needs — and you too." His father cocked his head.

Marsh picked up a small piece of wood and turned it over in his fingers. "I think Slattery's manipulating the Sweet Olive deal." He kept his face impassive.

"How might he do that?"

"He's bought land under a shadow company and is trying to keep the old Richmond leases active, even though some of those wells haven't produced in years."

His father waited.

"He stands to make a bundle if J&S drills in Sweet Olive, and there won't be wells anywhere near that expensive subdivision he's so proud of."

"Putting them in our backyards instead?" his father asked.

"Very likely."

"Don't worry." The rocker squeaked as his dad leaned forward. "Sweet Olive has lasted through tornadoes, hurricanes, floods, drought. The faithfulness of the artists won't be destroyed by a gas well or a sneaky land deal."

"I can tie Slattery up in legal knots over this — at least enough to get his attention."

"Then what's the problem?"

"I don't want Camille hurt in the process." He met his father's eyes, eerily similar to his own.

"Work with her on this. Trust her."

Marsh stood slowly, nodding. "You're wrong about one thing, Dad. Slattery's not the smartest man in North Louisiana."

He gave his father a tight hug and headed back to the office.

CHAPTER 35

Camille had trouble finding a parking place near the courthouse.

Several hand-lettered No Parking signs had been posted near driveways and someone had painted "Violators Will Be Towed" on a piece of plywood.

As she fed the meter, she reviewed the mental checklist of items she needed to research, hoping the office wouldn't be too crowded on a Friday.

Walking up a flight of steep marble steps outside the small but stately building, she turned and looked out on the street. If not for the dozens of new pickups and SUVs lined up in every available space, the town square would have looked like something from a hundred years ago.

The blue Louisiana flag flew with the United States flag from brass flagpoles. A monument to the Civil War dead stood guard at the base of the flags. Huge live oaks, the kind that suggested history and tradition, lined the street on the side of the courthouse.

Two men, dressed in khakis and polo shirts, wandered past. Camille's heart jumped into her throat when she saw that one was Jason Dinkins, who turned to speak as the other moved through a metal detector.

"Samford wasn't ready for the land rush." He pointed to the machine.

She nodded politely.

"They installed this thing a few months back when the crowds got so big." He took his change and keys out of his pocket and placed them in a small plastic bowl. "This used to be the quietest place in town, until word got out about the Sweet Olive shale."

"Has there been trouble?" she asked politely, watching her purse go through the scanner.

"Only an argument or two at the copy machine. The oil companies have pretty much worked out their differences. Staked their turf, that sort of thing."

"I see." She collected her things.

"Property records that way," the guard said, as though shooing her along. Jason fell in step beside her as she headed toward the hall to the clerk's office.

"I guess you must be about ready to head back to the big city," he said.

"We'll see."

"I don't see why anyone would want to live in Houston." Jason shook his head.

"Some people might say the same thing about Samford."

"I guess it all depends on where home is. Well, I look forward to working with you. No hard feelings, right?"

She narrowed her eyes as he sauntered off.

As she stepped inside the office, she was stopped by a crowd of people bottlenecked inside the door. A line wound around the edge of the room, and there was a number system, similar to one at the doughnut shop near her mother's house. Jason was chatting with an attractive woman in an official uniform on the other side of the room.

"It's been like this since the big shale discovery," a man in line in front of her said. "All that gas makes everyone a little crazy."

"Every clerk's office I've been in the past couple of years has been like this," Camille said.

"Everyone's searching for land to lease." He sized her up. "These lease hounds come in here, trying to steal business. Keep an eye over your shoulder."

"I'll be careful," she said, hiding her

amusement. She'd been in similar offices scores of times since college, when she'd researched the first records for Uncle Scott. She gazed around at the big logbooks in tall bins and glanced down at her white shirt. She'd be smudged and grimy by the time she finished this scavenger hunt.

Camille preferred the handwritten logs that showed property transfers through the years. They were like original paintings compared to laser-printer copies, full of nuances that digital records lacked. Her favorites were the hand-drawn surveys from decades before. Works of art with old-fashioned ink notations.

The Cypress Parish Clerk of Court's office, like many in the small towns where she had done deals, had signs pronouncing a host of rules, from how to request copies to the necessity to turn off cell phones.

This was a large room, filled with metal desks and lined with cubicles. Every computer was occupied, and every space covered with the massive books.

Verifying the last information on her index card of names would be the final step before the revised contracts, already drawn up, were put in the landowners' hands. If they wanted to sign, they would be handed their checks, also already printed.

If they didn't, she hoped their land would somehow, maybe through the grace of God, be protected.

She looked around the room. "Excuse me," she said to the man in front of her. "I'm supposed to meet Valerie Richmond here, but . . ." She gave a small laugh. "I didn't expect such a crowd."

"You're looking for Val?" Jason appeared from behind her. "I saw her in here yesterday but not today." The other man nodded, as though in agreement.

She debated whether to stay in line.

She had assigned Valerie to double-check descriptions and legal names for all Sweet Olive property. Based on J&S files, Val seemed to be proficient at legal legwork. Until now, when her findings lacked routine details.

After Janice Procell's comments at Ginny's house the other night, Camille wanted to see for herself — and had counted on Valerie to speed the process.

She checked her phone, her conversation with the man in line flashing in her mind. She scanned the office and found him, leaning against one of the bins.

"Pardon me," she said, and he looked up with a smile. "Did you say you saw Valerie Richmond here yesterday?"

He nodded, his expression puzzled.

"You're sure?"

"Yes, I'm sure." His voice was irritated. "It was my wife's birthday, and she sent her greetings." He stopped. "Is there a problem?"

Camille gave a quick shake of her head. "Sorry for troubling you," she said. "I guess Val and I got our wires crossed."

He turned pointedly back to the files, and she returned to the line. Valerie had told Camille she had spent yesterday working on an issue over in Ouachita Parish.

As the clerk finally called another person to the counter, Camille surreptitiously hit speed dial for Valerie. "Where are you?" Camille whispered.

"I'm not going to make it."

"What?" she said in a louder whisper.

"I had an e-mail from Mr. Stephens," Valerie said smugly, "asking for information on other Samford wells. Since we're about to lose our old leases on that land, he wants the information immediately."

Camille stepped out of line. The secretary gave her a small nod of approval. "Why would he assign that — especially when he said the Sweet Olive leases are the priority?"

"I handled some of these leases for my

father before I went to work for J&S. I guess Mr. Stephens knows I'm the best employee to handle them."

"Isn't that a conflict of interest?"

Valerie responded with a tinkle of laughter. "Apparently my father and J&S have cooked up a partnership." She paused. "I would have thought you would have been in the loop on that."

Camille rubbed her neck. "Is that why the records are so vague on these Sweet Olive plots? The surveys don't seem to match the land on the ground."

"Maybe you should ask your *Uncle Scott* about that. I have to run." She hung up before Camille could argue.

Three people had entered the clerk's office while Camille was on the phone, so she took yet another number and fell into place.

She heard the sound of the official seal as an employee stamped a piece of paper. The sound mirrored the anxious thumping of her heart.

By the time her number was called, she had imagined every possible scenario and waited anxiously while he pointed her to a gigantic record book. "You'll most likely find what you need there. If not, I'll pull another one for you."

Four other people were jammed into a

space about the size of her hotel bathroom, and each looked at her as suspiciously as she did them.

With the book spread open on one of the chest-high tables, Camille hunched over to cover the pages she was looking at and ran her finger through the columns. She didn't want anyone to see her checking the legal description of the Procell property. The last thing Ginny needed was another landman out there knocking on her door.

For almost an hour, Camille compared legal descriptions to surveys that went back to the turn of the century. Nothing matched Ginny's address.

Thirty minutes later, she found the deed and drew a deep breath, almost trembling with relief. An error with an earlier survey had been cleared up. Ginny's property was safe — but Camille couldn't follow the mineral rights.

A Sweet Olive survey showed another tract of land, a parcel that had not shown up in any of Camille's files.

Her eyes widened. She thought it was a vacant tract down the road from Evelyn's land, the perfect place to put a well. This could solidify the Sweet Olive deal — even give the artists some money — without tearing up the heart of the community.

She was about to make some unsuspecting landowner's day with a nice big offer.

Stepping out of the tiny room, she walked outside the courthouse and sank onto a marble bench, punching in Ginny's number. The phone rang several times, and Camille could picture it buzzing away, dogs barking and children painting.

"Come on, Ginny, pick up," she murmured.

"Sorry, Camille," Ginny finally said. "I have three new students today, and it's crazy around here. You're going to love their work."

"Ginny." She pitched her voice low, looking at people coming and going on the courthouse sidewalk. "I need to clarify a few details about your family property."

"Could we do this later? We've just started on the pottery project."

Camille jumped in the truck and raced to the Office of Conservation in Shreveport, thirty miles away.

Well files for the region were stored there, and she hoped she would find the answer she wanted. "Please, God," she pleaded, grinding the gears, "please."

She called Ginny again. "I know you're busy, but I need every record you've got."

Ginny gave a small laugh. "Could you and Marsh get together on this? I'm not the most organized person." She said something to one of the students and then spoke to Camille again. "Is there a problem?"

"I'm having trouble sorting out boundaries and the line of ownership." Camille's mouth got dry. "Let me do more digging."

"That's exactly what Marsh said." The state office building was an old-fashioned brick building, straight out of the 1960s. A polite guard searched her purse for the second time that day and directed her upstairs. The bland corridor made her feel as though she were walking into a trap.

The office itself was brighter, and Camille exhaled slowly, remembering.

An oscillating fan was perched on the window ledge, next to ivy in a pot. The green tile had been shined to a glow, but the office had a worn look. The room smelled like a mix of floor wax and old files, and its fluorescent lights flickered.

Very little had changed since she'd come here with her father, other than a new sign taped to the wall: "Please do not throw staples, etc., on the floor. Trash cans are available for your use. Thanks."

Rows of file cabinets filled the office, and she asked a clerk for guidance.

"You're a landman?" he asked. "Do you have any identification?"

Camille pulled the J&S office badge from her purse, and the man gave her grudging approval.

"You can pull the well files yourself. Put them in that box there when you're finished."

Digging through another file cabinet, Camille pulled out the files she needed — complicated records for each well in North Cypress Parish.

She opened them one by one and flipped through the pages. Each showed regular details, nothing out of the ordinary.

Until she got into the back of the third file.

She frowned and looked around the room, relieved that it was as empty as the clerk's office had been crowded.

She slipped pages out of the file and reread them as she walked to a copier that said, "Copies, 50 cents a page. Cash only."

Once finished with the transaction, she sat back down and put her head in her hands, leaning against a vintage library table.

"Are you praying or napping?"

Camille jumped and stuffed the pages back into the file. Snapping the folder shut, she straightened and chose another file.

Marsh stood so close he was touching her chair.

She shifted to block his view. *Does Marsh know?*

Half slumped against the table, Camille's eyes were wide, almost fearful, and her face was pale.

"Is your arm bothering you?" Marsh asked. "Maybe you should quit a little early today."

She sat up straight, focused on him. "What are you doing here?" she demanded, sounding almost . . . hurt.

"Let me think about that," he said, and then snapped his fingers. "Oh, that's right! I'm an attorney, and I come to this office several times a year."

She did not appear amused. "You happened to be here at the same time I am?"

"You think I'm following you?" he asked. "I thought we were working together on a final offer." He searched for a trace of the warm woman who was so thoroughly under his skin.

Camille shoved a file underneath another, and he pulled out the chair next to her. She flinched when he sat down and moved the stack of folders to her other side.

He kept his face impassive. "What wells

are you looking at?"

"As you're so fond of saying, I can't talk about my cases."

"Does the look on your face have to do with Sweet Olive?"

He could almost see emotions flit through her eyes. Confusion. Worry. And fear.

"Since I'm in the area, I'm auditing J&S wells in North Louisiana."

"If you were on the witness stand right now, I'd accuse you of perjury."

Her eyes narrowed. "Are you hiding something about the ownership of mineral rights up near Sweet Olive?"

Marsh put his finger to his mouth. "Could you lower your voice?"

"Don't shush me," she said, but her voice was quieter. "Someone's trying to cheat Ginny, among others."

Camille put a hand on his arm and shepherded him behind a row of file cabinets. "The records for Sweet Olive are mixed up. Did you know that Slattery Richmond owns a big tract of land adjacent to Sweet Olive?"

"His subdivision?"

"No, another tract . . . a key piece of property in Sweet Olive, filed through a company called Cotton Grove."

Camille drummed her fingers nervously on one of the olive-drab file cabinets. "I've got to go," she added abruptly. "I'll call you as soon as I know something."

"Let's figure this out together."

She gave him a sad smile. "This one I've got to handle on my own." With that, she dashed down the hallway.

"Camille!" he called out, but she did not look back.

Marsh slapped his hand against the file cabinet and walked directly to the records to be refiled. The clerk, frowning, stood next to the basket, his hands full.

"Wait," Marsh said.

The man, who had worked in the office since Marsh was in law school, scowled. "I beg your pardon?"

"Miss Gardner and I are working on a well together. No need for you to file the same files twice."

The clerk handed the stack to Marsh, his expression dubious.

Sitting at the table, Marsh began to flip through the files. He didn't know what he was looking for, but Camille's behavior confirmed the hunch that had led him here in the first place.

The first few files revealed nothing, and, frustrated, he dove into the last one, records for well number 291928. The well had not produced in years and had been plugged and abandoned, routine in this region.

But as he flipped the file shut, Slattery's name caught his eye, and he opened the folder once more and skimmed each page.

Slattery had been involved in the drilling of the well nearly sixteen years ago. But it must have been his partner's signature that had caused Camille to leave in such a hurry. *Johnny Gardner.*

CHAPTER 36

Walking quickly down a pretty boulevard, impatient to be back in running form, Camille twisted and turned, as if by retracing her steps in Samford, she could somehow make sense out of all of this.

Her shoulder and her head ached.

She had left the conservation office intending to face Ginny with the news that she didn't own the mineral rights to her land. But she knew she was headed to Marsh's house.

He had to be told that Slattery was undercutting his clients in Sweet Olive.

And that her father had been there when it had all started.

As she approached Marsh's neighborhood, she drew back at the scene at the Richmond house. Outdoor floodlights illuminated trees, and the chandelier in the foyer glowed through the transom. Cars lined the circular drive and —

She halted.

People were playing croquet on the lawn. *Croquet?*

Uncle Scott would have found this hilarious. She wished he would return her phone calls so she could talk about it, about the whole mess.

With people on the lawn, she thought perhaps she should turn around and hope no one noticed. Cemented to the spot, she heard the jingle of a dog's collar.

"Lovely home, isn't it?" a white-haired woman said, the dog sniffing at Camille's shoes. "Valerie borrowed my housekeeper for the evening. They're hosting some big oil guy tonight."

Camille gulped for air.

"Are you hurt?" the woman asked, studying her more closely.

Camille shook her head. "Catching my breath."

The woman threw her a suspicious look and tugged on her dog's leash.

Pretending to head the other way, Camille watched over her shoulder. The woman strolled up the walkway of a house across from the Richmond place. The dog sniffed at every inch of ground and the woman talked to him while he peed.

Camille took a quick inventory of the

handful of cars lined up on the driveway, recognizing only Valerie's. Her gaze moved on along the drive, and her heart plummeted. The little green MGB convertible was at the front of the line.

She heard the clack of a mallet when Valerie, with a sweater draped around her shoulders like it was February, hit a wooden ball. The shot must have been good because she threw up her hands in a touchdown sign.

Slattery sat in a brightly colored Adirondack chair, holding a drink. A waiter, wearing all white, was stationed at a portable bar.

Camille continued to scan the lawn, recognizing a couple of businesspeople. As casually as she could, she positioned herself to see better.

She'd almost given up when the door of the house opened, and Marsh's tall body stepped under the porch light. She couldn't read his expression but he turned to shake someone's hand. The door swung open farther and a slightly stooped man stepped out, vigorously returning the handshake.

Camille stepped into the street to get a better look, certain she couldn't be right.

Then she sank onto the curb, thankful for the cover of the shrubbery.

She'd never forgive Uncle Scott — or

Marsh — for this.

Camille marched into the office tower a few hours later, liking the way her cowboy boots clicked on the tile entrance.

"Must be something important going on," the weekend guard said. "It's been like a parade through here. Unusual, especially for a Friday night." He lowered his voice. "Even saw the big boss."

Stepping onto the elevator, she looked down at the jeans she had changed into. Only six weeks had passed since she'd stood here in a smudged skirt and uncomfortable pumps, but she felt like a different person.

As the door glided open, she stepped off, bumping into Slattery Richmond. He reared back. "Camille . . . What are you doing here?"

"This is my office. And you?"

He gave a nervous chuckle, shuffling a brown accordion file under his arm. "Got off on the wrong floor. Must be getting old." He punched the button three times and lunged into the elevator when the doors opened.

But Camille stuck her boot in, jamming the door open.

Slattery looked startled and moved to the rear.

"Did you used to work for J&S?" Camille asked, her voice cold.

He leaned forward and punched the button, but she didn't budge.

"Do I need to call security?" he asked.

She shrugged with her good shoulder. "Your choice."

His look shifted, almost admiring. "Scott knew what he was doing when he sent you here. Would you ever consider coming to work for me?"

"Not if I were stranded on a street corner with nowhere else to go. Maybe I should rephrase my question. *When* did you work for J&S?"

Slattery smirked. "It's old news that I worked as a roughneck with your uncle and your daddy in college. My father thought that job would encourage less drinking and more studying."

"That would have been in the early days of J&S," Camille said, this time her voice less certain.

"Very early. Those guys weren't much older than me." He grinned, showing a hint of the younger man he had been. "I lost more money playing cards than I made on the job."

"So you knew J&S from the beginning."

"Johnny and Scott," he said with a nod.

"But I moved on to the law business after that. Thanks to Louisiana's screwed-up mineral laws, I make a living without working in hundred-degree weather."

"Does Scott know you were running side deals with my father?"

Slattery calmly punched the button again. "Thanks to your friend Marsh Cameron, he does now."

She stepped back and watched the doors glide shut.

Walking to the J&S office, she tugged on the glass office door. She half expected it to be unlocked, but it held firm.

Sliding her badge, she opened it and the smell of Slattery's cologne hit her nostrils. "Hello? Valerie?"

She headed into the hall, but the offices were dark, other than the glow of computers. Flipping on the light, she half turned to push the door shut.

"Working late?" Scott's voice said from over near the conference table.

Camille shrieked, her legs almost giving way. She steadied herself, trying not to give her uncle the satisfaction of seeing how unnerved she was.

"Surprised to see me?" he asked.

"No," she said, her voice higher pitched

than normal. "Although it would have been nice of you to turn the lights on."

"We were in a bit of a rush. Thanks to you, Slattery and I had business to take care of."

"After your garden party?"

"Word travels fast."

"Not fast enough," Camille said. "Why didn't you let me know you were here?"

He sat in the chair where Marsh had sat during that first Monday morning meeting. "I heard you were getting a little too chummy with that clan of artists."

From across the room, she scanned the maps and other files she'd left out as she spoke. "They're good people."

He rolled his eyes and then gestured at the table. "Despite your soft heart, you're an ace. By letting that lawyer in on Slattery's shadow ownership, I struck a much better deal with Slattery. Needless to say, he doesn't want his legislative buddies — or the IRS — to know what he's up to." Scott grinned. "Although it would have been interesting to put a well right in the middle of his fancy golf course."

Pulling out one of the heavy chairs, Camille sat, her legs shaky.

Scott, chewing on a toothpick, walked over to the window and looked out at the skyline. "What a miserable town. I don't know what your father saw in it."

"My father?"

Scott turned and gave a hollow laugh. "He planned to settle here, but that fire got him." For a moment, she thought she saw regret on his face.

"If he'd have stayed with us, he wouldn't have been killed." Camille said the words she'd told herself so many times through the years.

"He didn't want to leave you, but I didn't have anyone else to send." Scott's words sounded defensive.

"Daddy always wanted to go. Wherever there was an oil well, wherever he could find a six-pack."

"He hated the travel." Scott strolled to the table and pulled out the chair at the other end. "The booze — and his love for a good poker game — made him easier to manipulate."

"Booze didn't get him burned to death."

Scott looked away.

"He was drinking, and you sent him anyway."

"I was needed elsewhere," he said. "I swore he could stay put if he'd just handle that one last crisis for me."

Camille ran her fingers through her hair, not surprised that they were trembling. "All these years you were my hero," she said. "You made me believe my father was the bad guy."

"You take after him. He was a dreamer like you, and he had the best instincts of any oilman I ever knew." Scott's voice was nostalgic. "We were a heckuva team."

"You sent him to his death," she said, her voice cold. "What kind of team is that? And then you used me just like you used him."

"Don't get dramatic on me. I've helped you out plenty through the years, just like I helped Johnny."

Scott pulled one of the survey maps to him. "I knew sending you here was a risk."

"Then why did you do it?"

"When I heard there was a group of people who were willing to walk away from oil money, I knew there was only one person who could make them change their minds."

"But I didn't."

"Thankfully I had Valerie to help. She was able to work with Drew Cross and one or two others. It's a start."

"Valerie is the kind of person you want working at J&S?"

Scott chuckled. "Ironic, isn't it? Slattery's and Johnny's daughters squaring off in the same deal. She's the kind of clever person we need on our team."

Camille choked. "Someone you can't trust?"

"*I* trust her. You have to learn how to work with people like Val. They're invaluable."

"Like my father learned to work with Slattery?"

Scott scowled. "That was a brief misunderstanding — and a poker game that got out of hand. Slattery could tie Johnny up in knots."

"Imagine my surprise to see the Gardner name on that lease," Camille said. "I wonder what happened to the money those wells paid after Daddy died. Did you pocket the royalties before that well quit producing?"

Scott shook his head. "Slattery got all of that," he said. "Your dad was a front for him."

"You two are despicable."

"I tried to teach you to look beneath the surface."

"My part in this stops tonight. Now." She pushed the heavy chair back. "That first interview I did was just the beginning. I'm calling every reporter I can find to let people know what you and Slattery did."

"I look forward to watching them," he said calmly. "You should have a good time telling how your father illegally fronted for those leases, that your family business is neck deep in all of this, that you've traveled around for years and talked people out of their mineral rights."

He stopped, and the silence thickened.

"Yep," he said, popping his knuckles. "You'll look every bit as bad as me and Slattery."

"I very well may, but I'll take my punishment — unlike you and that coward Slattery Richmond. I did nothing illegal."

"You try to make things black and white." He leaned over the table. "I am, however, willing to make a deal if you'll help me out."

"Why would I possibly help you?"

"For those goofy artists, of course."

She jumped to her feet, her boot toe catching on the carpet as she headed for the door.

"Camy, slow down and think."

Had he deliberately chosen the same words he'd used when she ran to his car all those years ago at Trumpet and Vine?

"You can make this right with everyone," he continued. She did not miss the satisfied look that moved across his face. "I'll honor your wishes for Sweet Olive."

"You don't know the meaning of honor," Camille said.

"Easy now. I'll only put up with so much."

She wavered. "What about the location of

the wells?"

He narrowed his eyes. "Where do you recommend?"

She moved toward the table, her mouth set. "Away from the row of artists' homes, Ginny Guidry's included." Leaning over, she pointed to a map on the table. "Put them here, or I'll see that every deal gets killed."

"If you kill the deals, your precious landowners won't get their money."

"Do you think J&S is the only company interested in Sweet Olive land? If it weren't for me, they'd have gone with Bienville long before."

"You sound like their attorney." Scott arched his brow. "You probably know he crashed our gathering this evening."

Camille's legs felt weak and her wrist ached.

"Marshall Cameron was mad as all get-out when he found out what was going on," Scott said, his mouth twisted, whether in anger or respect she couldn't tell. "He demanded a community grant for some art center — something you had suggested."

"Did you agree?"

"I told him you'd take care of it. Wrap this up, and do whatever you want." He swatted his hand at her, his gold-and-onyx ring shimmering. "I suspect Johnny would say you're doing the right thing."

Before Camille could reply, Valerie strolled into the office. In tight corduroy jeans and a knit top, she held a leather computer case. "I'm sorry it took me so long, Mr. Stephens."

"Perfect timing, Val," Scott said. "I was about to tell Camy that you've been promoted."

Camille studied the two, impassive.

"Valerie has agreed to head up a new community division in Houston."

"But . . ." Camille stopped.

"Val has a range of experience that will come in quite handy," he said.

"Thank you, sir," Valerie said and gave a mock curtsy.

"And she's convinced Jason Dinkins to move over to our side. He'll run this office, where we'll be able to keep a close eye on him."

"Are you firing me?" Camille asked.

"I'll let you finish off the Sweet Olive deal," he said, "but we both know it's time you moved on to something else." He paused.

"I get my bonus," she said. "And I keep the pickup."

CHAPTER 37

Marsh had his laptop on the dining table when the blue-and-white pickup pulled into his driveway.

The vehicle had barely stopped when Camille leaped from it, charging up to his house. He stepped away from the window and waited for the ding of his old-fashioned doorbell — but loud pounding on the door sounded instead.

"Marsh, it's me." Camille's voice was urgent. She kicked at the door as he opened it, catching his shin with her boot.

"Thanks," he said, resisting the urge to rub the spot.

She glanced at his leg, and then up at him. "I didn't know — about my father's involvement in Sweet Olive and all the deals Scott was working."

"I wish you would have confided in me that your father was the *J* in J&S."

"I was wrong not to."

Camille stood there, her sling and cast making her look like an upset angel with a lopsided wing.

Marsh opened the door wider. "Come on in."

Camille's emotions threatened to spill over the moment Marsh opened the door.

There had been nothing to be gained by keeping the secret — and much to be lost.

The hallway behind Marsh was warm and inviting, a Persian rug covering hardwood floors. Beyond that, the dining table was scattered with papers and law books. The living room was the way she thought a home should look — with its overstuffed sofa and pine coffee table and original paintings. A messy stack of books and magazines perched on an end table, and lamplight illuminated the entire space.

Marsh propped against the doorframe, and she couldn't believe she had ever thought he looked stuffy. His dark brown hair was messy, and he had a five o'clock shadow. He wore tight jeans and a red T-shirt advertising a "Skeeter Run" to eliminate malaria. He glanced down at his bare feet as her eyes lit on them.

"Another exciting Friday night," he said. "I wasn't expecting company."

"I would have called, but I wasn't sure you'd let me in."

He tilted his head. "You're a hard person to keep out."

Steering her to the cozy room, he pointed to the sofa, but Camille walked to the mantel. Looking to him for a nod of permission, she picked up a dog carving, stroking the smooth wood. A giddy feeling washed over her, but she wasn't sure if it was because of Marsh's art — or because of the way he made her heart pound.

"My father carved that for me right after my dog died."

"Oh," she said quietly. "What was his name?"

"Boudreaux. He was a good dog." His voice softened. "Why did you come here?"

"You talked Scott into giving up a big arts grant. Your work will change Sweet Olive forever."

He gave his head a quick shake. "I'd like to take credit, but Stephens agreed to that grant because of you."

"I don't believe that."

"You're not the most trusting person, are you?"

She looked him up and down. "I'm trying. This has been the most confusing experience of my life — and my life has included some doozies." She paused. "But it also has helped me see my entire life more clearly."

He gestured to the couch, putting a small cushion under her cast as she sat.

Her smile broke out. "I want to hear about the look on Uncle Scott's face when you busted into that meeting tonight. And then I'll tell you how I negotiated to keep the old pickup."

"I thought you hated that thing."

"It was my father's. I thought I'd better hang on to it."

CHAPTER 38

The paint-by-number of the juggling clown had been the work of Camille's father when he broke his leg on the neighbor's roof as a boy. It was the first piece of art Camille remembered, hanging in the ratty travel trailer that went from oil rig to oil rig.

Camille had tried to sell it in a garage sale after her father died, an unwanted symbol of his life. Her mother had snatched it out of the box and fussed at her.

The confrontation with Scott had inexplicably brought it to mind.

"Whatever happened to that clown picture Daddy painted?" she asked her mother on their early call Saturday. She tried for an indifferent note.

"That thing's up in the attic somewhere," her mother said with the soft little laugh Camille loved. "I haven't thought of it in years."

"See," Camille said. "We could have

tossed it after all . . ."

"I hoped you would want it one day. We don't have all that much of your father's."

Camille made a dismissive sound. "What an inheritance, right? That pickup and picture sort of say it all."

"Don't be disrespectful," her mother said, in a rare scolding tone. "Your father left far more than that picture — and that old pickup you talked Scott out of." Her mother's voice had a disappointed ring. "You're the fine young woman you are because of him."

"You raised me."

Her mother made a clucking noise. "Where do you think you got your adventurous spirit? Your brains? Your sense of humor?" She stopped for a moment. "I'm the dull, responsible one in the family. You are your father made over."

"That's not true. I'm . . . I work hard . . . I pay my bills — and I — I don't even drink." She sounded like she was a teenager again, arguing with her parent.

"Oh, Camille." The words were delivered with a heavy sigh. "Your daddy made a lot of mistakes — and he was taken from us before he could correct them. But he had so much life in him. He saw the best in people — even in that brother of mine."

"That's what I mean. Uncle Scott cheated Daddy, and he let him get away with it. And he's getting away again."

"Scott has to live with that," her mother said. "Your father forgave him. Johnny just didn't grow up as fast as you did. But he was a good man." She sniffed. "I'm the weak one. After he died, you had to take care of me."

"Don't be ridiculous," Camille said. "You've always been there for me."

"I made you turn to Scott for help. I let you down."

"Quit saying things like that. You're a wonderful mother."

"Be thankful, Camille, for who you are — for your father's influence. Put the past away, and move into your future."

Tears choked Camille's throat. "I'm trying."

"I love you. You're my one best girl."

"I love you too."

The line was silent for a moment. "Shall I pull that clown picture out?"

"That would be great," Camille said.

Ginny rounded her house, wearing overalls and a long-sleeved shirt. She held a large piece of metal and a can of spray paint. Her hair was smashed on top of her head, like someone had sat on a ball of yarn.

"I figured I'd see you bright and early," she said, "but I'll tell you right now, I can't take any more sympathy about my mineral rights."

She gestured to a table on the porch. A hand-turned wooden bowl sat next to a woven white-oak basket and a large ruby-colored vase filled with daisies. A piece of knitting stuck out of a gift bag, and a pastel painting of the nearby church was propped against the wall.

"I've had visits from nearly every person in Sweet Olive and more hugs than I can take. The kitchen looks like somebody died."

"Ginny, I'm —"

"You don't have to console me." She held up the piece of metal almost like a shield. "I'm disappointed, but I've lived through worse." Ginny stared from beneath the big glasses, her gaze matter-of-fact.

"You can take legal action. Marsh can file suit. Landowners do it all the time."

"No lawsuits, no legal action," Ginny said. "I've seen the records with my own eyes."

"Ginny, there's —"

"Let's talk about the real news around town. You're Scott Stephens's niece? Your dad owned an oil company?" She wiggled her thick eyebrows, her long earrings shaking back and forth. "Are you secretly rich?"

"Hardly. My father sold his J&S share to my uncle. He wasn't cut out for management."

"What was he cut out for?" Ginny asked curiously.

"I'm still figuring that out." Camille shrugged. "He seemed to wind up in the wrong place at the wrong time."

"He wound up in Sweet Olive," Ginny said.

"And look at what came out of that. You got hurt."

Ginny had a considering look on her face. "His time here set a lot of things in motion."

A cool breeze lifted Camille's hair and moved the whirligigs. She caught the fresh scent of sweet olive, heavier today. She smiled at Ginny's haphazard display of art gifts as they headed toward the porch swing.

"I know you don't want any more gifts, but you earned this one." Camille fished in the back pocket of her jeans with her good arm and handed a J&S envelope to Ginny.

"The art center grant?"

"I hope you're ready for another project."

"It was nice of Mr. Stephens to do that," she said. "Marsh said your uncle's not that crazy about your 'pigheaded' love of art."

Camille patted Ginny's leg. "Only you would say something nice about Uncle Scott after what he and my father did."

"I heard he's promoting Valerie. I hope she moves to Timbuktu and never shows her face around here again." Ginny rearranged her bun, tightening the clip. "So the community meeting will be next?"

"A week from Monday. Since most of the landowners declined to sign, a few things had to be redone."

"Will you be leaving then?" Ginny's voice held a note of disappointment.

"After I work out a few more legal matters. For the first time in my life, I'm not in a rush to leave."

"Since you have time on your hands — I mean hand." Ginny guffawed at her own joke. "I have an idea, and it doesn't involve gas leases."

"I'm in," Camille said with a smile.

"You've felt so bad about the art festival that I thought we might organize another art show, a quick one, just for fun."

The wind picked up before Camille answered, and Ginny's creations began to whir louder. "Ahh." Ginny twisted her head toward the sound. "God's at work even when we don't see Him."

CHAPTER 39

The purple-and-gold golf cart chugged across Ginny's yard a week later, balloons added to its decor. "What do you think?" Ginny asked. "Are you ready for our first annual Art with Heart?"

"Annual? Let's see how our impromptu show goes before you plan a yearly one." Looking around, Camille drank in the colors of Ginny's whirligigs against the blue October sky, the not-quite-red berries on a pyracantha bush at the edge of the house, and the fragrance of the sweet olive bush. "It's so pretty it makes my heart hurt."

Ginny gave a little laugh, not like her usual bold ones. "It's supposed to make you happy, not sad."

"It's a good kind of sad," Camille said as they puttered out on the road.

Ginny released a deep sigh, glancing in the rearview mirror and back at the house.

"You're looking for Kylie and Randy,

aren't you?" Camille asked softly.

"Their mother's bringing them, but . . ."

"You're doing the right thing," Camille said. "Janice will have them there in a few minutes."

"She's trying to do right, and it makes them happy to have her living back home again. I'm being selfish."

"You couldn't be selfish if you tried. How are you adjusting?"

"It's not as bad as I expected. She and I haven't always seen eye to eye, but my brother was important to both of us. That's a good enough reason — along with the kids — to make it work."

"She was upset about the mineral rights." Camille shook her head. "I wish that had turned out differently for all of you."

"There's a little good news from that," Ginny said. "Marsh thinks J&S's insurance company will pay the expenses we incurred when Todd was killed. That'll be a big help."

"You always see the good."

"Not really." Ginny scrunched up her face. "I can't see any good, for example, in you leaving us."

"It's hard," Camille said. They bumped along in silence for a moment. "But I'll have the pleasure of introducing your work to the world. Allison calmed down enough after all my delays to agree to take a few pieces."

"I don't want you to go," Ginny said.

"Those whirligigs are going to be a big hit in Houston, and then we'll have to talk all the time. You're going to be so busy filling orders that you won't have time for me anyway."

Ginny made a dismissive snort. "I'm having second — or third — thoughts about that. Who's going to want one of those? They're so primitive . . . not polished in the least."

"The world's full of polished," Camille said. "That's what makes yours special. Ginny, you have an eye for life. No one in the whole world sees things just as you do. That's true art."

"You're the first person who ever got excited about those things."

Camille held her arm out, narrowly avoiding Ginny's face. "I can see them in yards, parks, museums. You wait and see. Smithsonian, here you come."

"Not at those outrageous prices you want me to charge," Ginny muttered.

"You have a lot of time in each of them. You can't give them away. Trust me on this."

"So is Queen Allison going to give you any paying work since you'll soon be unemployed?" Ginny asked.

Camille groaned. "Not much, but I'm holding the Artists' Guild over her head. She's afraid if she ticks me off, she won't get your work."

They bumped ahead, past the small strip of fields to where the colorful houses dotted the road. "Oh, wow," Camille said. Lawn chairs and folding tables were spread throughout yards. Homemade signs lined driveways. "Art with ♡," one said. "Pray. Create. Celebrate," said another.

Familiar faces smiled as artists along the way greeted them. Lillie Lavender was setting up a table of free crocheted bookmarks, while Lawrence was changing out the bottles on one of his trees to reflect the oranges, yellow, and reds of Louisiana autumn.

"Fantastic idea, Camille," he said, strolling out to the cart. "I haven't seen everyone this upbeat in a long time." He reached his arms out toward her, his muscle rippling in the black T-shirt. "We needed you to get us out of our rut."

He looked at Ginny. "I have to tell you again how much I regret . . . I feel bad that you did all that work for nothing."

She held up her hand, her fingernails painted neon yellow. "I choose not to see it like that. I was called to do this work, to help you and your mother and Lillie and Bud get their fair share." She smiled. "A big, fancy gallery is going to show off my whirligigs. Janice has come to her senses. I'm thankful."

Before she could continue, Ginny's phone buzzed with a text. "Now here's important business." She gave her big laugh. "The Hot Dog King is looking for us."

"We'll see you at the church, Lawrence," Camille said, waving as they pulled off. She couldn't help wondering how Valerie had ever captured the heart of such a fine man.

The main gathering area had been set up on the front lawn of the quaint little white church, its steeple reaching to the autumn sky. Its old windows were a patchwork of opaque glass, recently repaired by Lawrence as a gift to the church.

The people who milled around, setting things up, were familiar to Camille now, and she smiled as she climbed off the golf cart to where the hot dog vendor was setting up, with his red-and-white striped apron and big red chef's hat.

Evelyn peered into the containers on the stainless-steel cart, and Bud, also wearing a striped apron, was telling a story.

Ginny's gaze followed hers, and she

smiled. "Bud thought it was a waste of good money to hire someone to cook. He insisted on helping the guy you brought in."

Camille gave a small laugh. "This is a special occasion. Wait till you taste one of the Cajun dogs he sells by the courthouse. That's what convinced me to hire him."

Another table nearby held a variety of birdhouses and other items made from gourds.

Evelyn was smiling as she walked over to the table. "Look, thingamajigs out of gourds!"

Camille's brow furrowed, and Ginny gave her big laugh. "Snowmen, Santa Clauses, all sorts of little guys. Bud grew those gourds in his garden and talked T. J. into helping him make a few things."

Behind the stand sat a table with free carved key chains and small pocket crosses. Bud smiled when he noticed Camille and Ginny and brought them each a small carved fish on a silver ring.

"A little reminder," he said with a big smile. His blue eyes, so like Marsh's, twinkled in the morning sunlight.

As Camille reached for the fish, she drew in a deep breath. The big sweet olive bushes on each side of the church door were in bloom, and their smell sneaked in underneath that of the hot dog vendor. She gripped the fish.

"Is Marsh going to make it?" Ginny asked, looking around.

"He plans to be here, but he's tied up on that . . ." Bud stopped and looked from Ginny to Camille and back to Ginny. "He has paperwork to wrap up on all the well business."

Ginny nodded, biting her lip. "Is he going to be able to get it done?"

"Sure hope so."

"Don't worry," Camille said. "We're all set to give you the grant money next week." She had to work hard not to say more.

"I'm not worried," Ginny said. "Things are working out better than I could have hoped."

After parking the cart on the gravel of the church's parking lot, Ginny and Camille climbed out and wandered over to the area where each artist had displayed a favorite piece of work. Lawrence had even helped Ginny mount one of her whirligigs on a pole to the edge of the church — Moses parting the Red Sea, people following with each puff of wind.

"Is this what you had in mind?" Marsh's deep voice said from behind Camille.

Turning slowly, she smiled. "It's better

439

than I imagined."

"Is everything set, Marsh?" Ginny asked.

He shook his head but turned to Camille. "Complications. We can discuss them later."

She dug her boot heel into the dirt. "I'm not going to put up with more of Scott and Slattery's meanness."

Marsh put his hand on her shoulder. "They'll get theirs one of these days."

"Aunt Ginny, look!" Randy ran from around the side of the church before Ginny could respond to Marsh. Holding a kite made from a paper plate and streamers above his head, he giggled. "See what Mama helped me make?"

Janice and Kylie followed more slowly, each also carrying a kite and each wearing a smile.

As Ginny moved toward the trio, Marsh put his hand on Camille's shoulder. "Have you done the Art Crawl?"

"Not really," she said, suddenly feeling a wave of melancholy sweep over her. "But I probably need to help with lunch."

"You sound like my father."

She laughed. "That's about the third time you've told me that since I arrived in Louisiana."

"It's a high compliment," he said. "Although you're a lot better looking than he is." Grinning, he nodded at her. "Did Ginny help you with that outfit?"

Camille looked down at the flowing, gauzy skirt, just touching her boot tops. Her lace top had a scoop neck. Her only jewelry was a pair of sea glass earrings that Lawrence had made for her as a thank-you.

"I got this at a thrift shop in Samford." She twirled around. "I thought I'd venture outside my comfort zone."

"You should do that more often." He reached up to touch her hair. "You look great."

"Maybe we should take a look at the art," she said, feeling shy at the intensity in his eyes.

"Lead on," he said but his gaze lingered.

She took a step forward and tried to memorize each sight — artists in their yards, demonstrating how they created their unusual work, Kylie and Randy squealing as they tried to get their kites in the air.

Her father's image came into her mind, driving down a dusty road, truck windows open, the wind blowing their hair. She had forgotten until now how he loved to laugh.

Her mother said he had brought them with him to Louisiana because he thought the people were the nicest he'd ever met.

He'd been right. When Camille left this time, it would be with a sense of deep regret.

CHAPTER 40

The For Sale sign on the house at Trumpet and Vine had been pulled up and was propped against the front of the house. The yard had been raked, and someone had hung a fall wreath on the door.

As Camille drove by, she gunned the truck, headed for Ginny's house before the final community meeting. The thought of the evening ahead felt like pulling a Band-Aid off too slowly, but she was excited about the announcements to come.

She slammed the heavy truck door and stood looking at Ginny's magnificent scenes, stirring in the evening air.

They would have sold well in the Houston gallery, but Ginny had been adamant when she'd called. She had decided against "shipping these things halfway across the country." Allison had been mad but insisted the work "didn't suit the gallery's brand" anyway.

Stepping onto the porch, Camille drew in a breath, the scent of sweet olive already fainter than it had been a few days ago. She inhaled, wanting to hold on to the fragrance as long as she could.

Children, at their regular Monday art lesson, were drawing at the art table, as they had been that first afternoon. Kylie and Randy's mother sat nearby, working with a lump of clay spread out on newspaper. When Camille tapped on the door, the children squealed, and Ginny hollered a boisterous, "Come in."

Janice met Camille's gaze and then looked down at the figure she was sculpting. She had started coming by after school once a week and staying to have supper with Kylie and Randy, part of the arrangement she and Ginny had worked out.

Ginny flitted around the room, her movements unusually jerky. She wore a pair of wide, blowing pants and a top that ballooned as she picked up keys, glasses, and phone.

"Are you ready?" Camille asked. "We have a lot to wrap up, and I hope it'll work out."

Ginny threw her an exasperated look and turned to Kylie. "Show Miss Camille your picture, Kylie."

The girl held up a drawing of a tall tree-like image with flames bursting out from it. Underneath there were two small figures holding hands and running. One wore a halo.

"Oh," Camille said, "the well fire." She hated thinking how the children had been affected by the explosion and evacuation.

"That's you, Miss Camille," the girl said. "Aunt Ginny says you're an angel."

Camille stared at the drawing.

"You saved Miss Evelyn."

Ginny shook her head when Camille opened her mouth to respond. "Listen to the children, Camille. Look what you've done for our community."

"I haven't done anything."

"Yes you have," Kylie said solemnly, going back to her seat.

Ginny bestowed one of her wide, generous smiles on Camille. "Want to help me get the snacks?"

In the familiar kitchen, the table was clear, except for salt and pepper shakers. The missing stack of papers caused a pain in Camille's heart.

"It wasn't meant to be," Ginny said, following her gaze.

"But you were cheated," Camille said.

"No," Ginny said, in much the same tone Camille had used earlier. "We didn't get the gas money, but we got Todd's settlement."

Camille pulled the snack tray out from a cabinet near the oven, something she'd seen Ginny use many times.

"You deserve more." Camille walked toward the children. "Life's expensive."

"God always provides," Ginny said. "Always."

Marsh helped his father arrange chairs in the small library meeting room, while Ginny, unusually quiet, made an urn of coffee.

"You're sure you want to stay for the check presentations, Ginny?" Bud asked. "We can do this without you."

"Of course she needs to stay," Marsh said, "for the grant."

"I've stuck with it this far," Ginny said. "I'll see it to the end."

Marshall's father gave a shake of his head. "I've always admired the way you conduct your business, Ginny. Take the high road. Slattery will get his just reward in the end."

"Marsh's right." She looked at Bud. "I want to get the grant check tonight and let us all move on. We've got big things ahead with our art. I refuse to mourn the lease money."

"Are things moving ahead with the gal-

sh asked.

much, wouldn't you say, Bud?"

looked from his father to Ginny.

er nodded. "I hope Camille's right have a shot at selling our work."

certainly believes in you," Marsh "Any luck buying the property?"

ot quite yet. Ross is working on it."

ny smiled. "I can't believe that it took many years for us to do this."

"We never had the gumption until Camille ame along," his father said. "Where is she, by the way?"

"I left her at the house with the children for a while. I told her they needed her, and we'd get a late start."

"Smart." Bud patted her knee. His father patting Ginny's knee?

"Is the art foundation paperwork all set, Marsh?" Ginny interrupted his thought and gave her booming laugh. "Listen to us, talking like we've got good sense. But if we want gallery space and room for classes and meetings, we need the foundation."

"Are you sure we shouldn't mention this to Camille?" Marsh asked.

"Don't frown, son. We wanted you to get the legal part done first."

"It's risky, bypassing her," Marsh said.

"You do your part," Ginny said, "and we'll

do ours."

"And we'll trust the good Lord to do H[
His father winked at Ginny.

As his father spoke, Camille stepped in
the doorway, a big smile on her face, an
they all turned guiltily toward her. "W
didn't hear you," Ginny said.

"We were discussing how the art grant wil[
work," Marsh mumbled, feeling heat creep
up his face. "And we hope you'll agree to
be on the Cypress shale field oversight com-
mittee — it will meet occasionally for
citizens to voice their concerns."

Camille looked troubled. "I'm not going
to be here for meetings."

Ginny shushed her with a wave of her
hand. "You can do most of it by phone and
e-mail."

Camille's emotions were more jumbled than
Ginny's art supply area as the room filled
with familiar faces.

She wiped her eyes behind her glasses —
she'd given up her contacts altogether since
coming to Louisiana — and tried to com-
pose herself.

"Ready to go?" Marsh slipped into the
metal chair next to her.

"I think so. I hope we're doing the right
thing by springing this surprise on Ginny."

He draped his arm around the back of her chair. "This bunch seems to like a surprise more than most," he said, trying to keep worry out of his voice.

Tonight he wore a light blue oxford-cloth shirt, making his eyes more startling than usual. Instead of his starched khakis, he wore a pair of jeans.

Camille could not resist reaching up and touching his hair, which had grown long enough to brush against the collar. "You look nice," she whispered.

"So do you. I like that new artist look you've got going."

She laughed, swishing the long skirt. "Between Ginny and Goodwill, I'm building a whole new wardrobe."

"I'm sorry we haven't gotten to spend more time together. With the changes at work and the last of the J&S paperwork, I seem to meet myself coming and going."

Ginny interrupted the moment by appearing by their side. "Come on, Camille," she said. "It's showtime."

"Wish me luck," Camille said to Marsh, and he leaned down and surprised her with a quick kiss on the mouth.

Kylie and Randy, dressed in their church clothes, stood near the front of the crowded room, which grew quiet as Camille made her way to their side. "Thank you, all, for coming," she said. "I'll admit that tonight's a lot more fun than the meeting we had at the gym."

"That's for sure," Drew Cross yelled out, LSU cap in place.

"Oh, shut up, Drew," one of the twins — Darlene, Camille thought — said, and everyone laughed.

"Tonight we'll distribute bonus checks to the three landowners who decided to sign," Camille said.

"Boo," someone said, and a few peopled hissed.

Holding up her hand, Camille smiled. "Everyone has to do what is best for him or her." She shook her head slowly. "I've had such a hard time learning that, but it's true."

She put her hands on Kylie's and Randy's shoulders. "Tonight is about the future and the many good things God has in store for Sweet Olive."

Lawrence let out an ear-piercing whistle, and most people clapped.

Camille knelt before the two children, a check in her hand. "Are you two young artists ready?" They beamed, and Camille looked to her side to see Janice snapping photographs.

"It is my pleasure," Camille said, reaching

for the oversized check, "to present this money to the Sweet Olive Artists' Guild for the development of a regional folk-art center, including art classes and a gallery."

The audience jumped to its feet, clapping loudly, yelling, and whistling.

"It wouldn't have been possible without your unwavering love for your neighbors and your joyful use of the creative gifts you've been given," she said.

Camille posed for a few more pictures with the giant check and the children, and then raised her hand. "Now, if I may, I'd like to make one more announcement."

Murmurs ran through the crowd.

"Marsh, would you join me?"

A few catcalls rang out. "You go, boy," someone said. "You'd be crazy to let her slip away," someone else said.

Ginny, sitting in the front row by Bud, looked puzzled.

"You too, Ginny," Camille said. "Will you come forward?"

Fiddling with her hair, in a fat braid slung over her shoulder, Ginny stood. "What are you two up to?" She pulled Marsh aside. "I thought we were waiting until it was final," she whispered loudly.

"Just go with it, Ginny." He pulled her back to the center of the room.

Camille reached behind her and picked up a manila envelope, similar to the one Uncle Scott had given her when he had sprung the Sweet Olive case on her.

"Ginny, everyone agrees that your leadership has made the difference these past few weeks."

"Thank you," Ginny said, "but everyone has done more than enough. I have casseroles to feed us through next summer."

The curious crowd twittered.

"This isn't a gift exactly," Marsh said.

Camille opened the envelope and pulled out a sheaf of paper.

"Some of you may have heard," Marsh continued, "that Ginny's mineral rights were signed over years ago."

The crowd grew quiet, as though a gift had been promised and then yanked from their grasp.

"But, as it turns out, the one well in that section, quite a ways from Ginny's home, has not produced in decades," Camille said.

"Louisiana's mineral laws are, shall we say, *different.*" Marsh looked at Camille, his blue eyes glowing, while the audience began to squirm.

"Here's the deal." Camille looked at Ginny. "Through a lapse by J&S, your well became available again. Because Louisiana allows a race to the courthouse to claim such rights, we were able to get yours back."

Camille extended the papers. "No one can drill on your land without your permission. And if you decide you're okay with drilling, the money will be yours."

Ginny rushed to the front but ignored the papers, sweeping Camille and Marsh into a bear hug.

The library erupted with clapping and tears.

CHAPTER 41

The night after the community meeting, Ginny insisted Camille ride with her to take the children home and then head to the artists' meeting.

Camille climbed into the front passenger's seat, moving a fast-food sack and a pile of newspapers before she sat down. Paper cups, coffee mugs, and a dried-out plastic bag of clay littered the floor. She appreciated that Ginny didn't apologize for the mess.

Ginny packed the artists into her minivan like a veteran school bus driver and played an art game as they drove. She asked questions about colors and shapes, and the children yelled over each other to answer.

"What's your favorite color for a butterfly?" she asked.

"Yellow," a child in the middle row of seats said.

"Orange," another yelled from the back-seat.

"If you could draw a butterfly a different color, what color would you choose?" Ginny asked.

"Purple," a little girl said.

"Blue," a boy said.

"Did you know there are blue butterflies?" Ginny glanced in the rearview mirror. "They mostly live down in South America."

Watching the last child dash into his house, Camille sighed and ran her fingers through her hair. "I'm going to miss them so much. My two months here feel like two years."

"Are you sure you have to leave?" Ginny asked.

"I'm sure I have to find a job."

"Couldn't you do that in Samford?"

Camille gave her head a shake. "Sadly, I don't think so," she said. "After the debacle with J&S, I doubt I'd be high on a hiring list."

"You won't consider it?"

"I'll consider anything," Camille said, "since I'm partial to food on the table." She looked out the window as they approached Ginny's colorful house. "I've been praying about it." Her voice was quiet.

"So have I." Ginny turned slightly in her

seat. "You did your best, Camille."

"It wasn't enough."

"Of course it was." Ginny put the minivan in gear. "Our best is always enough."

They pulled onto the small road. The lights of the closest drill rig shone like a skyscraper, but otherwise the setting was pastoral. The sun sank behind a stand of tall pine trees, and the air was almost cool when Camille let her window down a few inches.

"This is my favorite time of year," Ginny said. "You can almost feel change in the air."

Camille sniffed. "That's why I've never cared for it."

"Really?" The note of amazement in Ginny's voice surprised Camille.

"I like for things to stay the same," she said. "Change is overrated."

"Even when it's good?"

"I'm always waiting for something to go wrong." Camille hesitated. "Like your land deal. It seems like life's waiting to pounce."

"It worked out," Ginny said. "Most days things go right."

Something poked her, and Camille shifted in her seat, pulling out a paintbrush.

"You never know what you'll find around here," Ginny said with a laugh.

Camille rubbed the bristles on the brush

between her fingers and cocked her head. "Where are we going?" Camille asked when they passed Ginny's driveway.

"Oh, didn't I mention it? We're doing the Artists' Guild meeting differently tonight. We're taking a field trip."

"To look at art?" Camille asked.

"Not exactly."

"You're acting weird. Are you sure you're all right with me springing that on you last night?"

"Beyond all right," Ginny said. "When you came here for our mineral rights, I couldn't have guessed you'd hand mine back to me."

"Neither could I," Camille said.

They drove down the road through the artists' colony, porch lights on. Ginny slowed the van as they cruised by each house, going about as fast as the golf cart had during her first tour. Remnants of the "Art with Heart" day remained — signs in driveways, random tables not yet moved.

"Do you still think this art is special?" Ginny asked.

"Of course I do." Camille shifted to face Ginny. "One of these days, I'll work in a gallery, and I'll introduce Sweet Olive to the world."

"I sure hope so," Ginny said, driving on.

"Where's the meeting again?"

"In Samford," Ginny said, gesturing vaguely. "The artists want to show you something."

Dusk had settled by the time they reached the corner of Trumpet and Vine, and Camille was having a hard time catching her breath.

Bud's truck and Lawrence's car were in the driveway, and five or six of the artists had gathered on lawn chairs, a folding table covered with white sacks and cups. The For Sale sign was propped up against the house.

"I've always loved this house," Ginny said. "A lady from my church used to live here."

"It's nice," Camille said, "but I'm confused."

"It's the Guild meeting. I told you that."

"But you didn't tell me we were having supper at a vacant house."

Ginny waved her hand. "Wait until you taste the muffuletta sandwiches from that store across the street." She glanced around. "Parking might be a problem, but I guess we'll figure all that out."

"There's plenty of room there behind Bud's truck," Camille said.

"I didn't mean parking was a problem now. I mean it has the potential to be."

"Ginny, are you all right?"

"I'm great!" she chirped. "How about you?"

"I'm not sure."

"There they are!" the artists exclaimed as they climbed out of the minivan. "We were beginning to think you weren't coming."

"It took awhile to deliver the children," Ginny said.

"Maybe it'll be more convenient when we can have the lessons here," Lillie said.

Ginny threw her a frown, while Evelyn handed Camille a paper sack. "I hope you don't mind eating on your lap, Camille."

The round Italian bread and olive mix was delicious, and Camille chewed for a moment, trying to push the location out of her mind. She dabbed at the mustard on her mouth and ran her fingers along the coarse bread.

Ross's black pickup pulled up to the curb, and he strolled over to the table. "Here are the keys." He dangled one of Bud's carved key chains.

"For what?" Camille asked.

"We want to show you around . . ." Ginny's voice faltered. "We know there will be obstacles, but we think it can work. There'll be room for a small apartment."

Ginny nodded at Bud, who rose and

walked over to the For Sale sign against the house.

"We think we've had an answer to our prayers," Ginny said.

Evelyn nodded. "We hope you think so too."

Bud turned the sign around, which had been repainted.

"Future Home of the Sweet Olive Folk Art Gallery."

CHAPTER 42

The closing on the duplex was set for mid-November, and as they walked out of the title office, Ginny handed the keys to Camille.

"Are you sure?" Camille asked, her fingers gliding down the smooth wood of the key chain.

"If you utter those words one more time, I'm going to beat you with a paintbrush," Ginny said. "This is the perfect solution for all of us."

Camille's mind, with a voice sounding much like Uncle Scott's, told her all the reasons why this was a bad idea, but Ginny sounded determined and happy.

"Congratulations, again." Ross stepped out behind them. "I look forward to the grand opening."

"New Year's Day," Ginny said. "A fresh new start."

"But we'll be glad to have your manual

labor between now and then," Camille added. "There's a lot to be done."

"Is Allison still screeching in Houston?" Ginny asked.

"She calls every day," Camille said. "I told her we might be willing to let her do an exclusive Sweet Olive exhibit — if the price was right." She gave a mocking smile. "But she says the new volunteer is *eminently* more qualified than I was."

Ginny laughed so hard that she had to take her big glasses off to wipe her eyes.

Marsh, who had to make a rush trip to Baton Rouge for the week, didn't expect the crowd at Camille's new place on a Friday afternoon.

A gallery of lawn chairs lined the side yard. A giant flowering bush sat on the front porch, and he glanced down at the plant in his hands. So much for original ideas.

"Hey, Marshall." Evelyn waved cheerily from a lawn chair.

"Pretty impressive show of support, eh?" Lawrence came from around the corner, motioning with a large fork. He grinned. "We didn't expect quite this turnout."

"Hey, son." His father rounded the corner wearing his tool belt and stepped up next to

Lawrence. "How'd the interview go this week?"

"Dicey." Marsh gave his father a hug with his free arm. "They made it clear they usually appoint attorneys from larger firms. We'll see." He shrugged. "On the plus side, my computer system's up and running, and I've gained a couple of clients — thanks to you and Ross."

"Two more people called this afternoon." Lawrence grinned. "Not counting your mother, who wanted to know if you got the commission appointment."

The three men laughed. "You're going to make a great assistant," Marsh said. "You may decide to give up art for law."

"Part-time assistant." Lawrence shook his head as he spoke. "I'm working deals here and with Allison's gallery."

Marsh's father glanced at the plant in his hand. "If you're looking for Camille, she and Ginny should be here anytime."

"I'd better get busy, then."

His father winked.

Camille sucked in her breath when she and Ginny approached Trumpet and Vine.

"Surprise," Ginny said.

Someone had hung a string of bright little flags across the front porch. Two people were raking leaves, while three people held garbage bags and picked up trash.

Lawrence stood at a grill to the side. T. J. Aillet was up on a ladder, and Ross was handing him something. One of Evelyn's bright metal sunflowers had sprouted to the left of the steps, and someone — *Marsh* — was kneeling in the flower bed.

Before they were out of the pickup, the crowd had begun to move toward her. Evelyn was the first to reach Camille, wrapping her into a careful hug. "Your artists await you."

"What are you all doing here?" Camille asked.

"Earning shelf space in the Sweet Olive Folk Art Gallery." Ginny added her booming laugh to the end of the sentence.

"The light is going to be fantastic," Lillie Lavender said.

"I have just the carving for the mantel downstairs." Bud pointed to the part of the house that would house the gallery.

A minor commotion occurred at the corner of the house, and she looked up to see her mother coming toward her, arms outstretched.

"Mama?" Camille said, her brow creased.

"I'm so proud of you, honey." Her mother, a brown package wedged under her arm, gently held her for a moment, before putting her at arm's length and studying her. They both had tears in their eyes.

"But . . . what . . . how?"

"I'm thrilled for you." She kissed Camille on her cheek. "Our past is part of who we are, Camille, but we can't stay there forever."

"I finally realized that."

"Scott called today. He wishes you well, despite the new federal investigation."

Camille swallowed a lump in her throat. "I hope he'll be okay."

"He brought it on himself — but enough about that." Her mother handed her the package and helped Camille open it. The clown paint-by-number smiled up at her.

"The first piece of art for my new house," Camille said softly, hugging her mother again. "By Johnny Gardner. I loved him." She wiped at her eyes. "I love you. Oh, Mama, I'm so happy."

She searched the crowd and found Marsh watching from nearby. He brushed dirt from his hands and gave her a big smile. He looked much as he had her first evening in Samford, working in the yard, at ease. Her heart rate increased and her mother nudged her in his direction. Camille's eyes locked on his, sparkling blue in the late afternoon light.

"Am I ever glad to see you," he said as she stepped close, and he gave her a hard kiss. "Congratulations!"

"I missed you." Her voice was soft and sure. Marsh put his arm around her waist and walked her toward the porch.

When they stopped, a surge of joy unlike any she had ever known ran through her. Here, where she once thought her life was over.

Marsh pulled her next to him on the duplex steps, the spot of their visit a few weeks back. She scanned the crowd while soaking up the feel of Marsh so close. Her mother talked to Bud and Ginny across the yard, and Lawrence was laughing with —

"Is that *Allison?*"

"She flew in for the occasion." Marsh smiled. "And, I suspect, to try to get more of Lawrence's . . . work."

Her hand flew to her mouth to cover her burst of laughter, and Marsh gently removed it to give her another kiss.

The green leaves of a freshly planted sweet olive bush glowed in the flower bed. "Did you plant that for me?"

He nodded. "I want to help you put down roots."

"I'd like that."

He took her face in his hands. "I'll wait as long as it takes. Camille . . . I've fallen in love with you."

Her heart pounded. "I love you too."

That slow smile spread across his face as he drew her into another embrace.

She looked over Marsh's shoulder at the intersection of Trumpet and Vine. The traffic light flashed from red to green.

"Thank You, Lord," she whispered.

She was . . . home.

DISCUSSION QUESTIONS

1. Camille Gardner wants to follow her dreams as the book opens but is thwarted. Have you ever faced roadblocks on your journey? How did you handle those? How does she handle them? How does God guide us as we seek to do the right thing in life?

2. The artists in Sweet Olive have wavered in recent years, and they need a reminder of their talent. Why do you suppose Camille has such an impact on them? Which of the artists was your favorite? Why? Who in your life has been a catalyst for change?

3. Camille loves art and has found messages for her life in the creativity of others. What creative gifts do you see in your life and the lives of those around you? How might you share those with others?

4. The sweet olive bush entices Camille with its smell and becomes a symbol for the changes in her life. Do you have a favorite

flower that speaks to you? What season blesses you most?

5. Ginny Guidry makes joyful whirligigs, which become a reminder of God's hand in our lives. Why do you think these old-fashioned pieces of art move Camille so much?

6. Marsh wants to do the right thing, and he finds himself drawn to Camille. What do you think he learned during this story? How does he struggle with his mother and father?

7. Camille's mother is an important part of her life, even though they haven't lived in the same town for a long time. Why do you think they are so close? How do you handle long-distance relationships with family members?

8. Uncle Scott demands much of Camille, and she changes her life to accommodate his requests. Why do you think she does that? Have you ever felt an obligation to someone in your family? How did you deal with it?

9. Camille struggles with the memory of her father during her stay in Sweet Olive. How does that relationship unfold? Is there someone in your life who you have forgiven or need to forgive? How has that worked out?

10. The corner of Trumpet and Vine is where lives intersect. Is there a place in your life where you connect with others? Can a place, such as the old duplex, transform a community?

11. The community of Sweet Olive wants to pull together, believing that their strength comes in helping each other. Have you experienced the power of a small group or faith community helping you through a tough situation?

12. Each person in the book is, in some way, putting the past behind and moving forward. Who do you think changes the most? In what ways might God be moving you forward in your own life?

WITH GRATITUDE

I offer deep thanks to the many people who gathered with me at the corner of Trumpet and Vine:

To my agent, Janet Grant, and editors Sue Brower and Julee Schwarzburg, for welcoming Louisiana flavor;

To landman and author Tracy Carnes, who took me on a tour of the Louisiana Office of Conservation and visited for hours about Louisiana oil and gas; Attorney Lynn Estes Jr., who walked me through the intricacies of Louisiana law — and always makes me laugh; artists Brenda McCart, Carol Greening, and Judy Horne, who shared why creativity matters; although each of the above only suggested, and any errors or fictionalized facts are my own;

To friends (and early readers) Kathie Rowell and Jamie Chavez; Cedar Key artist Joan Morgan; the Montgomery family and their cabin; authors Lenora Worth, Lisa

Wingate, Betsy St. Amant, and Suzanne Woods Fisher; Stan Williams, who shares his "Moral Premise" wisdom generously; and Pulpwood Queen Book Club leader and friend, Kathy Patrick.

To Carol Vahue Lovelady and the memory of Helen Mack Vahue, who touched my heart as I wrote;

And, finally, always to my husband, Paul.